A RENDEZVOUS TO DIE FOR

by

Betty McMahon

ISBN: 978-1-257-93132-3

Printed in the United States of America

Self published with the wonderful tools and the support of the people at Lulu.com

For the Minnesota Rendezvous re-enactors who showed me how people at an 1830s rendezvous talked, dressed and acted – and who gave me lessons in how to properly throw a tomahawk. Also for the officers in the Wright County, Minnesota, sheriff's department, who made sure my law enforcement procedures were accurate.

For editors Susan Mary Malone and Nancy Johanson. For Bob Rockwell's great formatting job, and Vicki Stromberg who deserves many thanks for a fun cover!

And last, but far from the least, for my Minneapolis, Minnesota and Deming, New Mexico writing groups. Without your support, I'd never have finished this book.

A RENDEZVOUS TO DIE FOR

by

Betty McMahon

Betty McMahon

Prologue

After months of practicing and planning, it was finally going to happen. I had anticipated every possible problem and then eliminated them one by one. All I had to do was keep my cool. The rest would take care of itself.

I had already scoped out the sweat lodge, after he suggested it as our meeting place. Now, I was arriving plenty early, so I could do the necessary schmoozing. It was all part of my plan—as was carrying the only weapon I'd need. A trained warrior knows how to travel light and still get the job done. I smiled when I thought of how I'd do it. Thinking this one up was nothing short of brilliant. The weapon I'd leave behind would baffle the cops more than help them.

He made it so easy for me. "I've got that information you've been looking for," was all I needed to say, if I said anything at all. He'd kill for that information, but we'd see who kills for what information.

I checked out the lodge and its surrounds one more time. He thought it was so clever to meet in this particular place. He liked the irony of it, he said. But I couldn't have chosen a better location myself. It was isolated and the line of sight was just right for my purpose. Even the weather was cooperating. It was the land of mosquitoes, but not a single one was in evidence. All it would take is one mosquito slap to give away my position. I couldn't have asked for a sweeter setup.

I blew the air from my lungs through pursed lips. This was one venture I couldn't wait to pay off. I hadn't sat in all those god-awful city and county meetings for nothing, listening, always listening, while I collected the information I needed to formulate my plan. My plan was perfect. I knew my schedule right down to the last minute. I'd have a window of at least an hour where we'd be alone. Not that I needed an hour, but a good soldier always builds in enough room to maneuver, just in case.

I shook my hands in front of me to dispel the jitters and cursed the beads of sweat forming on my brow. I had nothing to be nervous about. All those hours of practice, practice, practice would pay off. It would be different for each one of them, but if they were all as easy as this one to set up, it wouldn't be long before my job was done. Now, I just had to wait and watch the little rat take the bait. I had no doubts he'd take it, either. Not for a minute.

What's that sound? Good, he's right on time.

Focus, focus, focus.

Finally, the last piece of the puzzle is about to be put in place. I have him exactly where I want him. He is in my power now and he doesn't have a clue, the little moron. We are connected, occupying a small part of the universe together. I'm the only one who can break the connection.

Look at him. The fool. Swinging up the path, thinking he doesn't have a care in the world; but, he's feeling the last breeze he'll ever feel on his face in this lifetime. He's probably dreaming about how he'll spend the cash he figures he'll get out of this little encounter.

I need to stop daydreaming. *Focus. Focus.*

He's coming closer. He's in the clearing now. Wait until he's absolutely in place before you do anything. There. He's kneeling. Getting ready to peer inside, just as I knew he would do. Does he really think he'll find me in there?

Stand still. Don't move a muscle. You've got time.

His eyes are still adjusting to the light. Now he's standing. Probably wondering where I am.

Now . . . before he turns around! Ready. Aim. FIRE!

Ah . . . perfect. *Perfect.*

Not that I ever doubted it would be anything less.

One down. Four to go.

Chapter 1

Sunday

It's mind-boggling how a day that starts so beautifully can end up so disastrously. The beautiful part started when I stowed my camera gear into the back of my Jeep and climbed into the driver's seat. It was barely dawn on a lovely Minnesota June Sunday. The disastrous part started not long after I entered the grounds of the Prairie River Trappers' Rendezvous.

I take pictures to pay the rent, but when I'm fed up to my f-stops with wedding gigs, I look for opportunities to indulge my passion for "real photography." That's what I was doing as I headed north on the almost deserted highway.

The idea of grown men and women reenacting an 1830s gathering site of fur traders and Indians fascinated me, and my friend Anna Sanders had been adamant about my taking in the event. "Cassandra Cassidy, you absolutely *must* go to the Rendezvous," she had said. "You'll get some great pictures of black powder shooting, tomahawk throwing, and blacksmithing.

Sunday is the last day, so don't dawdle in making your decision to attend."

I figured I'd burn through a few megs on my digital cameras and fill up some rolls of film on my good old 35-mm. I'd also be able to add to my personal collection of Indian photographs, as some members of the Prairie River Band had a couple of sweat lodges and some teepees on the grounds. I've been interested in Indians ever since reading about them in the third grade. Then, after attending a powwow with a school group my junior year with camera in hand, I had become hooked. At the Rendezvous, the Indians would be "trading" with people masquerading as trappers, military men, and buckskinners. Buckskinners! I pushed my vehicle up to seventy-five, anticipating the day's possibilities. Weather reports promised a warm, sunny day.

I pulled into the parking lot about seven. Early for me. The Rendezvous covered a generous eleven acres, with more than a hundred encampments. I threw my camera bag over my shoulder and set out to find the nineteenth-century equivalent of a Starbucks.

The entrance to the trading post was flanked by a ten-foot tall palisade-type fence. A gate was open to allow the paying public to enter. I produced my photographer's press pass and slipped in, immediately noticing several permanent buildings within the palisade walls. A clerk's quarters and company store were made out of hewed logs and had twin fireplaces bookending the building.

Like an early-day multipurpose room, a couple of sleeping bunks were attached to a far wall. The storekeeper had to simply tumble out of bed and walk the few feet to his "store"—a super-sized log slab balanced across two huge upended logs. From shelves in back of him, he could pull off goods, such as tomahawks, knives, knit hats, gourd dippers, animal skins, blankets, buckskin shirts and dresses . . . whatever anyone wanted to buy or trade.

At a blacksmith shop, the 'smith stirred up embers, preparing to fire up his forge for the day. I made a note to stop by on the way out.

In a corner, I saw long-skirted women pulling wonderful-smelling bread loaves out of a clay oven. With my nose pointed in the bread-bakers' direction, I almost tripped over an Indian, squatting with a knife in his hand in front of a half-finished birch-bark canoe. "Oops, sorry," I muttered, as he threw out his arms to keep me from plunging headlong into his lap. I pushed myself up, dusted off my jeans, and peered around to see who had witnessed my less-than-elegant spill. Then, as composed as I could manage, I flashed a smile at the guy and proceeded on my way.

Event participants were beginning to stir from a motley assortment of wall tents, teepees, and lean-tos that had been erected beyond the palisades, forming "streets" throughout the encampment. The acrid smell of wood fires mingled with the pungent smells of frying bacon and fresh-brewing coffee. Tin cups rattled to the accompaniment of pots being taken on and off the spits erected over small cook fires.

As a photographer, I could usually walk through a crowd as an almost-invisible observer, snapping pictures and chatting up the people I photographed. But in this crowd, dressed in twenty-first century clothing, I was as conspicuous as a stockbroker at a jugglers' convention.

A trio of mountain men passed by, yakking and spitting. They wore pants made of the hide of some kind of animal, cotton shirts, leggings, and moccasins. They nodded to me and, when one peeled off from the trio, I snapped a few pictures of him. "Who are you?" I asked.

"Name's Ground Kisser," he said. "Got the name twenty years ago when I kept fallin' down after a particularly unrestrained night of imbibin'."

I photographed him as he turned to spew a stream of tobacco juice on the ground and then swipe his mouth with the back of a hand. I resisted the urge to say "Yuck," and asked, "And, what's that?" I pointed at a rawhide bag hanging around his neck.

"My 'possibles' bag," he said, opening his mouth to reveal a few gaps where his teeth should have been. "Got a knife, some powder and shot, some fire-startin' stuff, and a little tobaccy in it."

Ah, yes, "tobaccy," the cause of the little wet brown spots I kept trying to avoid as I wandered the grounds. To complete the man's frontier ensemble, a small ax dangled from a leather string around his waist. "What do you use that for?" I nodded toward it.

"My tomahawk?" He patted it. "Come 'round to the 'hawk games, and you'll see what we do with 'em."

I zeroed in for a close-up of the dangerous-looking implement. "So, you compete with it?" I wanted to keep him talking. "Is it made especially for competition? Is it special?"

The tail of some kind of animal that was attached to his furry hat wiggled as he shook his head. "Nah, my 'hawk's not too different from everyone else's 'round here. 'cept for Tomahawk Pete's. He takes 'hawk-throwin' pretty serious. Has his made special. Might be somethin' to it, too, 'cause he usually wins."

Walking on, I noticed a wildly bearded man in a flashy outfit—headband, loose-fitting shirt, vest, trousers with a bright red waist sash, and moccasins—perched in front of a teepee, smoking a hand-rolled cigar. Eager to talk, he told me he was a *courier de bois*. "I was reared up with the Ojibwe," he said, in what was becoming an irritating accent most of the reenactors seemed to have adopted. "Got plumb tired a givin' up ever'thin' to the French fur companies, so's now I'm a free trapper. Some a

9

them folks say I'm a outlaw and they put a bounty on my head. I hafta keep a lot a light between me 'n them." He winked at me, while chuckling, then spat a ubiquitous stream of tobacco juice off to the side, missing my right boot by a hair. I jumped back a couple steps.

The trapper was drinking something from a tin cup and it reminded me that I hadn't eaten breakfast yet. "Do you know where I could buy a cup of coffee?" I asked.

"Wal," he said, lifting his cup. "Made this coffee from some green coffee beans I traded with a fella', oh, 'bout six month ago. Jest roasted a coupl'a handfuls in the fire last night so's I could throw them into coffee water this mornin'. I'll pour ya a cup." He reached for a smoke-blackened coffee pot. Seeing my look of distress, he grinned. "Or I could rassle up a cuppa coffee from this Maxwell House pouch, if ya like." He poured some water into a paper cup he had stashed behind his antique utensils and then tapped a couple spoonfuls of instant coffee into it. "Enjoy," he said.

Grateful and about to be fortified with a shot of caffeine, I sipped the tepid brew and waded out into the city of tents again. As I photographed a wiry little guy—also missing his front teeth—he held forth about his life as a Long Hunter. He pivoted to display all his worldly possessions, while he launched into his memorized lingo. "It's all here, on muh back. A tarp, ground cloth, foldin' skillet, tent stakes, rope, tin pots and cup, wooden bowl, horn spoon, fork, squirrel cooker, a pouch for my fire kit, muh possibles bag, haversack, 'hawk and two knives, a camp hatchet, salt and pepper horns, jerky, parched corn, cornmeal, coffee, dried fruits and veggies, powder horn, priming horn, smooth bore gun, two blankets, and a spare shirt or two."

I laughed. "And I thought lugging my cameras was a challenge. Why are you here, Long Hunter? What draws you to participating in these weekend events where you leave the comforts of the twenty-first century behind?"

He squinted at me. "What you talkin' about, ma'am? We always come to Ronnyvous. How else you think we're gonna peddle our hides?" He turned away, shaking his head, his persona still intact.

I strolled through the encampment, marveling at the sounds and sights that were missing. No blaring rock music. No buzzing cell phones. No sign of soft-drink cans or Styrofoam fast-food containers, candy wrappers, or cigarette butts. The transformation to the 1830s was almost complete. About midmorning, I was kneeling before a little girl swathed in a coat fashioned from a red-and-white-striped Hudson Bay blanket. Her mother, in a long cotton calico chemise, was leaning over her with a corn cob, preparing to scrub off a morning's indulgence in sticky candy. As I clicked the shutter, someone called my name.

"Hey, Cassandra."

Glancing over my shoulder, I groaned. It was Eric Hartfield. "Hello, Eric." I pushed myself to my feet, bracing for his opening salvo.

"Looking to shoot a few Indians today, C.C.?" He smirked.

"No, you little prick, I'm shooting rocks. Where's the one you crawled out from under?" I struck a hands-on-the-hips, legs-firmly-planted stance. I'd been in "Nice Minnesota" mode long enough. The man always had a way of irking me and I was immediately on guard.

"Now, now, Cassandra, I just don't know what to make of a remark like that." He stepped closer, his scrawny five-foot-seven frame a mere foot away. His breath smelled of stale coffee and menthol cigarettes. I saw the blood pulsing at his temples and pulled myself up as tall as I could manage, distracted for only a moment by my reflection in his wire-rimmed glasses.

"What are you doing here, Eric?" I backed up a step.

He reached into his shirt pocket, pulled out a package of cigarettes, and tapped one into his hand. "Not that it's any of your business, sweetheart, but I'm on assignment for the Duluth paper. They want a write-up on this event."

That stopped me cold. How could a respected daily newspaper hire a scumbag like Eric? I'd seen road kill with a more appealing personality. "How'd you manage that?"

"It's called freelancing, honey." He cupped his hand around the cigarette, lighting it. After taking a long drag, he squinted down at me. "Some newspapers appreciate the skills of an experienced journalist."

"Unlike others that shun the shenanigans of unprincipled ones."

"That little incident with the *Star Tribune* was only a bump in the long, sometimes rocky road we journalists must endure."

"I wouldn't call being fired from a major newspaper only a bump in the road!"

"And I suppose your part in that little charade makes you the Fourth Estate's Joan of Arc."

"I didn't ask to be part of that."

"No? Well, you sure as hell made the most of it to advance your own agenda." Red-faced and barely controlling his anger, Eric waved his cigarette in my face.

I shifted my weight and flapped the smoke out of my face. "All I stated was my professional opinion."

"Your 'professional opinion' huh." He spit on the ground, purposely aiming as close to my shoe as he could. "That's what I think of your professional opinion. It carries about as much weight as a fencepost."

"The jury didn't seem to think so." Our voices had raised considerably and I noticed that both visitors and participants in the Rendezvous were glancing curiously at us as they passed by.

"It didn't take a professional to expose an amateur's work," I added, turning to leave. I'd had enough of Eric Hartfield for one day.

He grabbed my arm and spun me around. "We'll see who ends up being exposed as an amateur," he said, his face turning a shade redder with each decibel of his raised voice.

"Should I interpret that as a threat?" I wrenched my arm away.

"Interpret it however you want, you lying bitch!" He sprayed saliva into the air and shook a fist at me. "Nobody does what you did to me and gets away with it!"

I leaned toward him. "Are you talking about revenge, Mr. Hartfield? That should be great for your already sputtering career. I can see it on your résumé . . . right under the part about your photo-doctoring skills."

He glared at me, spun around, and stalked away. He'd gone about ten steps, when he turned back. "If I were you," he shouted, "I'd watch my back."

I lifted my chin. "The next time I see you, I'll fire two warning shots . . . straight into your head!" I pointed my index finger and wiggled it, imitating the pulling of a trigger. Immediately, I was annoyed with myself for engaging in such a juvenile reaction. No one else had the ability to raise my hackles in such a way, but that was no excuse.

Eric Hartfield was a columnist for the *Minnesota Issues Review*. He used whatever clout he had to attack anyone or anything outside his narrow political comfort zone. American Indians were one of his favorite targets. Shortly after I moved to Colton Mills, Frank Kyopa was running for his second term as tribal chief of the Prairie River Band. Eric wrote about it, as a reporter for the *Minneapolis Star-Tribune.* In one of his news stories, he ran a picture of Frank entering the building of a land developer in Chicago, implying that Frank was secretly meeting with the developer to make deals. Because I had often photographed Frank, he knew about my photography-computer skills and asked if I could determine whether or not a photo was a fake. His attorney hired me, and it was easy to prove that the photo had been rather crudely doctored. A photo of Frank had been super-imposed on the picture of the developer's office entrance. Eric was discredited and fired. When I testified against him, he blamed me for his fall.

I displayed a few Indian photographs in a Minneapolis gallery, and, because I had access to the Indian community, I became a "go to" person for photos to accompany American Indian newspaper and magazine stories. Every favorable gallery review and photo credit rubbed more salt into Eric's wounds. He pestered me regularly. His telephone calls and e-mail messages belittled my photos and became so frequent in numbers, I could have sued him for harassment. Unfortunately, my work often took me to events he was covering, so I hadn't been able to avoid him.

Although he said he was working as a freelancer, I wondered what had really brought Eric to the Rendezvous, a nonpolitical family event. He usually went where there was news . . . or where he intended to stir some up. Feeling uneasy, I resented the pall he had cast on what had been a promising day.

The 'hawk-throwing competition was slated for 10:30, so I made my way to the edge of the encampment where targets had been erected away from the main Rendezvous traffic. I arrived too early. Officials had postponed the event for a half hour to wait for one of the competitors. *Must have been a short list of competitors,* I thought. 'Hawk throwing was definitely not ready for prime time.

The break gave me much-needed time to run back to the parking lot to replace my battery packs and get some fresh CF cards. I had three digital cameras with me: one to shoot newspaper-style photos, one for my own use, and a smaller one I was testing. Crossing the field to the parking lot, I compulsively shot up the last few megs remaining on the small digital. I usually separated the CF cards into envelopes. Since I had brought only two envelopes with me, I pulled out the card from my small camera and tucked it into the watch pocket of my jeans. Then, with new cards inserted into each of the cameras, I headed back to the contest grounds, arriving just in time to see the contest get under way.

It probably wasn't written in 'hawk throwing rules, but every contestant sauntered in an identical walk to the throwing line. The all-male group stood motionless for a few seconds, squinting at the target. Then they swiveled their heads and, to a man, spit out a brown arc of tobacco juice. The spitting ritual over, they wiped their hands on their trousers, and then held their long-handled 'hawks in front of them shoulder high, while they took a bead on the target. The target was about fifteen yards in front of the throwing line. I'd seen one like it in my landlord's yard—a foot-thick cutout from a fat, ten-foot round tree, propped up on its side.

Once they had sized up the target, the marksmen stepped forward, at the same time lifting their throwing arms above their heads. Depending on each of their personal styles, they took either two or three steps and then threw the ax with a powerful swing. The axes flew end-over-end toward the target. About one out of three struck the target and remained imbedded.

Finally, Tomahawk Pete was announced—the thrower I'd heard about from Ground Kisser and the one who had held up the competition. I watched as a husky, bearded man strolled up to the throwing line and began the same ritual as the contestants before him. I focused my long lens on the thrower and suddenly did a double-take. Tomahawk Pete was my landlord, Marty Madigan! Now I knew why his weird backyard hobby was throwing tomahawks.

Today, his aim seemed to be off. Maybe he was flustered because, as the latecomer, he had held up the competition. His throws were only good enough for third place. After the points were tallied and announced, I searched for him on the sidelines. "Too bad about the contest," I said. "I heard you were the favorite to win."

He snatched off his slouch hat and ran his fingers through his wavy gray hair. "Aw, hell," he said, "I'd have had a better chance if I could have found the tomahawk I usually use. I searched high and low for it. Couldn't find it." He slapped his hat across his knee.

"Isn't one 'hawk as good as another?"

"Mine's special," he said, leaning his elbows on his knees. "I have my 'hawks made by a blacksmith in town. The blade is weighted and shaped the way I want it. I even have him tap some nail studs in a particular design at the end of the handle. When I'm not using it in competition, I hang leather fringe on the end of it."

"Don't 'hawk handles break easily?" I asked, drawing on the little information I'd gleaned from other onlookers of the competition.

Marty fingered the 'hawk he'd used that morning, stroking the wood. "Not mine. My handles are made out of black walnut. I've had the same handle on that 'hawk I lost for more than a year. I expected to have it for another year . . . or even more than that."

"Well, I hope it shows up," I said, turning to leave. "Better luck next time."

Eager to take a break from the Rendezvous events, I decided to maneuver towards the tribe's encampment to "shoot a few

Indians," as Eric had sarcastically suggested. One good thing . . . I hadn't seen anything of that menacing creep since our earlier confrontation. Maybe the Rendezvous was big enough for both of us.

I strolled along a well-worn path that cut through the woods surrounding the clearing and found it enjoyably quiet, after all the Rendezvous activity. Birds were singing in the chokecherry trees and I could hear the rippling river somewhere to the left of me, making its way to the mighty Mississippi.

As the pathway petered out, I could see a couple of teepees that had been erected in a stand of tall pines on a rise above the river. No one seemed to be around. I searched for the sweat lodge, knowing it should be closer to the river, but I couldn't locate it. Since sweating ceremonies are considered sacred, Indians never consented to being photographed while in a lodge. I felt my excitement rise. Maybe, if I hurried, I could take a few pictures while no one was about.

I found a narrow, rocky path that led directly to the river and followed it through the brush. In less than a minute, the lodge emerged in a clearing only a few yards ahead of me. It was little more than a dome-shaped hut made of hides draped over a willow-branch frame. The door was merely a flap of deer hide. The lodge would accommodate only four or five adults, who would sit around a pile of rocks in the center. During a "sweat ritual," they heated the rocks white-hot, then poured cold water on them to create very hot steam. Depending upon the ceremony, participants burned bunches of sweet grass, smoked or passed a "sacred pipe," talked, prayed, or pursued visions. After they had sweated long enough, they headed for a dip in the river while rubbing themselves with sage.

No smoke was rising above the lodge. I figured the ashes must have been left to burn out after the previous evening's ceremonies.

I hurried to the structure and peeled back the hide from the opening to peek inside. Because the hides formulating the lodge were made of thick hides, the sunlight couldn't penetrate them. It was rather dark inside, but I noticed a few wadded-up blankets near the fire pit. I paused to adjust the lens on my camera and then pointed it at what I hoped would make an interesting picture. The flash went off, illuminating the scene for only an instant. That's all it took. A second of illumination. I jumped back, trembling, and smothered a scream with the back of my hand. *It . . . it's not a pile of blankets,* I thought. *It's a . . . a man!*

I backed up and swung my head in every direction to examine my surroundings. Not a single leaf on any tree stirred. I saw no one. It was unbelievably quiet. I shivered, knowing I was utterly alone. *What should I do? Maybe my imagination has gone wild.* Slowly, I turned to take another look. *God, no!* I thought. *It . . . can't be.*

But it was. The man by the fire pit was Eric Hartfield. A very dead Eric Hartfield. And a familiar weapon was buried deep into the base of his skull.

I had a sick feeling I'd found Marty's missing tomahawk.

Chapter 2

Monday

There was nowhere to turn, no place to run from my tormentors. I was penned in by flying tomahawks that swirled around me in a shower of spraying blood. Rhythmic undulations and incessant drumming pounded on my eardrums. I sank to the ground and wrapped my arms tightly around my body, trying to make myself as small a target as possible. One 'hawk landed directly in front of me, another to my right, another to my left. There was no escaping them. I was doomed. An earsplitting, piercing scream forced me to lift my head.

I awakened sweating and shaken, the scream persisting, despite the realization that I had survived an all too realistic nightmare. Why wouldn't the shrieking stop? I sat up and shook my head. The sound changed to something more recognizable. It was my bedside telephone!

"Cassandra, are you okay?"

"Anna? You heard—"

"Yes and I've been worried sick! My friend Willis was at the Rendezvous." Her voice was unnaturally high. "He just left the store. He told me what he knew about that horrible, horrible incident yesterday. I'm so sorry, Cass. I should never have urged you to go to that event." She paused. "How are you, honey? Never mind. I'm coming over. You can tell me then. I'm going to bring you something. Coffee? Something stronger? How can I help?"

I rubbed my eyes and swung my legs off the bed. "I'm all right, now that I'm awake. Don't come here, Anna. I'll come to your shop and see you in about an hour." I hung up and sat motionless for several minutes. I couldn't shake the image of Eric wrapped around the fire pit with that ghastly hatchet in the back of his head. Maybe coffee would help. I showered, dressed, ran a comb through my curly hair, and headed toward town.

A lot of elements make a town livable, and Colton Mills had enough of them to make me rein in my Jeep, when I first passed through a year ago. Returning from a photo shoot in Duluth, I had decided to take the slow route back to the Twin Cities where I had lived for a couple of years. I still remember how the approach to Colton Mills had taken my breath away. A two-lane paved road passed through a forest of pines and descended a mile or more into a valley cut through by the Oxbow River. Then, suddenly, the town simply "appeared," like something out of a nineteenth-century picture post card.

I couldn't resist stopping to photograph the downtown area's brick and stone facades that marked Colton Mills as a once prosperous grain and lumber milling center. Then, places, such as the wooden grain elevator on the edge of town, which sat by long-abandoned railroad tracks, charmed the photographer in me. I was hooked. It was such a contrast to the traffic-blocked city I wanted to leave behind that, before leaving town three days later, I had rented a second-floor studio. Heading south, I had purposely overlooked the unsightly subdivisions sprouting in the soybean fields and the year-round brick McMansions displacing the tiny summer clapboard cabins around Oxbow Lake. After all, a working photographer had to get her potential clientele from somewhere.

Now, and in retrospect, I knew I'd have had to reconsider my decision if it weren't for The Grizzly Bar. All the town's qualities wouldn't be worth the paper the Colton Miller newspaper was printed on, without a decent place to get a real cup of coffee. Although a resistor of trends, I was fully in favor of the Starbucks craze.

This morning, as usual, Roxy, a fellow refugee from the rat race, was working behind the counter. "Morning, Roxy," I said. Roxy and her husband Mel, transplants from Minneapolis, had transformed a building that once housed a machine shop into a coffee shop with a northern Minnesota feel. A six-foot cardboard cutout of a grizzly bear holding a steaming cup of coffee loomed over me as I entered. The coffee bar's tag line was emboldened on the bear's cup: ROARIN' GOOD COFFEE. The shop looked as if a chainsaw demon had been turned loose in a pine forest. Whole trees—stripped of their bark, cut into ten-foot lengths and shellacked—flanked the counter from floor to ceiling. A half dozen booths, faced with pine slabs, lined one wall. Throughout the shop, several square tables and chairs, also made of pine, had been conveniently placed for relaxation. Near in a cozy seating area, Northern Minnesota *objets d'art* graced shelves interspersed with used books and magazines.

Roxy greeted me the way she did every time I came into Grizzly's, as the locals called it.

"Hi, Cassandra." She leaned her forearms on the tall counter. "What'll it be? The regular?"

The relationship I had established with Roxy, while exchanging pleasantries over my morning coffee order, made her one of my closest acquaintances. Thankfully, she hadn't yet heard about Eric's demise and my involvement. "I'll take two to go," I said. "The flavor of the day and one extra-large hazelnut, with a shot of espresso." Minutes later, I stashed the steaming paper cups in the Jeep's cup holders and headed across town to the Vintage Clothier.

Anna's store was located on the edge of the business district, one block off Main, where the old buildings were being turned into shops that drew tourists to Colton Mills every weekend. It was situated in the former Ames Ladies Wear store, between Ye Olde Fudge Shoppe and Embroidery Heaven. With the weekend tourists gone, I had no problem snagging a parking place.

Before entering the store, I paused to check out the show windows. Anna had dressed the window mannequins in long white summer frocks, featuring balloon sleeves, high neck-hugging collars, and tiny, cloth-covered buttons that would have taken an hour to fasten. They were appropriate for a game of tennis at the old Minneobi resort, circa 1880, but simply looking at them made the perspiration bead up on my forehead. Of course, my usual jeans-and-red-shirt uniform, was contributing to my discomfort as well. It was a combo I might have to abandon in the already too intense June heat.

The antique wooden door that opened into the store featured an oval of stenciled glass. It immediately set the tone for what was to come. I pushed the door handle with the side of one hand, while juggling the two coffee cups. As I entered, a bell chimed to announce my presence.

Anna was behind the counter talking on the phone. She tipped her elegant head and peered over the rims of the half glasses perching near the tip of her nose to acknowledge me, rolling her eyes upward in gratitude, as I set a coffee container on the counter and pushed it toward her.

Like Roxy and me, Anna was one of the "new people" in Colton Mills. About to celebrate the two-year anniversary of the Vintage Clothier, she'd been a resident a year longer than I. Anna reminded me of my foster mother, Mrs. Andrews—Crazy Mrs. A, as most people called her. Instead of trying to disguise her considerable bulk, Mrs. A flaunted it, with swaths of bright purple and red fabric. I can still see the discs of silver, bigger than half dollars, that always hung from her ears, and the silver-crafted squash-blossom necklace that splayed across her ample bosom. She swept her gray hair high on her head and secured it with combs. Wisps of it would escape and frame her round, unlined face, as she expressed whatever outlandish opinion she had on any subject that particular day. As I came up in the foster care system, Mrs. A was the closest thing to a real mother I ever had.

I'd taken to Anna, because she exhibited Mrs. A's zest for life. She would be about the same age, but where Mrs. A was big and loud, Anna was slim and sophisticated, gliding through her vintage shop as if it were a Paris salon. She wore her hair slickly pulled back from her lovely face and fastened with a pearl barrette. Today, she was dressed in a black silk sweater over a long, slim mauve skirt. "Yes, yes," she said. Her refined voice ran counterpoint to the clicking keys on her computer perched anachronistically on the antique wood counter, looking as out of place as a motor on a stagecoach.

I strolled around, waiting for the conversation to end. Anna's shop was crammed with racks of period clothing. Prim hats with fragile netting, pointy-toed shoes, turn-of-the-century under things, and other items I couldn't identify were neatly displayed on shelves. Scarves and gloves were draped out of dresser drawers or over period furniture. It was all a part of Anna's artfully designed jumble. Whenever I saw what women a hundred years were subjected to wearing, I worshipped anew at the altar of Levi Strauss.

My own closet consisted of a row of shirts in various patterns and shades of red. I used my creative brain cells behind the camera, not in composing outfits to wear every day. I never deliberated about the day's outfit . . . only whether I'd tuck the shirt in, wear it unbuttoned over a tee-shirt with the tails out, or whether I'd roll up the sleeves. Pair any shirt with my jeans and boots and I was ready to go. When the occasion called for it, I'd trade in the jeans for a pair of slacks, but the red shirt with jeans and boots ensemble had become a uniform.

Many of the pieces in Anna's shop were copies of the real thing. Anna had learned early on that few modern women fit into the small sizes that ladies of the past wore. She had turned her business into a reproduction clothing establishment, when she opened the Vintage Clothier. Now, she also had a thriving business on the Internet.

"Cassandra, dear," she said, finally off the phone and gliding over to my side. She gave me a big hug and pulled me onto a red velvet settee beside her. "Tell me exactly what happened." She listened without comment as I filled her in on the details.

Anna had introduced me to the Rendezvous concept when I visited with her about a month ago. I had come to discuss a client's project. Heather Wilson, who was planning a 1920s theme wedding, was renting clothing for the event from Anna, who had carved out an area in the back of her shop where people could pose in their vintage clothes. I had photographed several groups there and also called on Anna for props suitable for other occasions. Because I had acquired a reputation as a wedding photographer of the different-drummer variety, I attracted my share of nontraditional projects. As nontraditional went, Heather's was pretty tame. Nothing like the ceremony I photographed the previous spring, while scrunched shoulder to shoulder in the dinky basket of a hot air balloon with a couple, their minister, a witness, and the pilot. Recording the momentous I-dos in a vehicle that was gliding a thousand feet over the Oxbow tested more than my photographic skills.

Anna had suggested props for Heather's photo shoot. "This velvet settee (the very one we were now sitting on) will be perfect, don't you think, dear? You could pose the wedding party just so around the bride and groom."

"Maybe so." I had stepped around her to find something more appropriate to the occasion, and that's when my destiny jumped up and bit me, as something furry brushed against my face. "What the hell is *this*?" I had thrust the thing away from me.

"A fox pelt!" Anna had seemed surprised that I wouldn't recognize such a varmint. "There's a huge market now for frontier clothes, and fox pelts are one of the accessories most often requested. So, I stocked a few." Sure enough, she had added racks of buckskin dresses and pants, calico dresses, plain dresses, boots, kerchiefs, beaver hats . . . and the fox pelts.

"Where on earth would someone wear a getup like that?" I had asked, pointing to a brown-fringed number hanging on display.

Anna was way ahead of me, as usual. "Cassandra, you really must get out more. There's a whole culture of people they call reenactors. You've seen them at restored forts and old houses. They dress and act the part of people from some other era. It's quite fascinating." She had held up a skimpy bustier that must have been worn by a lady of the night "Old clothing styles can be very 'in-style' when worn by someone like you. This would look very sexy with your Levi's."

I had grimaced and walked away. "A thirty-something Britney Spears look. Just what I need. What kind of animal trapper would wear that little number?" I had pointed to what looked like an animal hide with holes for arms.

Anna had patted her hair and grinned. "Even trappers needed diversions now and then. And he would probably wear that to a Rendezvous."

"At a meeting with his girlfriend?"

"No, no, no." She had laughed at my naïveté. "A Rendezvous is a place where trappers meet once a year to trade their furs for supplies. If you're interested, you can read about the era. I've got several books on the subject." She pointed at her book wall, where a shelf carried books with titles such as *1800s Rendezvous Clothing* and *Fur Trade Fashion*.

When Anna got interested in something, Anna became the expert. She was the one person who could grasp the trauma eating me up inside. "Anna, I've never experienced anything even close to this," I said, holding my head in my hands. "I thought I'd photographed all kinds of scenes. I've been to many accidents. I've even covered other crime scenes, but it's never been, oh . . . *personal* . . . not like this. What am I going to do?"

"How did the sheriff treat you?"

"Law enforcement was fine." I massaged my forehead. "A deputy put me in the back of a squad car for privacy and briefly interviewed me. He followed me all the way home to make sure I could drive safely." I gave her a lopsided smile. "But the sheriff's not going to be too happy with me. The contents of my stomach became part of the crime scene."

"For once in my life, I'm speechless," Anna said. "I don't really know what to say to you, except this will eventually be over. Whoever would have thought something like this would happen, when we discussed the Rendezvous a short month ago. Do you have to talk with the sheriff today?"

"Uh-huh." I stared emptily at the wood floor. "Well, actually, I have an appointment with someone from Clayton County . . . a deputy sheriff. He's using space in our police department to interview me. I'm sure it's just routine, but—"

A man entered the store and disrupted my pity-party discourse. Anna went to greet him. "Hello, Mr. Lansing."

"Good morning, Anna," he said, bowing slightly. "And please call me Willis. Mr. Lansing was my father."

The old joke fell flat coming from a man who looked as if he wouldn't know a joke if it jumped up and bit him. Tall and slim, he carried himself rigidly erect. A well-trimmed gray goatee framed a square chin that was set off by a thin mouth. Steely, focused eyes glared out under severe brows. Doffing his Greek fisherman's cap, he revealed a stubbly salt and pepper crew cut. He looked to be Anna's age or older. I had the urge to add a thin mustache and photograph him in a World War I German Kaiser uniform.

Anna gestured toward me, to bring me into the conversation. "Willis, this is Cassandra Cassidy, a dear friend."

"I am happy to make your acquaintance, but I wish it were under more auspicious circumstances," he said stiffly. "I am so sorry for your terrible experience yesterday."

"Willis was here earlier and told me what happened," Anna explained, taking Willis' arm. "He reenacts the part of fur trade characters." She glanced up at him. "Those of you who participate in such events take your characters very seriously, don't you? It seems that most of you have meticulously researched everything—how your characters would talk, what they would eat, and so forth."

I examined Mr. Lansing more closely, while this exercise in adoration was going on. "Yes, I remember seeing you there," I said finally. "You took part in the tomahawk competition."

"Yes . . . yes, I did." He tore his gaze away from Anna. "And did well this time, since Marty was inconvenienced by not having his favorite tomahawk."

My ears perked up at the mention of my landlord. "Do you know Marty well?"

"He has deep roots in this part of the country," he said, his gaze drifting to the back of the store. "His father was a town lawyer or politician, or something of that sort. He was successful enough to build a lovely house outside of town. Excuse me, please. I see what I came to purchase." He moved to walk around me.

"I rent Marty's carriage house," I said, starting to follow him.

He stopped and turned. "I am sure he is a fine landlord," he said. He smiled with his lips closed and continued on his mission.

"Marty was a helicopter pilot in Viet Nam," Anna said, fussing with a dress hanging on display. "He suffered even more, after he returned, because his wife had taken their son and disappeared."

"You never told me you knew Marty," I said.

She glanced at me and then resumed her activity. "I know of him mostly through what I read about him in the newspaper. He runs a helicopter business in our county . . . mostly emergency stuff. You know, flying people to the hospital in the Cities and sometimes around the country. He's also on one of the town commissions."

"Sounds like an upstanding citizen," I said.

Willis Lansing was rifling through a rack of military uniforms. Anna patted my arm. "I'll be back after I see to Willis," she said.

"No, no," I said, swooshing her away. "That's okay. I'm okay. Really. Take care of your customer. I'll talk to you later." I examined my watch. I had just enough time to make my meeting with the Clayton County deputy. Arriving late would not put me in his good graces.

Chapter 3

On the way to the police station, I reminisced about how I had met Marty. When I first saw his house, it had loomed out of the Minnesota pine forest like a prop in a "B" horror-movie set. As I drove around the circular driveway, its gloomy image was heightened by the specter of unclipped, still spindly hollyhock skeletons drooping forlornly against the foundation. Above them, a peaked roof jutted over the stone sidewalk, like a crouching animal about to pounce.

I remember wondering how could I have lived in Colton Mills for almost a year and not known the place existed? I had checked the newspaper ad again: CARRIAGE HOUSE FOR RENT. WITH STUDIO. A two-story brick building stood about a hundred yards to the right of the main house. Ivy crept up one side toward its shake-shingled roof. It looked perfectly charming.

But getting to the "charming" entrance meant I had to walk up several wide wooden stairs. My five-feet-four inches weighed in at about 125 pounds, and I wasn't one to throw my weight around when I felt a little spooked. I had no more guts than the bear making up the rug under my coffee table, who regarded me glassy-eyed out of his beautiful six-foot-long pelt.

I stepped out of my Jeep and stared up at the house. For some inexplicable reason, it gave me the jitters. The stairs led to two curtained double doors opening onto to a shadowy front porch that wrapped around the front and east side. The vision of my studio apartment, tacked onto the end of a dingy hall above the hardware store, flashed through my mind. It was broad daylight on a lovely sunny day in a safe, post-card-perfect small town. What could possibly go wrong?

I ascended the stairs. The porch and steps were in good repair and freshly painted. A good sign. I rang the doorbell. No response. I tried it again. Still no response. From somewhere in the back, I heard a peculiar sound. *Thunk. Thunk. Thunk* I retreated down the stairs and crept along a stone walk that led to the back of the house. The walk ended at a weathered iron gate. I opened it and peered around a massive lilac bush that could have been planted when George Washington was a child.

Thunk.

A burly man was throwing an ax at a foot-thick ring cut from a massive tree, which he had propped up on its side. He took aim and flung one ax after another. Some stuck into the tree-trunk target, while others bumped off and flew into the bushes. He stopped throwing and went to retrieve the implements.

"Hello!" I called out. Not too loudly. If he didn't hear me, I could turn around, get into my vehicle, and forget I'd ever seen the house. But he had heard me. He turned and waited for me to speak. "I called earlier about the carriage house for rent," I yelled, never taking my eyes off him as he marched toward me.

Tall and well-built, he looked as if he could model for a middle-age Marine recruiting poster, if there were such a thing. A gray bushy beard framed his weathered face, suggesting he was as old as my father would probably be, but I had no way of knowing that. "I'm Marty Madigan," he said, extending a meaty hand over the gate. He had a deep, gravelly voice. His intense gray eyes didn't quite meet mine.

"Cassandra Cassidy," I said, grasping his hand.

Offering no explanation for his ax-throwing activity, he got right down to business. "Come this way." He led me back along the walk toward the carriage house, reciting history as he went. "The carriage house was built in 1880, the same time as the first part of the main house. Originally, it had three bays that provided housing for the Swanson family's carriages. That area has been converted into a modern garage. Olaf Swanson had the first and biggest flour mill near here and built this place five miles out of town, because he liked the view. He must have been a determined fellow to manage this kind of construction so far out."

"Sounds like he had a long, bumpy road to town for a sack of sugar."

Marty nodded, ignoring my attempt at humor, and continued with his commentary. "Swanson's flour mill was located in the area where the bridge crosses the Oxbow, about two miles toward town. The river was dammed up there to provide power for the mill. So, his place was really not that far from where he worked every day." He opened a side door that led into the garage and fingered the end of the exposed wall. "You won't find another building with brick walls this thick," he said, caressing the side of the wall. "I don't think a tank could take them down." He gestured around the interior of the garage. "Plenty of room here for a couple of vehicles." He turned in my direction, but still didn't meet my gaze. "How many do you have?"

"Just one," I said, nodding toward my ten-year-old Jeep sitting in the driveway.

"Well . . . that will leave plenty of room for storage. If you're a pack rat like me, you can never have enough room for storage."

The garage spanned the front of the building. A door at the rear led into a hall. Light filtered down from an open stairway at the end leading to the second floor. Another door led to what had been the harness room and was, for me, the clincher. The area had been converted for the former tenant into a darkroom. It was large enough for all my equipment and then some. I asked questions, such as whether the water was filtered. But I could already picture my enlarger on the shelf against the far wall.

"The tenant who left a couple of months ago was a nature photographer," Marty said, leaning against the door jamb. "He'd pack up and take off for weeks at a time. He finally decided to move further north, closer to the places where he took most of his pictures. He even produced a calendar that's sold in Books on Main." He glanced my way. "You take nature pictures?"

"Not on a regular basis." I chose not to elaborate. Somehow, taking wedding pictures paled next to Mr. Former Tenant's beautiful nature calendars for sale on Main Street.

We mounted the stairs and emerged into a bright, sunny loft. The wall opposite was white-painted brick, with a fireplace halfway down the wall. White ceilings arched toward a peaked roof that was punctuated with brown wooden beams running horizontally wall-to-wall, about three feet beneath the peak, producing a dramatic effect. Three skylights let in the afternoon sun, adding to the light filtering in from the oversized windows above the staircase. The sitting area blended into the narrow kitchen at the back of the room. A door led to the bedroom and another to a roomy studio/office, also lit by a skylight.

Resisting the urge to shout, "I'll take it!" I had put on my businesswoman's cap and strolled back through the kitchen, opening the refrigerator and checking out the dishwasher and cabinets. I didn't tell my soon-to-be landlord, but my mishmash of unmatched plates and mugs would barely fill one cabinet. My baking equipment—consisting of one flat round pan big enough to bake a frozen pizza—would be lost in the other cabinet, and I could fill one small drawer with my discount-store silverware and assorted kitchen tools. I inquired about heating and lighting costs.

Marty had listed those for me. "You can see it's move-in ready," he said.

"Yes, I see that." He hadn't known it at the time, but as long as the kitchen had an electrical outlet for the coffeepot and a microwave oven, it was move-in ready. "The lease on my downtown studio is up in a month, but I'd like to begin moving my things in here this weekend, if that's okay."

He had presented me with a lease. My prudent self had said I shouldn't sign it, but my audacious self had whipped out a pen, trumping the twinges that were running down my spine as I signed it.

Now, as I turned into the parking lot of the police station, I wondered if I had signed that lease a little too hastily. What did I really know about Marty, except that his favorite tomahawk had somehow found its way into Eric's scalp.

Chapter 4

Monday—Police Station

The murder hadn't made a big splash in Colton Mills, a hundred miles or so south of Clayton County. Regional TV ran a short clip on the Sunday night news and the Minneapolis paper had covered it briefly in its Monday edition.

Reporter Killed at Rendezvous Event

Eric Hartfield, a columnist for *Minnesota Issues Review*, was killed Sunday in Prairie River Township, at the site of the annual Prairie River Rendezvous. The Rendezvous is an annual event in which participants portray authentic characters of a nineteenth-century fur post.

Hartfield's body was discovered in a sweat lodge that had been erected by the Prairie River Band and periodically used for ceremonial purposes. The apparent weapon was a tomahawk of the kind that Rendezvous contestants use in tomahawk throwing competitions. The sheriff has not named any suspects.

So far, my name had not surfaced as the one who had discovered the body, and my hope was that I could remain unidentified. What I wanted most was for the sheriff to return the "tools" he had confiscated, because they held all my cameras and the envelopes of exposed film and CF cards.

When I arrived at the police station for my interview with the Clayton County deputy sheriff, the police directed me to, of all things, a bomb shelter under City Hall. "I'm Cassandra Cassidy," I said to the receptionist. "I'd like to see Deputy Shaw."

"Deputy Shaw?" A hint of amusement flashed across her fleshy face. "Oh, yes. You mean Deputy *Sheriff* Shaw." She punched the air above her head with her forefinger. "We're short of space in the police station and had to give him a room downstairs." She pointed to a staircase. "Take that to the basement, turn left when you get to the bottom of the stairs, and walk to the end of the hall. He'll be waiting for you."

The cold, clammy walls made me shiver despite the hot day outside. I wrapped my arms around myself and tried to relax on the flimsy folding chair where I sat next to a gritty little table. It was impossible, of course. My mind churned over the details of my experience, causing increased anxiety. When my name was called, I actually stumbled into the smaller cell-like room, which was furnished with nothing but two chairs and a decrepit wood table, about the size of a teacher's desk.

My expectations for a quick and routine interview were dashed in the first five minutes. The kindly deputy from the Rendezvous had been replaced by one with a Perry Mason complex. Far from being the personable small-town Barney Fife I expected, Deputy Sheriff Bertram Shaw went by the book. He had folded his scrawny six-foot frame onto a dusty wooden chair, his pen poised over a clipboard. Before he uttered a word to me, he rubbed his nose and made a face in reaction to the room's musty smell. Then, without any niceties, he began his questioning. "How did you came to move into the house next to Mr. Madigan?" His eyes were cold and his voice told me this was to be a no-nonsense interview. I peered over his shoulder to avoid making eye contact.

"I moved there because I liked the accommodations." My eyes caught sight of a spider web in the corner of the concrete room, directly behind his right shoulder. I wondered how long would it take the spider to drop onto the cardboard boxes stacked helter-skelter against the wall.

"Did you know Mr. Madigan prior to living in his rented house?"

"No, sir, I simply answered his ad in the paper."

"Did you ever see anyone coming or going to his house?"

"No, sir. I can't see what goes on at Marty's house from the carriage house."

"Were you ever concerned for your safety?"

Was I? The day I rented the place, it occurred to me I had signed a lease to live next to an ax-wielding landlord who lived in a remote house, five winding miles from the nearest town. "No sir, I can't say that I was. Nothing untoward has ever happened in the time I have lived there." I felt fidgety, for some reason, and drummed my fingernails on the table.

Shaw stared at them and seemed to lose his train of thought. "You're a photographer, I understand."

"Yes. I make my living selling the photographs I take." I shifted in my chair.

"Doesn't that involve carrying heavy equipment?"

"Sometimes."

Shaw rose from the chair and paced back and forth in the tight space. The dust from the chair clung to his black sheriff-uniform slacks, outlining his skeletal buttocks. I forced myself not to giggle hysterically. "You must be . . . shall we say . . . a strong lady, to haul all that equipment on a regular basis."

I glanced up at him to gauge his intention with such a question. His gaze raked across my body. "I'm strong enough, I guess."

"Do you do anything special and deliberate . . . to keep fit?"

"I lift weights."

He scribbled a notation on his clipboard and then, without warning, leaned over the table to stare into my eyes. "How well did you know the deceased?"

Taken aback by his closeness and abrupt switch in subjects, I shrunk back in my chair. "Eric? I . . . I knew him only on a professional basis."

"Is that so. Hmm." He was silent for several seconds and then slowly lowered himself onto the chair opposite me again, crossing one leg over the other with equally slow deliberation. "Apparently, you knew him well enough to engage in a rather strident argument at the Rendezvous."

I bit back a defensive retort. It finally dawned on me that Sheriff Shaw was treating me like a suspect. Should I refuse to answer his questions? Or would that look like I had something to do with the crime? I felt like a character in a gangster movie. Make that a gangster cartoon . . . Simpsons-style. I was in a windowless basement bomb shelter being grilled by a brusque-speaking sheriff's deputy. Ironically, the scene even included the ubiquitous light bulb dangling from the ceiling.

"Did you or did you not threaten Mr. Hartfield with bodily harm, Miss Cassidy?" The deputy's jaw muscles worked overtime in his hairless baby face.

"I'm sorry. I . . . I'm not sure what you're talking about." I squirmed on my chair.

"Of course you do. Several witnesses heard you say you would harm Mr. Hartfield, if you ever saw him again."

I was momentarily speechless, as my shouting match with Eric returned in vivid memory. It was merely the kind of stuff angry people say in a moment of passion. It wasn't real, but evidently when a murder has been committed only minutes later, chit-chat takes on a life of its own.

Shaw was becoming impatient.

"Well . . . what would *you* say, if someone told you to 'watch your back'?"

"*I* ask the questions, Miss Cassidy, and I'm waiting for your reply."

I lowered my head and stroked the scar on my neck. Before I could utter another word, the door opened. "Excuse me, sir, there's someone here to see Miss Cassidy." A uniformed policeman gestured toward my interrogator. "Sheriff, if you please, you may wait out here."

Sheriff Shaw stalked out of the room, and a slender man dressed in a dark blue-striped business suit entered to take his place. He shut the door, took in the room at one quick glance, smoothed down his thin mustache that matched a full head of striking white hair, and finally smiled at me. Probably in his late sixties, he didn't appear frustrated by the surroundings. He extended his hand and presented me with a business card. "Cassandra Cassidy, I presume?" His speech was precise and firm.

I nodded.

"I am Lawton Sanders, your attorney," he said. "Anna sent me."

Chapter 5

Tuesday

Monday's interview had left me rattled. I wondered what direction Shaw's questioning would have taken, if Attorney Lawton Sanders hadn't shown up. I would be eternally grateful to Anna for sending her brother to me. Sanders had called at the crack of dawn and was in my kitchen with his briefcase open, ready for business. "At this point in the investigation, *anyone* connected with the crime scene is actually a suspect," he said, spelling out my predicament and attempting to relieve my fears.

"But, how could Sheriff Shaw possibly think I am the one who murdered Eric?" I shoved a mug of coffee toward him and sipped at my own. "I've never even *held* a tomahawk, let alone thrown one. I'd never been to a reenactment before either, and I had no idea hatchet-throwers would be competing. He didn't ask me any of those questions. What about Marty? It was *his* tomahawk in Eric's skull. *He's* the one Shaw should be questioning, not me."

Sanders' gaze was steady, his voice calming. "I'm sure he's questioning Marty, too, and he'll reach the conclusion that you couldn't possibly be the murderer, when all the facts are in." He pulled out a legal pad. "Now, if you want me to act as your attorney, start at the beginning and tell me exactly what happened from the time you entered the Rendezvous grounds."

Minutes later, he stuffed the legal pad into his briefcase. "I'll field any media questions, Cassandra. Also, when the deputy contacts you again, refer him to me. Don't do any talking to anyone, unless I am present."

That seemed like an impossible order, but I nodded anyway. As soon as Sanders left, I paced the floor. I don't handle uncommon stress well. I handle stress with chemicals. The darkroom kind. The digital revolution consigned some photographers' darkrooms to antique status, but I used mine often . . . whenever I wanted an effect I couldn't get through my computer software. I decided that concentrating on the development of the black and white photos from Heather's wedding might help me think more clearly. I headed directly to my darkroom, thankful, once again, that the carriage house had come equipped with such a luxury.

As I plunged developer paper into the chemical baths, my mind raced through the possibilities. The sheriff would investigate my past combative connection with Eric. Worse, he would take my so-called threatening statement at the Rendezvous seriously . . . especially since I was the one who found Eric dead minutes later. Who else hated Eric as much as I did? Marty? Did he even know Eric? One thing I knew for sure about my landlord . . . as his war experiences attested, he was capable of killing. And, he had attended the Rendezvous, as he had for many years, he was an expert with tomahawks, and it was his so-called "lost" 'hawk that felled Eric in the sweat lodge.

As soon as that thought entered my mind, I brushed it aside. It would be stupid for any sane killer to use an easily identifiable weapon to commit a crime. Not only that, it would be equally stupid for someone intent upon murder to be seen by so many people at nearly the same time the crime was occurring. Marty wasn't stupid.

A million other thoughts crowded my focus on developing quality prints for Heather. I couldn't begin to sort it all out all the details, but I intended to make an effort. Passively waiting for someone else to solve my dilemma wasn't my style. At least it hadn't been my style since Mrs. A had taken me under her wing.

* * *

When I was about the age of four, I was placed in foster care. I wasn't sure how or why, because people have always been light on the specifics. In fact, almost secretive. I have some hazy moments of memory when pictures of people—maybe my parents—swim into my consciousness, unrecognizable and contorted, like figures swimming underwater. Why was I separated from them? Were they still alive and somewhere without me? Did they ever wonder about where I was and what I was doing? Did they know that I had been shifted from one home to another for ten years?

I was the Browns' little girl, until Mrs. Brown became too ill to care for me, and I was snatched away to join the Youngmans. I remember the Youngmans. In order to fit into their household, I had to coexist with Peggy, their precious princess of a daughter. When anything went wrong, it was always my fault. The final straw came when Peggy lifted money from her mother's purse and shifted the blame to me. Before the week was out, and despite my protestations of innocence, I was on my way to live with another family. It became a pattern— packing up and traipsing to another house of strangers. I'd have to deal with new schools, having no friends, and trying to establish a relationship with faux siblings, recreating myself to fit into each new situation.

I moved often, until Mrs. Andrews accepted me as her foster daughter. I was thirteen. By then, I had adapted to so many different families and situations I felt like a chameleon . . . with multiple personalities. Over the years, my once sunny disposition had completely eroded. I no longer expected good things to happen. I had withdrawn into a wimpy, scared little rabbit.

Most people called my new foster mother crazy. She was certainly different from your typical PTA-type mom. I can see her still, stalking J C Penney's on the trail of the perfect pair of stretch pants. Not just any stretch pants. Following her own fashion drummer, she favored anything with purple and red in it. Flowers, stripes, solids; it didn't matter, as long as it was purple and red. Even with my stunted fashion sense, I perceived she was a bit over the top in her wardrobe choices. I groaned whenever she put the stretch fabric to its ultimate test, pulling the pants up over her lumpy thighs. As if that weren't bad enough, she paired the pants with pink or green patterned shirts.

My foster mom teased her gray hair into a mini-mountain, shellacked it in place with hair spray, and then applied her makeup mask . . . heavy on the mascara, a generous swipe of deep-plum lipstick, and matching blobs of blusher on both cheeks. She thumbed her nose at social conventions of all sorts. I never figured out how she was accepted as a foster parent. But if she hadn't been—and if I hadn't been sent to live with her—I'd have ended up on welfare or in prison, as did so many foster home "graduates." By the time I got to Mrs. A's, I was the ideal target for anyone who wanted to test his mettle on a pushover. She sent me to school in clothes that attracted the class bullies like a three-legged rabbit did a coyote. When they found out I was a foster child, it gave them even more ammunition.

One day, however, my personality got a transplant. Whenever I got off the school bus, the kids' jeers followed me as I shuffled toward home, my chin meeting my chest. "Prairie chicken!" they taunted. "Cluck, cluck, cluck." And I suppose I did look like one. I was dressed that particular day in an oversized flowered dress with clunky shoes and white socks—Mrs. A's idea of how an eighth grader dressed. "Cassandra is a reject," one of them shouted, singsong-style, while hanging out the bus window. "Her parents didn't want her. Her parents didn't want her."

Mrs. A heard them. She brought me into the house, sat me down, and forced me to tell her what was going on. I tearfully related how I was continuously ridiculed me about my clothes and my family. "My dear," she said, "it's my fault about the clothes." She wiped the tears from my face. "We'll shop tonight for some updated duds. Then we'll talk about how you're going to defend yourself against these playground Nazis."

The very next day, I put her first lesson to the test. "Hey, look, it's old sourpuss," Tommy the Tormentor taunted, approaching me on the playground with two other boys in tow. "Hey, sourpuss, ain'tcha ever gonna smile!"

Feeling more confident in my newly purchased Levi's and Lacrosse shirt, I sucked in a deep breath, lifted my head, and spit out what I'd rehearsed in front of my mirror. "I don't know what makes you so stupid, Tommy, but it really works!" The little bully opened his mouth to retort, but before he could say anything more, I straightened up and delivered the junior high equivalent of a *coup de grace*. "You've got the personality of a bowling ball!"

It wasn't a David Letterman comeback, but I had learned the power of verbal bravado, thanks to Mrs. A. I have never forgotten her words of wisdom. "All you have to do is utter courageous words, Cassandra. The courage itself will follow."

My smart mouth put enough starch in my backbone to get me through the rest of my childhood and teenage traumas and, by adulthood, I was as well adjusted as the next person. Feeling the presence of Mrs. A and hearing her guidance was as effective as any session with a $200-an-hour psychiatrist. The only time a crack appeared in my carefully constructed identity was when stress reared its ugly head as the result of a conflict I was powerless to resolve.

That was the kind of stress I was experiencing right now, in Colton Mills, Minnesota. It wasn't that I didn't have confidence in my attorney. I was simply accustomed to taking matters into my own hands. For some reason, I felt deep in my bones that Sheriff Shaw would rather make me the hatchet murderer than spend time searching for another possible suspect. I sensed he'd stay on me like Velcro on wool. Circumstantial evidence is a powerful convincer. I was the only one who knew for certain that I wasn't the bad guy. Even though it required skills that weren't on my résumé, I knew I'd have to play amateur detective. The best place to start my investigation was with Marty.

That was easier said than done. I had paid no attention to Marty's comings and goings. I hadn't even seen him, from the time I moved into the carriage house until our paths crossed at the Rendezvous. On a normal day, I spent half my working time keeping appointments and the other half in my office or darkroom. The activities of my landlord never came to mind.

I examined the quality of the photographs I had been laboring over and dumped them all into the trashcan. Trying to work, while worrying about my future, had been a total waste of time and energy. It was a good thing Heather was still on her honeymoon and wasn't expecting finished prints anytime soon. As I exited the darkroom, I snapped off the red ceiling light and slammed the door behind me, thinking I should become a reenactor myself and specialize in 'hawk throwing. The skill might come in handy.

Chapter 6

Tuesday Evening

Since it was still early, I decided to make use of the evening to fulfill another commitment. My next wedding gig was to take place at Patriot Stables, and I needed to check the layout. It would be fun to be around horses again. They liked me and didn't talk back.

By the time I reached the stables, it was after seven in the evening. I strolled through the barn, clipboard in hand, as I scouted places to effectively pose the bridal party. I took my time, stopping now and then to inhale the fragrant aroma of hay and listen to the comforting sounds of horses placidly munching their evening meal. The peaceful ambiance took me back to the Evening Star Stables in southwest Minnesota, where I had first started my love for all things "horse" by mucking stalls at the age of seventeen. By the time I was eighteen, I was exercising the horses and, eventually, halter-training the owners' colts. Those hours in the stable brought a little sanity into my life.

I made notes on my clipboard and stepped outside the stables, ready to head back home. Suddenly, a familiar crackling sound caught my attention. Fire? I stepped toward the noise and my nose immediately registered "smoke." Within seconds, I saw flames shooting into the air. I clutched the notes to my chest and dashed back into the barn, falling into a crumpled heap on a bale of hay. Frozen in place and with my eyes tightly closed, I shivered uncontrollably.

Without warning, I felt someone shaking me. "Hey, hey, it's okay. Stop screaming! The fire's out." A man pulled me to my feet.

Still trembling, I pushed the hair out of my eyes and composed myself. "I-I'm all right. I'm all right," I said, sucking in a huge breath of air and expelling it through pursed lips.

"All it needed was a fire extinguisher," the stranger said, sitting me down again on the bale of hay. "Some ignorant cuss tossed a half-burned cigarette into a pile of loose hay and didn't stomp it out. I find out who and the guy's history. Wait here a sec and I'll be right back. I want to make sure there aren't any embers left to do more damage." He strode over to the barn hydrant for a pail of water to throw on the still smoking mess.

I stood up again and found my knees were still wobbling. Frustrated, I shook them one at a time. I wanted to leave, before I'd have to explain my reaction to the easily contained fire.

The cowboy returned, with a swagger and a grin. "Now that you're better, we can start over," he said. Slimly built, he was attired in jeans, boots, and a well-worn cowboy hat. His gaze traveled over me briefly, before meeting mine. "I thought I'd met all the pretty gals around here." He looked me up and down again. "Yes, ma'am, you sure do those jeans justice."

The voice, the lame pickup line, and even the swagger were familiar to me. I tilted my head and studied him. "Jack?" I squinted and shaded my eyes from the glare of the setting sun with a cupped hand. "Well, for . . . you're Jack Gardner!"

He pulled off his cowboy hat and bowed. "The one and only. Am I lucky enough to know this lovely lady?" He stroked his cheeks while thinking and closed his eyes. They flew open and his grin widened into a dazzling smile. "Cassandra Cassidy—all grown up, with short, curly hair?"

Our responses tumbled out in stereo. "I thought you were in New York," he said, at the same time I said, "I thought you were in Texas."

"You go first." I waggled my fingers at him.

"I've been stable manager and trainer here for six months," he said. "Wrangling cows was fun for a few years, but I was getting busted up down in Laredo."

Laredo. That explained the twang he'd acquired since I knew him, and probably the slight limp, too. I had noticed it, when he walked toward me. "I take it Texas ranch horses aren't like pampered Minnesota Arabians."

"You got that right." He sighed and lifted his finger to tip his hat off his forehead. "They laid injuries on me too numerous to mention. But I didn't get *too* busted up, if you know what I mean." He winked and rested an arm on one of the barn's vertical supports right behind me.

Still an incorrigible flirt, Jack couldn't help himself. The minor-league pitch he'd perfected years ago was still working for him. At one time, it would have landed in my strike zone, but, now, it wasn't even in the ball park. I'd eaten up the cowboy lothario line when I was his fling *du jour* one forgettable summer in our younger days. But . . . even though the romantic attraction had worn off, I couldn't help but appreciate the figure he cut in his form-fitting Wranglers. "Exactly what do you do here?" I asked.

"I mostly train Quarter Horses and teach some roping."

"Roping?"

"Yeah, roping," he said, "I gained a pretty good roping reputation in Texas and have some belt buckles and even a fancy saddle to prove it. How about you? You sure haven't changed much after all these years. The braids are gone, but I'd know those blue eyes anywhere." I had brown eyes. "I heard you went off to New York to study art or something." He glanced toward the horse stalls and lowered his voice. "I heard you got, you know, married."

Since my circle of acquaintances was small, I was very seldom confronted about my past. But here it was. "I was in New York for a while. To study photography, not art. As for marriage, well . . ." I peered over his shoulder toward the approaching darkness behind the opened barn door.

"Well?" Jack prompted.

I shrugged. "Let's just say marriage to a musician isn't all it's cracked up to be."

"So you ended it?"

I reached for my clipboard, which had fallen to the floor of the stables and swept clinging straw with my hand. "Sort of. He went on a tour out west and didn't come back."

"Geez, that's too bad, Cass. Then you came back to Minnesota?"

"I missed the place." I smoothed my hair. Could my stomach be fluttering? Annoyed with myself, I asked, "So how come you're working here so late?"

"I was practicing with the Patrol and just got back."

"Patrol? That would be the—"

"The Mounted Horse Patrol. I rode with them years ago. They had an opening this spring and I joined up again. Sometimes I serve as a reserve deputy sheriff."

I pictured Jack as a county crime fighter on horseback. My recollection of the Horse Patrol was that most of the riders spent their time touring the county fairs in the summer or searching for the occasional lost or missing person. "Sounds like fun."

"It is. Actually, I'm at the stables to play veterinarian. Midnight, one of the horses stabled here, cut a big gash in his leg when he kicked out a piece of the wood fence in the south pasture. I have to treat the injury a couple times a day."

"That black gelding over there?" I pointed to its stall. "I noticed him when I was snooping around. Will he be okay?"

"He'll be himself again in a week, ten days."

"How come you're nursing him? Where's the owner?"

"He belonged to a girl who died not too long ago. Her father keeps up the board, but nobody has ridden Midnight or paid him much attention in months."

"Bummer," I said. Then I remembered a conversation I'd had the previous week with one of my wedding clients. "I might know someone who'd be interested in the horse. Let me know if he's for sale."

"Sure, I'll check it out." He crossed his long legs and leaned his backside against the wall, chewing the end of a hay stem. "Anything exciting in your life these days?"

Anything exciting in my life. Talk about understatement. I took a deep breath. "I'll give you the short version," I said, and related the events of the past few days. "You hadn't heard about any of this?"

"Not a word. But I don't have much time to follow the local news." He narrowed his eyes. "By any chance, does that bad experience at the Rendezvous have anything to do with your reaction to the fire I just put out?"

"It's a lifetime phobia," I said, massaging the scar on my neck. "Fires terrify me."

"That was pretty obvious." He walked beside me, as I headed for my car. "You know, Cass, Prairie Township is my old stomping grounds. For what it's worth, some of my buddies are deputy sheriffs there. Keep me informed about what's going on. You may need some help."

When I didn't respond, he continued. "I'm holding a cutting clinic on Thursday afternoon. Why don't you stop by?"

Despite my reluctance to expand our re-acquaintanceship, my "photographic opportunity" antenna went up. Cutting cows was a regular chore at real working ranches and catching on as a sport in Minnesota. I could pad my photo portfolio with some horse-action shots that could eventually turn into "hay." Not one to turn down the thought of making more money, I nodded and even managed to grin. "Thanks for the invitation, Jack. I might stop by," I said. I slipped under his arm, which was holding the door to my Jeep, and slid onto the driver's seat. "At any rate, I may see you when I hold my next wedding photo shoot here."

* * *

Wednesday

Lawton Sanders called me bright and early Wednesday morning with jarring news I could have done without. "Deputy Sheriff Shaw would like to interview you again," he said. "Today."

I slumped against the wall of my kitchen. "That guy doesn't sit well with me. Do I have to go?"

"I'm afraid you do," he said. "I'll be there, too. Shaw asked for a meeting this afternoon. Is that too soon for you?"

I sighed. "No, that's fine. Let's get it over with."

This time, the police had managed to free up a regular interrogation room. No more questioning in the basement bomb shelter. However, the more conventional surroundings didn't make Deputy Sheriff Shaw any more pleasant. He greeted us curtly and launched right into his questions. "Did you know where your landlord, Mr. Madigan, kept his tomahawks?" He chewed on the inside of his bottom lip.

"No, sir," I said.

"You said you observed him throwing tomahawks in his backyard prior to the tournament. Is that right?"

"Yes, sir. I did see him practice with a couple the first day I met him, but I was focused on the possibility of—"

"Then you're saying you *did* know about his tomahawk throwing." Shaw nibbled on the inside of his left cheek this time.

"Not really. Not to the extent you—" I glanced at Sanders, who barely nodded.

"And you live directly next door to Mr. Madigan, on the same property. Is that correct?"

"Yes, sir."

"So, theoretically, you would have access to his tomahawks, since he stores them outside his dwelling and in a shed near the carriage house."

"Well, theoretically, I suppose." I glanced at Sanders again and wished he would stop the questioning.

Shaw flipped to another page on his notepad. "Did you know Mr. Madigan would be at the Rendezvous?"

"How could I have known that, if I never saw him and hadn't talked with him since the day I signed the lease for my apartment?"

Shaw slapped the table with his hand. "*I* ask the questions, Miss Cassidy. I repeat, did you know he would be at the Rendezvous?"

"No, sir, I didn't."

"Did you acquire a list of the participants in the 'hawk-throwing competition?"

"When I entered the gate of the Rendezvous, I was given a schedule of events and locations."

"Then you *did* know your landlord would be a tomahawk-throwing participant."

"*No*," I countered. "The participants' names were listed in their Rendezvous character names. I had no idea what his Rendezvous name was . . . or anyone else's."

Shaw made a notation on his clipboard. "You've photographed Indians for several years, haven't you?"

"Yes, sir."

"Ever photograph Indians throwing tomahawks?"

"Not that I remember, but—"

"Is this your photo?" He held up an eight-by-ten photo.

I took the picture from him and studied it. "It could be."

"And what is the subject of the photo?"

"An Indian throwing a tomahawk."

"Now do you remember where and when you took it?" The look on Shaw's face indicated I'd better remember, or else.

"I photograph many Indians at many events. This one . . . escapes my mind."

"It escapes your mind." Shaw made a few more notes on his clipboard and peered up at me without moving his head. "How well do you know Frank Kyopa, the head of the Prairie River Band, Miss Cassidy?"

I glanced at Sanders, who was scribbling notes of his own. Shaw's question had startled me. "I . . . I see him fairly often at the Indian events I attend, and I've photographed him a few times."

"And . . . how would you characterize your relationship?"

"No 'relationship,'" I said. "I know him enough to greet him, if we're at the same event, and to photograph him at the various public events we attend. He would recognize who I am and he has purchased some of my photographs."

"Don't you know him well enough to testify on his behalf . . . *against* Eric Hartfield?"

I sighed inwardly, hating for my interrogator to see me feeling rattled. I shouldn't be surprised that he had done his homework. Expecting more questions about my court testimony, I fidgeted with the ring on my right hand, glad that my shaking hands were hidden under the table. "Can you explain to me how your hair was found on Hartfield's body?"

"My hair *couldn't* have been on Eric's body!" I said, literally sputtering.

Now Shaw had my attorney's attention. Sanders peered closely at the deputy. "You've got proof, I assume?"

"Initial investigation strongly suggests it's Miss Cassidy's," Shaw said. "We'll know the results when the lab work comes in." Shaw pushed back his chair and slammed his notebook closed. "We are still in the investigative phase, Miss Cassidy, but I'd strongly suggest you don't leave town. Our questioning isn't over. Not by a long shot." He glanced briefly at Sanders and left the room.

I rubbed my temples. A massive headache was already in progress. "Do you have any idea what that was all about, Lawton? I felt like I was on trial."

Sanders packed up his notes. "He's definitely playing hardball," he said. "But I think he's fishing."

His reassuring words offered small comfort. Feeling decidedly defeated, I shuffled out of the police station, feeling for all the world like an already convicted felon.

* * *

Running full speed on my treadmill, an hour later, somewhat calmed me down. At least enough to think rationally. I had run the interview through my mind several times. Things weren't looking good for me. The only thing I had going for me was that Shaw hadn't yet arrested me. Nevertheless, I was still free to figure out the real killer. I had to find out more about Marty. That was a given. Anna had told me his wife had left him, never to be heard from again. In light of recent events, I wondered if she had left him, or if he had something to do with her turning up missing. The idea that Marty may not be the victim in his wife's disappearance, but the one who caused it intrigued me. If he could do in his wife and son, he could certainly kill Eric. But why? What could his motive possibly be? Motive was key.

After clocking five miles, I still hadn't come up with a plausible way to conduct my investigation. I wasn't accustomed to snooping into people's lives, but my own was at stake. I'd have to get over any reticence I had.

Jack, of all people, gave me my first lead. I was pretty sure that I hadn't heard the last of him. I had opened too many opportunities for him to insert himself into a murder investigation, especially when the female who hadn't responded positively to his charms was knee-deep in the outcome. His call came as soon as I hopped off the treadmill.

"Hey, Cassandra, are you still trying to find out what you can about your landlord, Marty?"

"Well, yes, I guess so," I said.

"I might be able to help you out." Jack sounded cheery and confident.

"You know him?"

"Not personally, but my friend Randy works with him in the city's emergency services department. He's told me that Marty has a hot temper. I'll set up a meeting with him tomorrow, if you want."

"That would be great, Jack. Thanks. And Jack . . . let's not tell anyone I'm doing this. All right with you?"

"Sure. No problem. I aim to please."

Chapter 7

Thursday

I woke up the next morning drenched in perspiration again. I had experienced the same dream that had plagued me for years. I was being carried, kicking and screaming from a fire. The fire was so real, I could feel the heat and smell the smoke. I could even feel the rawness in my throat from crying and breathing deadly fumes.

As a child, I would wake up crying when the dream came. Now, I wake up in a sweat, relieved to know it's only a dream. I would keep the dream in the "fantasy" category, except the scar on my neck continuously reminds me that the fire may not be only in my imagination. Even though no one has ever said, "I know a fire separated you from your parents," I know I'll never get the dream to go away until, someday, I smoke out the story behind it.

But not today. And probably not tomorrow. I was used to me the way I was. If I threw real parents into the mix, I'd have to recreate myself . . . again.

I was drinking my second cup of coffee, trying to put my dream behind me, when Lawton Sanders rang my doorbell.

"Cassandra, the sheriff's department has issued a warrant to search your house," he said.

"When and what for?"

"They're searching for anything that might help them in their investigation. I advise you to cooperate with them."

"Can I expect to see the deputy sheriff from hell again?"

Sanders gave me a stern look. "Don't underestimate Deputy Shaw, Cassandra. His kind can be very dangerous."

"Why's that?"

His frown deepened and his gaze became more intense. "A low-ranking, but ambitious law-enforcement officer looks forward to making his reputation on a case such as yours. He may be much more aggressive than seasoned members of the force and read much more into so-called evidence that he uncovers. The police humiliated him when they put him in the basement for your initial interview. He's got a lot to prove."

I ushered my attorney into the living room. "I still can't believe Shaw has his sights set on me. If he read that entire case against Eric, he'd know all I did was use my expertise to show that the incriminating photograph had been doctored."

"He's young, and he's playing the odds. He knows that the person who discovers a victim is often the person who perpetrated the crime. I expect you'll hear much more from him."

Right on cue, the doorbell rang. "I have a warrant to search your premises," Shaw said, when I opened the door.

"Be my guest," I said, accepting the warrant and sweeping my arm into the house to motion him inside. What could he find? I had no stash of tomahawks. No bloody clothes. No weapons. He was wasting his time.

Nevertheless, it was hard to keep from worrying, as Shaw and his crony pawed through my cabinets and pulled items off the shelves. As soon as they were gone, I'd launder every item of clothing they touched and thoroughly clean the whole place. My only consolation was knowing they'd find nothing incriminating.

Two hours later, Shaw asked for access to my computer. The request had the effect of slapping me upside my smug, complacent head. Eric Hartfield had not only tweaked me in person every chance he got, but he'd sent me irritating e-mails whenever the spirit moved him—or whenever my Indian photos were in the newspaper or on TV. I led Shaw to my upstairs office and opened my computer. I had deleted the majority of Eric's e-mails, but there were enough left that when Shaw found them, he thought he'd hit the Big Bear casino jackpot. I read the first two from the monitor:

Date: Mon, 14 Jun 18:14:54 -0500
To: Cassandra Cassidy <ccas@yahoo.net>
From: Eric Hartfield
<ehartfield@hotmail.com>
Subject: Sunday's Star Tribune review

CCAS: Read Sunday's review of
your latest. Some reviewers are
too easy to impress. <<Powerful
and irresistibly moving.>> What
a bunch of tripe.

Date: Sat, 28 Aug 21:11:23 -0500
To: Cassandra Cassidy <ccas@yahoo.net>
From: Eric Hartfield
<ehartfield@hotmail.com>
Subject: Another fool's been sucked in

CCAS: I have walls that are more intelligent
than the guy who wrote that <<there's not a
false or sentimental image anywhere in this

show.>> Have they all fallen for the <<Noble
Savage>> crap.

I thanked my lucky stars I'd had the sense not to enter into a
cyberspace shouting match with Eric and had never responded to
his messages; there were no threats from me to Eric in my outbox.
However, I did live to regret my habit of storing files on my
computer to avoid paper clutter. Shaw immediately pounced on a
folder I'd foolishly entitled ERIC and added more arrows to his
growing mass of evidence. Right there, in plain sight, was a years'
worth of Eric's columns.

Shaw's face was virtually gleaming with this discovery. By
the time he'd copied those articles and e-mails onto CD-R disks
he'd brought with him, I felt tried, convicted, and sent up for the
murder of Eric Hartfield.

"Damn!" I said to Sanders, after Shaw and his buddy had left.
I threw a displaced pillow back onto the sofa. *"Damn* him! My
lovely, comfortable carriage house will never be the same, now
that it has been dirtied by Shaw pawing through my personal
belongings. How could I have allowed myself to be so
blindsided?"

"Keep telling yourself this is routine business, Cassandra. You
know you're innocent and so do I. Trust me to do my job and
don't let Shaw draw you into a verbal war." He headed for the
front door. "I'm going back to my office now. I'll keep my eyes
and ears open."

As soon as he had left, I furiously sprayed shelves with a
household cleanser, spritzed furniture with polish, and did
whatever it took to wipe away all vestiges of the deputies'
intrusion into my life. I couldn't help but think of all the television
shows I'd seen where innocent citizens had been railroaded for
murder, only to be exonerated years later. Could that happen to

me? I wouldn't let it. I'd conduct my own investigation and beat Shaw to the punch.

Jack's friend, Randy Pearce, was meeting me at Leo's Bar at noon. It was a good place to start.

* * *

Leo's Bar was like a hundred other roadhouses strung out along Minnesota's rural roads. The one-story building hugged a row of spindly pine trees. Its walls were a nondescript gray that looked as though they hadn't been repainted since the building was erected thirty years before. The windows were filled with the ubiquitous neon beer signs and appeared dreary in the noonday sun. Only three pickup trucks were parked in the gravel lot.

I knew who Randy was as soon as I entered the place. Tall and slender and decked out in jeans and boots, he could have been a Jack Gardner clone, except for his shy demeanor. He couldn't meet my eyes when I introduced myself and shook his hand. I prattled on, trying to put him at ease, after we were seated across from each other in a red, cracked-vinyl booth. "Are you self-employed like I am, so you can get time off in the middle of the day?" I sipped my fourth cup of coffee for the day.

"Self-employed. Guess that's a fancy way of sayin' I work when there's work to be had."

Sensing Randy's reluctance to engage in small talk, I cut to the chase. "Do you sometimes work with Marty Madigan?"

"I drive the ambulance for the city. That's one of my jobs." He picked at his fingernails. "It's pretty chancy work. You don't need an ambulance every day in a place like Colton Mills."

I waited without speaking, as he took a drink of his Coors.

"Now, Madigan, he's another sort altogether." He glanced at me briefly, then focused on the suds topping his beer. "Not like us grunts, workin' for a livin'. He shows up only when the rescue operation needs a chopper. You know . . . after a bad accident, when someone has to be flown to a big-city hospital. That's the only time I see the guy. We're not like friends or nothin' like that." He attentively wiped the condensation from his beer bottle.

The waitress heated up my coffee. "So . . . you drive the ambulance—"

"I see Marty, maybe three, four times in a year." He played with his napkin, twisting it around his finger.

"Is he easy to work with?"

"He's a grumpy kind of guy, know what I mean?" He glanced at me again. "Maybe he don't mean nothin' by it, but he can be rude as hell. And demandin'." He motioned for the waitress to bring him another bottle of Coors.

"Like when?"

"The last time, I thought he was gonna throw a punch at one of the EMTs." He took a long swig from the bottle.

"Why? What happened?"

Randy rested his elbows on the table and leaned toward me, making eye contact for the first time. "It was an accident out on County Road 113. Remember it? Middle of the winter? Colder 'n a witch's tit."

"I can only imagine."

He dropped his gaze and ran a finger around the rim of the beer bottle "A mother and her son went off the road and plowed into a snow fence. Both had to be airlifted out of there. We had the two bundled up when Madigan set his chopper down in the road. The guy insisted on seein' their faces before he'd take 'em on board."

"Was that a problem?"

Randy folded his arms and leaned back in the booth, gazing in my general direction. "I'd say so. They'd been bandaged up and

64

covered to keep from gettin' frost bite and goin' into shock. Usual thing is to just load 'em up and fly the chopper to the hospital. Every minute counts. You know?"

"So what happened?" I leaned toward him to make sure I caught every word.

"Madigan kinda spazzed out." He rubbed his forehead. "He's a big guy, you know? He pulled his arm back like he was gonna hit the EMT guy, then yanked the cover off the woman, took a quick look, and told the EMT to load 'em up."

"Was the EMT concerned that Marty might not transport them safely?"

"Well, yeah, but he wasn't about to challenge him. He's got the only chopper for miles around. Nobody's gonna make Marty mad."

"Thank you for telling me about this, Randy. I really appreciate it." I reached into my pocket and handed him my business card. "Just in case you think of anything else," I said.

All by itself, Marty's behavior probably did seem strange, but if his family really did disappear without his knowledge, maybe he was still focused on searching for them. As much as anyone else, I knew the powerful pull family can have on a person. While Marty had a family and lost it, I remembered a time when I didn't have a family and yearned for one.

Foster mothers would tell me, "Any day now, a family is going to swoop you up and take you home for their very own!" What I really wanted was for my own parents to come back and reclaim me. I imagined them "somewhere." Whenever I went into a public place, I looked for my "real parents." I'd check out every passing couple and listened to how they talked to each other or to their kids. I even studied their eyes, to see if they were like mine. But every year, my fantasy family faded further into the background, and months passed into years. Over and over again, I packed my meager belongings and moved on to another foster family's house. Always abruptly. Always without discussion.

I remembered the oft-repeated scenario, as if it were yesterday. My social worker would come to school to pick me up. She'd take me out to her car, and my clothes would be there, in plastic bags. Once, I was allowed to keep a toy stuffed horse I'd gotten for a birthday. But in ten years, I didn't own anything that couldn't be put into a Hefty bag.

One day, I started looking forward to a permanent new family, not backward to the ones who'd abandoned me. As each placement ended, I would think that maybe the next one was the real family, the real mother, the real place I could stay forever. I still had my stuffed horse with me when the concept of "family" took on a whole new meaning. Mrs. A took me in and kept me with her until she died, when I was seventeen. I knew I was luckier than most of the foster kids I had bunked with over the years. I had four years of "family." I had my own closet in my own bedroom filled with clothes Mrs. A had bought me. Soon, I was living the way I imagined "regular" kids lived—in a life filled with swimming lessons, picnics in the park, and pedaling a new bike through the streets. Because Mrs. A had no other family, it was always only the two of us, and I hoped the arrangement would never end. Mrs. A encouraged me to forget my past.

I thought about what I knew of Marty Madigan. Maybe he was still locked into his past, fixated on events that had occurred nearly forty years ago. Had his sadness or bitterness driven him to such anger that he'd kill the person who got in his way? Had Eric uncovered something about his past that he wanted kept buried? I wanted—needed—to know.

Chapter 8

Thursday mid-afternoon

On the way back from my meeting with Randy, I stopped in at Sanders' office. He had persuaded the sheriff's department to make a second copy of the photos they'd confiscated from me. He not only had my cameras and several fat envelopes of color prints, he also had an envelope with the photos from my digital camera copied onto a compact disc. Once again, I thanked God and Anna for sending Sanders to me. If I had depended on my own resources, I would probably never have seen the pictures again.

At home, an hour later, I loaded the disc into my computer and clicked through some of the photos. Images of people having a good time at the Rendezvous filled my screen and I forgot, for a moment, the last horrendous one taken at the door to the sweat lodge. When I flipped through the color prints, I stared at it, trying to see and remember any details that might provide a clue as to the identity of the murderer. When nothing seemed out of place, I gave up and stashed the photos in a folder in my file cabinet for future reference.

Since it was only 2:35 p.m., I decided to take Jack up on his invitation to visit his cutting clinic. The smell of horses and saddle leather had always been a good way to re-ground myself and I was ready for a diversion. Too much deep thinking was decidedly depressing.

I didn't mind that the sky was overcast as I drove to Patriot Stables, because cloudy skies always produce more interesting photos. Already in a "downcast" mood, I wasn't about to let the lack of brilliant sun deepen my gloominess. I focused on the types of photographs I could produce. By the time I reached the stables, my disposition had changed considerably. I was the always interested professional.

Several horse trailers, still hitched to their pickups, were parked in the field surrounding the fenced arena situated a short distance from the barn. I parked on the other side of them, grabbed my camera and headed toward the group of mostly young riders—more girls than boys—who were focused on grooming the animals. The adults, who had driven the trucks, milled about drinking coffee and reading newspapers. The pounding rhythms and undecipherable lyrics of some new rock song intermingled with whinnies from one horse to another. I counted about fifteen horses. Jack was nowhere in sight.

A half dozen red and white Hereford calves drifted around the arena, occasionally bawling for their mothers. Teenage girls chatted while they saddled their horses, in their inimitable murder-the-English-language that always made me feel middle-aged. First girl: "Me and him went to the concert alone this time." Response: "The concert was, like, you know . . . awesome."

The overnight drizzle, which had produced the lingering overcast sky, had made the arena muddy. No one seemed to mind, although it appeared to be a messy day for both animals and riders. Once the horses were saddled and ready to go by their riders, they were taken to the gate. By now, I had snapped several photos and was searching for Jack. No one else seemed to mind that he wasn't immediately available.

Five minutes later, Jack sauntered over to the group, leading his horse. He looped the bridle reins to the fence and greeted his students. He went from horse to horse, checking the tightness of the girths and the rest of the tack. "Lookin' real good," he said to the "concert" girl, obviously impressed with the figure she cut in tight jeans and spandex top. The girl beamed, and it took me back to the summer I was seventeen. I'd gotten sucked into Jack's orbit, too, naively thinking he'd singled me out as someone special.

When the gear was checked out, Jack returned to his horse. "Cowboy up!" he shouted, and as if it were choreographed, fifteen jeans-clad legs swung across saddles in unison and, once all riders were astride their horses, they turned their attention to the arena. Jack exuded "Texas cowboy," from his battered Stetson to his muddy chaps. The best pix are in the details, I thought, and zoomed in to photograph his well-worn cowboy boots poking through the stirrups.

Jack was uncharacteristically earnest as he addressed the riders. "The idea behind cutting is to separate a cow from the herd," he said. "You're going to teach your horses to mirror the cows' moves, until an individual cow goes where you want it to go. That's going to require good reining skills on your part and good athletic ability on your horse's part. The first thing we're going to do is introduce your horse to a cow."

Well . . . calf, I thought to myself.

It didn't take long to realize that Jack's characterization of the event as a "cutting clinic" was a gross exaggeration. The horses hadn't been trained for anything more than pleasure riding and the riders hadn't the slightest idea as to what was expected of them. I moved into place, scoping out some interesting angles.

The riders had entered the arena and were maneuvering their horses close to the calves, who bunched together at one end of the arena. I continued snapping pictures, wishing for a little more action. Suddenly, I bumped into someone leaning on the wooden fence watching the activities. "I'm so sorry," I said. "I wasn't paying attention to anything other than what I see in my camera."

"That is quite all right."

As soon as the man straightened up and faced me, I remembered him as the one I'd wanted to photograph in a Kaiser uniform. "Mr. Lansing? We met in the vintage clothing shop on Monday."

"Yes, yes," he said, taking my hand between his two hands. "You are Cassandra Cassidy, the photographer who lives in Marty Madigan's carriage house."

"That's right." I eyed him with open curiosity. "I remember your saying that you know Marty quite well. Do you see him often?"

"Not often, but enough to say we're more than acquaintances. We are both involved in reenactments. We will take it up again, when things settle down for him."

"When and how do you think that will take place?"

"I have no way to know that, but as soon as the authorities discover who killed the reporter, Marty will no longer be under suspicion."

"You sound certain that he's not guilty. It was his tomahawk in Eric's head."

"My dear, Marty cannot be guilty." He shook his head with vigor. "He is not the kind of person who could perpetrate such a crime."

"How do you know that?"

"Over the years, Marty has very generously shared information about the Rendezvous with me." He gazed across the arena toward the horizon. "He knows a great deal about the manner of dress, the language, activities, skills and even the weapons used in that time period. I have always found him to be nothing but a gentleman."

"Did he ever say anything to you about Eric Hartfield?"

"Oh, no, our acquaintanceship is based primarily on subjects related to the Rendezvous. I have not talked with him since the event. I will, of course. I am simply giving him time to deal with the tragedy of the situation. I want him to know he has my support."

My mind shifted into high gear. "Mr. Lansing—Willis—would you consider allowing me to accompany you on your visit to Marty, when you're ready? I'd like to go to Marty's house, but . . . you know, I'd like someone with me."

Lansing threw back his head and laughed aloud. "Oh, Cassandra, Marty is not a dangerous person. But if it will make you feel better, I will do that for you."

"Thank you," I said, breathing a sigh of relief. We exchanged cell phone numbers.

"And how about you?" Lansing stroked his jaw and peered more closely at me through narrowed eyes. "This has been a frightful ordeal for you as well, has it not?"

I nodded. "Yes, well—"

"You, too, will soon be exonerated. You must practice patience. Were you able to take some good photographs of the event, before the unfortunate incident ruined it for you?"

I nodded again. "Fortunately, yes. They were confiscated by the sheriff, but my attorney was able to negotiate their return just this afternoon. I've only had a few minutes to go over them, but I'm pleased with many."

Our attention was drawn to the pounding of hoof beats from the other end of the arena and the shouting of the young people in one loud cacophony. I broke into a run along the fence to see what was happening. Without warning, a calf bolted by me and headed straight for the open pasture beyond the arena. Behind it, following every move the calf made, cowboy Jack Gardner rode to the rescue.

Jack twirled a rope above his head, while I snapped away. Finally, I'd have some action shots. As the horse closed in on the running calf, Jack's lasso sailed into the air and slid over the calf's neck. Jack's horse came to an instantaneous stop. The action tautened the rope and the calf toppled into the grass and then scrambled to its feet and stood waiting. Jack towed the subdued animal safely back to the arena. I gave him a thumbs-up as he passed by and had to grin at the expressions on his students' faces as they cheered. They were probably dreaming of the day they could repeat the action and with the same degree of skill.

I turned to resume my conversation with Lansing, but he had left the scene. I filed away his comments about Marty and congratulated myself for enlisting yet another ally in my quest to learn more about my landlord.

When the young cowboys and cowgirls had loaded up their horses and the last trailer had lumbered down the road, I set out to find Jack. He was in the tack room, putting away the last of the ropes, saddles, and bridles. "I got some good shots, but the best were of you," I said. "Your students are rather green in calf cutting."

He grinned. "Yeah, well, you work with what you've got. We're a long way from Texas up here. Nary a real ranch in sight. They're all caught up in the idea of playing cowboy though. They want to call it a cutting clinic. I let them get away with it."

"Nice roping anyway."

"You liked that, did you?" He looped his arm around my shoulders. "So you got some good pictures of me. To decorate your walls, I suppose."

"I doubt it," I said. "Maybe I'll do a feature on you for *Texas Monthly*. A Minnesota cowboy. They'll eat it up." I squirmed out from under his arm. "I really came to tell you about my meeting with Randy today."

"What do you suppose that was all about?" he asked, when I told him about Marty pulling back the tarp from the victims' faces.

"Not sure. Unless it has something to do with his lost wife and child."

"Where do you go from here?"

I sighed wearily. "Not sure. I've never done this before."

"Why not talk to Randy again? Maybe he can give you some new leads, now that he trusts you. I know he's home today."

"Getting him to talk at all is like pulling teeth from a bunny rabbit, he's so dang shy, Jack. What else could he tell me?"

"Anything is better than nothing. Don't give up now." Jack scribbled Randy's home address on a scrap of paper and handed it to me. "I'll call and tell him you'll be stopping by later."

* * *

All I knew about being involved in a murder was what I'd seen on television and in the movies. Watching a suspect squirm on film has little in common with being the squirmee. If I dwelled on my troubles, though, I'd go mad. Keeping appointments kept me sane and gave me the illusion that, at least temporarily, my life would go on.

I had no idea what else I would ask Randy and I couldn't imagine what else he'd have to tell me, but visiting him would shorten the evening hours I had to spend alone. The sun was finally setting as I approached his house on the other side of town. He lived in the same farmhouse in which he had grown up. I reviewed what Jack had told me about him. One of six children, he had remained in the farmhouse as his siblings left one by one and after his parents died. The farmland had long ago been sold off. The house stood by itself on a smaller parcel of land surrounded by the now towering pines and maple trees his parents had planted fifty years ago. The encroaching housing developments suggested that Randy would have to make a choice about staying put or selling out in the near future.

I parked in the driveway a few feet from the front porch. A light reflected through the drawn shades in what I assumed was the living room. As I trotted up the three steps of the porch and eyed the peeling paint of the front door, I was relieved to hear the rather loud sounds of the TV projecting out through the slightly raised window. I knocked three times and waited for Randy to come to the door. I knocked again, louder this time and with the flat of my hand, reasoning that with the elevated television sounds, he probably couldn't hear me. It seemed rather odd that he wasn't watching for me though. I was sure Jack would have called to tell him I was on my way.

When he still hadn't answered a few seconds later, I turned the doorknob and pushed the door open a few inches. "Randy? It's Cassandra Cassidy. Sorry I'm so late!" I entered the house and stepped hesitantly into the living room. "Randy?" Inadvertently, I shivered. Something wasn't right. I could sense it. Feeling stupid, I shook off my unease. I was acting like a ninny, instead of a self-confident woman determined to be her own investigator. I was simply visiting a new friend in a typical Minnesota farmhouse.

"Randy? I'm here." I walked more determinedly into the room and peered about me. Several lamps were lit, casting bright light on the furnishings, which were well worn. It was to be expected. Six kids had a way of wearing out anything upholstered and few men would go shopping for replacements, if they were comfortable with things the way they had always been. *"Randy,"* I called out again, literally bellowing this time. I felt like an intruder. I headed around the couch toward a doorway to what I assumed was the kitchen. As soon as I passed it, I came to an abrupt halt. "Randy?" My hand flew to my face and my shaking fingers covered the scream erupting from my mouth. With my heart in my throat, I clutched my chest and then reached out to brace myself on an end table. This was no time to pass out.

Randy lay sprawled across the coffee table in front of the sofa, face down. A knife protruded from his back. His shirt was stained with matted blobs of blood.

I don't know how long I stood frozen in place. Trembling uncontrollably, my instinct for self-preservation finally kicked in. In mere seconds, I ran through the options facing me. I could simply leave and let someone else discover Randy. I could touch him, to see if he were still alive. I could . . .

There was only one choice I could live with, no matter what the future dictated. I fumbled in my shoulder bag, spilling half its contents on the floor, pulled out my cell phone, and with a shaky finger punched in 911.

Chapter 9

Friday

By 7:00 a.m., the next day, my doorbell was ringing. Persistently. Still clad in pajamas and far too glum to protest, I shuffled through the kitchen and the living room to open the door. It was Anna.

"I heard what happened, Cassandra," she said, proffering one of Grizzly's magical elixirs. "I doubted you'd be sleeping, so I came as soon as I could." She wrapped her arms around me in a warm hug. "You're shaking, girl. I'm so sorry."

"You're right about my not sleeping," I said, yawning. "I don't think I'll ever sleep again without being haunted by Eric and Randy. The cops. The questions."

Anna guided me back to the kitchen, where I sank onto the first chair. Shoving my coffee container onto the table, I propped my elbows next to it and dropped my chin into my hands. I felt listless, sick at heart, and completely doomed. Not even the smell of the steaming coffee or the knowledge that I would undoubtedly enjoy it got me out of my funk.

"Do you want to talk about it?" Anna asked, her voice infused with concern. "Or has the whole ordeal worn you out?"

"No. I'll talk about it," I said, blowing my nose on a tissue. "I *need* to talk about it . . . with someone who doesn't think I'm a double murderer." My eyes flew to meet hers "You *don't*, do you?"

She scowled and pinched her lips. "Of course not! You were in an unfortunate place at the wrong time." She paused for a sip of her coffee. "What were you doing at Randy's, by the way?"

I told her about my initial interview with Randy, and of how I thought he might remember more valuable facts about Marty's connection to Eric. I blinked away a few tears. "You told me Marty's wife and child left him while he was serving in Viet Nam, and that he hasn't seen them since. When Randy told me about Marty's reaction at the accident and that Marty tends to blow up easily, I thought there might be a connection to Eric's killing. You know . . . that he has unsettled issues and he copes by inappropriately blowing his stack. I wanted to talk with him about it."

"And when you got there, you found him—"

"Dead. I found him *dead,* Anna." The wailing sound of my voice startled me, but I continued with my rising tirade. "He had a knife in his back! Why would anyone want to kill him? He was a shy, hardworking guy who helped the community by driving an ambulance."

Anna patted my hands. "It's . . . unimaginable. What do the police think?"

"Two murders in Clayton County within four days and *I* turn up at both of them?" I pushed myself to a standing position, but feeling weak-kneed, slumped onto my chair again. "What else could the police think, but that *I'm the perp!*"

"Did they actually say that, Cassandra, or are you reading something into their questioning, because you're, understandably, upset?"

"They didn't have to say, 'you're the lying perp'," I said, weary to the bones. "I could tell by their questions and the way they handled me that I was the only one on their radar." I swiped the tears from my eyes with still shaking fingers.

Anna looked puzzled. "By the way they *handled* you? Did they mistreat you? Didn't Lawton—"

"No, no . . . they didn't have the opportunity to do any serious mistreating, thanks to Lawton. He arrived just in time. I'll be forever grateful to him. And to you, of course, for having an attorney for a brother."

"What will you do now?"

I shrugged. "Would you believe it, Anna? I have all the law enforcement in Clayton County on my back. First, I had only Deputy Shaw, with the sheriff's department. Now, the city police are going investigate me, too." I pushed my chair away from the table and rose to a standing position. This time, my knees clicked into place. I paced back and forth, while thinking of my strategy. "I can't simply wring my hands and let things happen willy-nilly. It would drive me crazy. I've got to find out what's going on in this town. Someone has a serious grudge."

Anna pursed her lips and wiggled them from side to side while she thought about my outburst. "Is that wise, Cassandra?" she asked, finally. "Isn't it better to leave this to the professionals? They can't charge you with anything until they have proof. That's the way the court system operates."

I stared out the kitchen window at a robin that was returning to its nest after finding the early worm. She was free to go wherever she pleased, whenever she pleased. "You have no idea how it feels to be in my position," I said.

"No, I don't, so I shouldn't be offering advice." Anna managed a tight smile. "For at least a few hours today, however, you should close the blinds, turn off your phones, and try to get some sleep. You can think better when you're rested."

I rolled my eyes, a habit I'd developed only recently. "Yeah, sure, after all this coffee I just downed."

She took my arm and guided me to my bedroom. After pushing me onto the rumpled bed, she grinned. "I brought you decaf . . . and I may have dropped a little something more into it. It should begin working within the next few minutes."

* * *

By the time I awoke from Anna's drug-induced sleep, it was already 2:00 in the afternoon. I wasted no time in continuing my private investigation. I set out to find Jack.

His somber demeanor was unlike the Jack Gardner I'd seen in the last couple of weeks.

"I'm . . . well, I can't adequately express how I feel. I'm beside myself with grief." He hurled a bridle onto a tack room hook. When it hit its mark with a plunk, he cast a fleeting glance my way. "I'm sorry as hell you had to be the one to find him, Cass."

I shrugged and nodded, waiting for him to continue.

"Try as hard as I can, I can't come up with anyone who'd want to hurt Randy, let alone kill him." He hung his head and scrubbed his forehead with restless fingers. "He didn't have an enemy in the world. None that I know of anyway."

"How well did you know Randy?" I paced the stable floor, pausing to kick at a few hay bales. From the sides of my eyes, I observed Jack. Since I wasn't an expert in body language, his grief appeared entirely authentic.

His stricken gaze met mine. "We played the same rodeos a few times. He'd gotten to where he almost always finished in the money." He stomped his foot and pulled off his cowboy hat. "Damn! What a despicable thing to happen to him."

"I don't suppose you've heard any particulars from your law-enforcement connections."

He smacked his hat against the stable door and then fiddled with the brim. "As a matter of fact, I did. This morning." He glanced at me again. "You already know that Randy was stabbed in the back. They think the knife was thrown from across the room and he probably never knew what hit him. It has something to do with the angle of the blade and the deepness of penetration."

I stuffed my hands into the pockets of my jeans. "Any sign of a struggle?"

"Probably not."

"Robbery perhaps?"

"Who would know if anything is missing? He drove the ambulance part time for a job, so he barely made a living." He wiped his forehead with a bandana pulled from his back pocket. "His entire net worth was probably his saddle and the chaps and trophies he won while on tour."

I kicked at the loose straw on the floor of the stables. "I don't suppose you found out anything more about the weapon?"

Jack grabbed a brush and began forcefully brushing a mare that had been tied in the aisle between stalls. "Only that it was handmade and old. A hunting knife." He flipped the horse's mane out of the way as he agitatedly groomed her.

I leaned across the horse's back. "You say the knife was old. Old, as in, say a 1950's kind of old?"

Jack stopped brushing. "More like an 1850's kind of old." He peered directly at me for the first time. "Have they been interviewing you, too?"

"Interviewing? I'd say more like grilling. I'm their prime suspect."

"Damn, Cass, I'm so sorry."

"I'm sorry, too," I said, suddenly straightening and raising my voice. "I'm sorry that a so-called friend of mine sent me over to a murder victim's house!"

Jack's head jerked toward me. "What the hell is that supposed to mean?"

"I'll leave that to your own interpretation," I said, turning to leave.

Like everyone else in Colton Mills, I triple-checked my locks that night and seriously entertained the idea of buying myself a Rottweiler.

Chapter 10

Saturday

I was out of bed by 6:30 the next morning and went right to work on my weight machine. As I had told Deputy Shaw, it takes muscle to haul around lenses and heavy photographic equipment. In addition to maintaining and even building muscle, the workout produced the endorphins necessary for sanity. On my mind throughout the entire sweat-session was the fact that it had been almost a week since the beginning of the worse week of my life.

It was hard to imagine photographing a wedding, with everything that had happened. The idea of calling in "sick" quickly passed though. It wasn't Lori's fault her photographer was up to her ears in two murder investigations. I'd made a commitment to do her wedding and I would follow through. I checked and rechecked my gear and drove the now familiar route to Patriot Stables. I took several standard wedding shots before the ceremony—if you call "standard" posing the bride and groom against the front of a horse stall while cuddling their horse's head between them. That done, I schlepped around the ranch with my camera, photographing family members and the bridal party on bales of hay, by the white-painted fence, and in other sites I'd previously identified.

The wedding itself was to take place on a strip of land that had been carved out of the ranch by the Oxbow Creek when it cut through a slice of the property on two sides. A grove of cottonwood trees had grown up there and formed a picturesque site, especially with the covered wooden bridge, which allowed visitors access to the location. It was definitely a Minnesota summer-perfect spot. I'd photographed lots of theme weddings and this was one of the more fully realized ones. Guests who had paid close attention to the invitation, which encouraged "casual cowboy dress," perched on bales of hay. Those who didn't used folding chairs.

Living in small-town Colton Mills and photographing costumed affairs sometimes made me feel as if I were in a time warp. But, I'd wanted to get as far away as possible from the Big Apple, and to that end, I'd succeeded.

As I zeroed in on some of Lori's western-themed touches—a horseshoe archway, a pair of saddles flanking the entrance, bandanas on the chairs—I could hear my city-born-and-bred photographer mentor groan at the idea of participating in such a kitschy event. But artistic New York-training-be-damned, I'd been enjoying my Colton Mills career. As a foster kid, I was used to being the perennial outsider, so photography suited me perfectly. I could mingle among people as an integral part of the event, but be separate at the same time. That's the way I liked it.

As usual, the guests murmured among themselves as they were seated, their chatter playing in the background like elevator music. I can't pinpoint the exact moment I realized the conversation had taken on an entirely different cast. Instead of commenting about the weather, the bride, and the occasion, they were chatting about Randy's murder . . . and I was the center of attention. I caught the gaze of a gray-haired lady guest, as she whispered behind her hand to her friend and my heart skipped a beat. I turned away, pretending to snap another photo over her shoulder.

A rare sense of panic swelled inside my chest. If the murders were not solved soon, I may not have a professional life. Thankfully, before my wild thoughts could stifle my ability to focus on the wedding, I ceased to be the center of attention. I heard the Cowpokes' rousing rendition of "Boot Scootin' Boogie," and over the music the pounding hooves of a horse. The groom, decked out in a white western tux, with black boots and Stetson, circled his black Arabian around the entire site containing the seated wedding guests. He trotted to the front, made a spectacular 360-degree spin, dismounted with a flourish, and strode into position before the altar. It was one of the more dramatic entrances I'd seen, and I scrambled to get it all on film.

When the band switched to "Love Can Build a Bridge," the attendants strolled up the aisle in their Western dress and the wedding was under way. With the strains of "Here Comes the Bride," the guests turned heads to take in the bride's entrance. I was stunned to see that Jack was leading the white mare holding Lori, who was seated sidesaddle in her Victorian wedding dress. Lori's father strode next to the horse and smiled up at his equally beaming daughter.

I was continuously on the move for the next several minutes, snapping pictures of the ceremony and guests from every angle. I sustained this pace into the evening at the country club reception, where the cowboy theme continued. The Cowpokes belted out country-western two-steps and waltzes for at least two hours. I went through the process automatically, but with an edge of nervousness I hadn't previously experienced. Clearly, I was a subject of interest.

When I finally packed up my gear, it was late and I was both physically and mentally exhausted. I stowed everything in my Jeep and headed for home. A long, hot shower would feel divine. As I pulled up to the carriage house, I punched the remote to open the garage door. Nothing happened. *Damn! What a night for the opener to fail.* I parked and strode to the side door, feeling slightly irritated that my homecoming wasn't as welcoming as I'd wanted it to be. Feeling around for the lock, I cursing myself for not turning on the deck light before I had left the house. Then I remembered the little laser light on my keychain and trained it on the door.

Without warning, my heart was drumming against by ribs as my mouth turned dry as a year-old deer bone. I swallowed the gagging lump in my throat. The door was already open! Not only open, but the wood was splintered around the lock. *Someone has broken into my garage.*

The hairs on the back of my neck bristled as I dashed back to my car and locked the doors. That "someone" could still be in the garage, hiding in the dark. I whipped out my cell phone and started to punch in 911, but my fingers refused to make the connection. The idea of inviting the police to my place had me paralyzed. There would be more questions. More stares. More silent accusations. I sat perfectly still for several minutes. Thinking. Thinking and searching every inch of the property outside my confines with restless eyes. *I'll have to handle the situation myself.*

Trembling and feeling clammy from sitting in the car with no windows open, I slowly opened the door and stepped onto the pavement of the driveway. Hearing nothing, I dashed to the outside wall of the carriage house. Then, hugging the bricks, I inched my way back to the side entrance, pushed open the door with one outstretched hand, and then quickly stepped back. I had seen cops do that in the movies. Nothing happened. No gunshots. No blinding light. No escaping burglars. No inside noises. I reached around the corner of the doorway to flick on the lights. I tried several times. Nothing happened. The intruder had either unscrewed the bulb or turned off the power connection.

I switched on my hopelessly inadequate laser light and played it around the inside of the garage. Since I had little to store in the cavernous space, it didn't take more than a few seconds to see it was untouched and no one was in sight. I slithered over to the stairway and crept up the stairs to my apartment, hating the eerie silence. Staring at the door, bathed in only the thin beam from my keychain light, I finally gathered the courage to reach for the doorknob and give it a turn. *The door is still locked.* Breathing an audible sign of relief, I inserted my key into the lock, pushed the door open and reached inside to flick on the light switch. Light flooded the room with daylight luminosity. I tiptoed cautiously throughout the apartment, searching behind furniture, under my bed, and in every closet. From what I could tell, no one had entered the premises.

Returning to the kitchen door to lock it, I stumbled into the living room and flopped onto the couch. My once thoroughly fatigued mind was pumped with a new supply of adrenaline and it was difficult to focus. Someone had definitely broken into my outside door to gain entrance to the carriage house. Why? And why hadn't this person used the same ploy to gain entrance to my apartment? Nothing seemed out of place.

Minutes passed as I went over every possible scenario. Then the answer hit me. *It's not my apartment. It's my darkroom. Someone wants what I have. But what? Photographs? Photos that may absolve me from complicity and pinpoint the real murderer?*

Of course! Photographs of Rendezvous events! I leaped off the couch and dashed to the kitchen, purposely making a lot of noise. I stomped from one end of the room to the other and finally thrashed through one of the drawers. If the intruder were still hiding downstairs, I wanted to give him the opportunity to make his getaway through the broken garage door.

Armed with a more powerful flashlight, I knew I couldn't delay any longer. I started the long descent down the same stairway to my darkroom, located on the far side of the garage. I whistled and sang "The Yellow Rose of Texas," hoping my off-pitch rendition would scare away any boogiemen. My hunch was right. The darkroom was in shambles. I groaned aloud. As my eyes roamed over the mess, I realized nothing was salvageable. Chemical powders had been pulled off the shelf and sprinkled over mountains of photo paper strewn across the floor. Drawers had been pulled out of my filing cabinet and their contents dumped. Mixed into the heap, I saw scissors, tongs, and other tools. When I nearly stepped on an X-acto knife, I gave up and returned to my living quarters. There was nothing I could do now that couldn't wait for morning.

Minutes later, with a cold beer in hand, I stewed over the latest tragic event in my life. *At least one person knows I'm innocent. That's a given. I have to assume that person wants to ensure anonymity. Who? WHO? And the bigger question . . . was the break-in successful? Am I in danger?*

Too frazzled to think straight, I triple-locked my apartment door, then called and left a message for Marty, asking that he repair the garage door and get electrical service restored to the downstairs as soon as possible. I made no mention of my destroyed darkroom.

As I dressed for bed, I peered into the bathroom mirror and saw my face of despair. Within one week my whole life had changed. I was now both a pursuer and the pursued.

Chapter 11

Sunday

After a fitful night of sleep, I rolled out of bed, walked zombie-like through my morning routine, dressed in a pair of well-worn jeans and a tank top, and then forced myself to go back downstairs. For the next couple hours, I sorted through the rubble in my darkroom and carried one boxful of ruined photos at a time into the garage. Several of my favorite enlarged Indian photos, which I had positioned on an easel, were destroyed beyond repair. Although I'd scanned the negatives into my computer, it would take time to reprint them.

As the morning wore on and the stacks in the garage grew higher, my frustration increased. I couldn't account for a single missing photo. I stepped gingerly around the darkroom and, unexpectedly, caught sight of an envelope that was pasted to the floor. I recognized it as one I had picked up from Sanders' office a couple days earlier. It was empty. All of the Rendezvous photos had been removed. Apparently, when the intruder opened the second drawer and found the photos he wanted, he had left the rest of the drawers intact. My one consolation was that, although the intruder would know whether or not he had been photographed, I could still get copies. Deputy Shaw had the originals in his office.

Finally giving up any notion that I could handle this new situation on my own, I called my attorney. "You can't withhold this information, Cassandra," he said. "After you inform Shaw of the break-in, I'll go to his office and get new copies of all the photos for you."

"I'll trust your judgment, Lawton," I said, heaving an exaggerated sigh. "You know I can't stand the guy, but I'll call Shaw right now. If he wants to meet with me, I need you to run interference for me. Will you be available?"

"It's Sunday, Cass. I doubt he'll want to see you until Monday morning. Let me know, though. I'm here to see you through this ordeal."

Fortunately, I was able to inform Shaw of the break-in and the missing Rendezvous photographs through his voice mail. I added that Sanders would be visiting him on Monday to make a new set for me, to replace the stolen ones. I didn't bother to suggest that this might prove I wasn't his murderer.

Later, with a stale cup of coffee, I collapsed on the sofa. I felt drained, yet strangely wired at the same time. I had a starting point for my own investigation. As soon as Sanders brought me a new copy of the photographs, I would spend hours poring over every detail. I would see who was at every event. As I was mulling over my plan, the doorbell chimed. "Who's there?" I called down the stairs, one hand clutching my throat as I swallowed my fear. It was silly, of course. If my nighttime intruder was both Eric and Randy's murderer, he wouldn't ring my doorbell in broad daylight. Or would he?

"It's me. Jack."

Dashing down the stairs, I pulled open the door and stared at him, thankful to see a friend.

He shifted uncomfortably from one foot to another, seemingly unsure of his reception. "I was in the area, so I decided to stop by," he said. "I didn't like the way our last conversation ended."

I motioned him inside and we climbed the stairs to the living room. "Make yourself comfortable," I said, examining him from the sides of my eyes. I perched on the edge of a club chair facing him, where he sat stiffly on the couch.

He rubbed his hands nervously over his jeans-clad knees. "I'm on your side, Cass. I'm not your enemy. You can trust me."

After studying his face, I rose to stand at the window. The leaves on the old maple tree that obstructed my view of Marty's house fluttered in the breeze. "Right now, I'm taking everything at face value, Jack," I said. "And if something smells a little 'off,' it goes into the 'suspicious' file I'm carrying around in my head." I turned to see his reaction to my not-so-friendly words.

He nodded. "That's fair. I'd probably feel the same way. I just hope you can file away that I'm your friend and available to help you, if I can."

"I'll do that. Thank you." I absently straightened magazines on the coffee table.

"Good." He scanned my apartment. "Nice place." He rose from the couch and pointed toward the Indian pictures hanging on the fireplace wall. "Very nice. Your work, I'm sure. I can see why you like living here . . . but you don't have the best security. The downstairs door doesn't have a lock on it."

I managed a smile. "Well, at least the doorbell is working. Which means Marty's got the electricity back on."

"Electricity?" He scowled. "Shouldn't that be a given?"

When I told Jack about the break-in, his eyes lit up with the possibility of a "law-enforcement issue" to pursue. "Did they take all the photos of the Rendezvous?"

"They took all the color prints."

"A damn shame. You spent hours on that project. Have you got any more?"

"I have a compact disc of photos the sheriff returned to me. They're in my computer." I nodded toward my office.

"Shows that the intruder wasn't tuned into contemporary times," he said, shaking his head. "Bet he thought he had cleaned you out."

I straightened a pillow on the couch and moved across the room. "I should take a look at the ones in the computer right now. They might give me a clue as to what he was looking for."

"I'll help, if you want. Two sets of eyes are better than one."

"Sure, I'd appreciate the company. I'm still a little on edge." I led the way to my office. Once settled in front of my notebook, I opened the file that included the photos.

"Holy shit! There must be hundreds of pictures in your computer!" Jack said. "This is not a ten-minute job."

I laughed. "It's easy to take a ton of digital photos when you don't have to think about film costs." I started up the slide show, which displayed each individual photo full screen.

"What specific things are we looking for?" Jack pulled his chair closer to the table.

"Don't have a clue," I said. "But for openers, I'd say shots of anyone we know. Eventually, I can organize them by subject, but not today."

We viewed photos of people and events taken from several angles and various distances—close-ups, long shots, some with backgrounds out of focus, others in clear context. "Some nice shots of my landlord," I said, displaying the photos of Marty. "Here he is, in the 'hawk-throwing contest."

I leaned closer to the screen. It was hard to see Marty's features, because he wore a wide-brimmed hat, pulled low over his eyes. The rest of his face was shadowed by his bushy beard. I had caught him in one moment of short-lived jubilation when the 'hawk landed where he wanted. He had pulled off his hat and was waving it in the air, while he kicked out one of his boot-clad feet. I had zoomed in to get a close-up, but he turned just as I clicked the shutter. I regretted I hadn't photographed him standing on the sidelines after the competition. And, unfortunately, I had taken no pictures of him *before* the contest either.

In another photo, Willis Lansing was drinking coffee at a vendor booth in the early morning light. He was dressed in the costume of a trader—white cotton shirt tucked into pants held up by red suspenders. His pant legs were tucked into leather boots. He carried his beaver hat under his arm, as he used one hand to wipe away perspiration from his brow.

I especially liked some of the people shots and knew that Photoshop magic would turn them from okay shots into very good ones. "Isn't that Eric behind the Indian woman doing the weaving? Yes, it is! I'd recognize him anywhere." I marked the photo. "And, there's Randy, over by the horse corral." I felt my shoulders droop. "Both dead," I murmured. "Both murdered in the same week. I can't stop asking myself why." The slide show had run its course. I turned to face Jack. His eyes were glazed over and he looked ready for la-la land. "See anything suspicious?"

"Not a thing. It looks like a big party to me. Everyone's having a good time. It's hard to believe a murder was being committed nearby at the same time some of these pictures were taken. A murderer is loose in our town. A murderer who was probably in your house last night."

Chapter 12

Monday—Week Two

I was up at the crack of dawn, after a night of tossing and turning and sitting up to hear sounds that weren't there. Clearly, my Saturday night visitor had me spooked. I had relived every hour of every day since finding Eric's body in the sweating lodge. Nothing special stood out, except something Deputy Shaw had said in his last questioning session. He had asked me how well I knew Frank Kyopa, the head of the Prairie River Band. Although I had testified in his favor, by labeling the photograph Eric had taken of him entering a land developer's building in Chicago as a fake, I hadn't mentioned it. I had passed off my knowing him only as a casual business contact. I hadn't been convincing. My dancing around the mulberry bush had kept me firmly on Shaw's suspect list, especially since the episode I had failed to mention on my own was the one that ended Eric's career at the *Star-Tribune*. But why was Shaw so interested in connecting me to Kyopa?

Certainly he didn't think Frank and I were in cahoots and out to get Eric.

Only one way to find out. Ask the man himself. I dialed Frank's office and reached his assistant, who told me Frank was a busy man. I cut to the chase. "This is Cassandra Cassidy. A deputy sheriff is linking me to Frank in the matter of Eric Hartfield's murder. It is critically important that I be able to talk with him about it. This morning, if possible."

Thirty seconds later, I was given my appointment. Frank would see me as soon as I could get to his office. It was in northern Clayton County, not far from where the Rendezvous took place. I was buckling the seatbelt in my Jeep by 8 a.m., to allow myself plenty of time in case I got lost.

Frank Kyopa made a memorable impression. I'd photographed him in his reservation office, after he'd been elected president for his second term. In one picture, he was seated in a high-backed leather desk chair, his forearms resting on the massive mahogany desk. Dressed in a custom-tailored gray suit like the CEO he was—a man who steered the sizable fortunes of the tribe's casino—he gazed confidently at the camera lens. The pinstripes in no way disguised his muscular physique. In my favorite photo of him, he was standing near the window in three-quarter profile, with the outside light reflecting on his sharply chiseled face, brown as a walnut. The light bounced off his black hair, shot with gray, and delineated the dozens of facial fissures formed from a lifetime of smoking Camels.

By the time I arrived in Colton Mills, Frank had already served as tribal chairman for four years. He was respected by all factions . . . Indian, business, and government alike. But his path to tribal respectability hadn't always been pretty. I'd learned that much from trying to winnow fact from fiction in Eric's news stories. A decade ago, the tribe was wallowing in debt, a not uncommon condition for reservations before casino gambling made some of them rich. Frank had left the rez after high school graduation and received a business degree, thanks to an athletic scholarship from the University of Minnesota. He worked for a couple of corporations to learn the ropes, then started a manufacturing business in the eighties. That company now employed several hundred employees. During all this time, he had remained connected to the reservation, returning for family events and to stay current with the rough-and-tumble political shenanigans that characterized the community. Trouble was, those who got the upper hand, politically speaking, used their positions to line their own pockets.

In 1990, Frank cut his ties to the company he had founded, pulled up stakes, and moved to the reservation. His return was not universally applauded, according to articles printed in the *Minnesota Review*. Entrenched tribal leaders resisted his "interference" and, sometimes, the going got rough. Articles also documented the political carnage and trail of victims, as Frank clawed his way through the ranks.

Eric hadn't taken either side in his articles. He had mocked the entire state of affairs, calling tribal government a "Laurel and Hardy way to run a government." He had painted Frank as an opportunist, no better than the leaders who had been feeding from the tribal trough for decades. He had scoffed at Native American sovereignty, feeling the entrenched system was bogus and most problems would be solved if the tribes were governed by the U.S. government and managed by "professional managers."

Frank and I had become friends as we ran into each other at powwows where I photographed the events. He had bought several photos of urban Indians I'd taken in Minneapolis. Our friendship had culminated when he consulted me about Eric's doctored photo a year ago.

Frank's sense of power came through, as I shook hands with him now in his wood-paneled office. "Cassandra, good to see you again, in spite of the circumstances." He motioned for me to be seated in the chair fronting his desk. Then he took his place in the high-backed leather desk chair. "My assistant told me Deputy Shaw has you on his list of murder suspects and I am, somehow, linked to you in some sort of subversion, I suppose. Tell me your version of the events."

I filled him in on what I knew and included the details of my unpleasant encounter with Eric at the Rendezvous. He fiddled with a silver paperweight on his desk, thinking. "Does anybody know why Eric was in the sweat lodge in the first place?" he asked. "He must have been going there to meet somebody, don't you think?"

"Beats me," I said, shrugging. "And it's as mysterious to me that Shaw is interested in exactly how friendly *we* are. What's that all about?"

"I'm also on Shaw's list of suspects."

Stunned, I stammered out a response. "I-I . . . I don't know what to say, Frank. Because of . . . your past history with Eric? Or . . . or that fake picture fiasco?" Their shared history was volatile, to say the least. I suddenly remembered a confrontation between the two that had taken place in March during a hearing about the proposed development at the reservation. Eric had been baiting Frank with questions.

"Why do you think the Indians have more right to this property than tax-paying American citizens do?" he had said to Frank, who was leading the meeting.

Frank had responded angrily. "You know damn well we may own a small portion of the land around the lake, Hartfield, but that is because the land was unfairly taken from us a century ago." He had shaken his finger at Eric not two inches from his smirking face. "When we try to buy it back, asking prices go higher and higher. Now this development corporation comes in with its money and its plans to build houses for a few rich Americans. If it turns into houses for city people, they will bring their noisy, polluting jet skis and motorboats. They will clog the winter ice with their ice houses. It is our right to enjoy the same clean water, natural resources, and pristine environment as our ancestors enjoyed. And we don't need a creep with the morality of a fencepost to come up here and tell us there's a better use for that land than leaving it just like it is."

Frank's voice jolted me back from my daydreaming. "From our past dealings, Deputy Shaw could surmise I had a motive to see Hartfield dead, I suppose. Everyone knows we had no love for each another. Our war of words was always made public."

I nodded. "You were quoted in the paper, once, as saying you'd just as soon slit Eric's throat as look at him." I tapped my pen against my notebook and grinned wryly. "That gives the sheriff a lot of ammunition."

"A lot of people would have liked to slit Eric's throat," Frank said, pulling on an ear. "He was always out to agitate people and start a controversy." He scratched a cheek and gazed directly at me. "They've got something else on me, too, Cassandra. I was in the vicinity about the time of the killing."

"You were at the Rendezvous, too? I didn't see you."

"You know that I participate in traditional ceremonies whenever I can. I was at the sweat lodge the night before the Rendezvous and had returned in the morning to retrieve a hat I forgot in one of the teepees where I'd changed clothes. Somebody evidently saw me in the parking lot with the hat in my hand and informed Shaw of my presence."

"I know you've got a thing about an old Stetson with a beaded hatband. Is that the one you left behind?"

"The very one. Kind of a lucky hat, I guess, and I didn't want to lose it."

"So, because of *that* you're a suspect, too? But, why are they connecting you to me?"

He tented his fingers and brought them to his chin. "Has to be the court thing where you identified Eric's fake photo. That's the only connection I can think of. It's also widely known that Eric didn't take kindly to the verdict and losing his job at the *Star-Tribune*. He blamed both of us for the demise of his career."

I sighed and slumped in my chair. "Whatever happened to that development business? It sounded like it was going through, even though you were adamantly opposed to it."

"That development got postponed, maybe even cancelled."

"How'd that happen?" I evidently hadn't kept up on county events.

Frank stood and walked to the wall of windows in his office, a frown on his face. "Not the way you'd think. The county hosted an open house in the spring. Complete with little sandwiches, cheese balls, and stuff like that. Whenever there's free food, Kenneth Good Heart shows up. You know him, Cassandra. Big mouth. A lot of stories."

I did know him. I'd been hearing about his stories ever since I came to Minnesota. I could see his craggy face. Long, gray, stringy ponytail. Dancing, impish brown eyes. He always wore a derby-like hat. He'd long ago gotten false teeth, but usually left them in his pocket. I pictured him with his head back, roaring about some joke he'd just made, his hands slapping against his skinny jeans-clad knees.

"Ken is eighty-five, you know," Frank said, turning to face me. "I think what's kept him going all these years is bugging government bureaucrats. Last year—it was really dry, if you remember—he and two of his cousins performed two rain ceremonies in front of city hall to end the drought. When rain finally came, the last week of September, they sent a bill for $32,000 in expenses to the county, pointing out that their ceremonies had created the rainfall."

I chuckled. It could have happened that way. "Did they pay?"

"Hell, no. But it's typical of the way Kenneth tweaks the government. Anyway, at this particular city event, Kenneth got to gabbing about the old days. In the early 1950s, the tribe got a grant and built a paint manufacturing company on the reservation. It hung in there for about five years and went belly up. But here's the clincher." Frank returned to his desk and pounded a fist onto the surface. "Kenneth said the plant disposed of its wastes on the property outside the reservation. It amused him to contemplate the developers' reactions when they discovered the mess they'd have to pay to clean up."

"And did they?"

"Well, it didn't get that far." Frank reseated himself. "One of the commissioners at the event overheard the conversation and used the information to derail the whole development. I knew all about the paint factory and always assumed it was common knowledge. I did *not* know about the illegal dumping."

"So what happened?"

"At the next meeting, this commissioner—Marty Madigan—dropped Kenneth's bombshell on the entire commission board."

I nearly choked when Frank mentioned Marty. This was the connection I was looking for. *Marty knows Eric!*

"Madigan had been against the development from the get-go and used Kenneth's information to force the county to prepare an Environmental Impact Statement based on evidence that chemical wastes were dumped into the very wetlands that was slated for development."

"Why was Marty against the development?"

"Two reasons, as far as I can tell." Frank lifted his hand and extended his index finger. "One, Madigan's kind of an ornery bastard and just likes to make waves."

"And the second reason?"

He lifted a second finger, punching the air with his hand. "He didn't trust Guy Strothers, the president of the Bridgewater Land Development Company. He had swept the commissioners off their feet with his fancy charts and promises of tax revenue. They never took the time to thoroughly check him out. Anyway, the time it will take to research the EIS could sidetrack the project until it's too late to do anything about it this year. And if the outcome is finally negative, it could scuttle the project for good." He folded his arms on the desk.

I settled back in my chair. "I imagine that didn't sit too well with the developers."

"Guy Strothers was livid."

"Do you by any chance remember when that commission meeting took place?"

"I might." Frank closed his eyes and drummed his fingers on the desk. "It was before Memorial Day weekend, but after my wife's first day of work. That would make it about May 25th. Somewhere around there."

I did some quick arithmetic in my head. That meeting was two weeks before the Rendezvous. Had Marty and Eric planned to meet at the sweat lodge? Maybe the meeting got out of control and Marty' temper got the best of him. I considered other possibilities as I drove back to the carriage house.

Both Marty and Frank had tempers that erupted spontaneously, if they were pushed too far. Both found Eric exceedingly irritating. Eric had publicly humiliated both of them by working to expose a project they were against in a negative light. If Shaw had this information, why was he working so hard to involve me? And if Shaw had acquired knowledge of their verbal wars, why was he singling out Frank as Eric's murderer and me as his accomplice? Randy's name kept popping into my mind. What did either of these men have against Randy?

Other questions came to me, too. What was the motive? It was unlikely that two murders only days apart could be assigned to an eruption of temper. And, lest I forget, how would Frank have gotten a hold of Marty's tomahawk? And why, if they were on the same page, would he deliberately set Marty up to take the fall? Maybe he simply found the lost tomahawk and didn't know it belonged to Marty.

Of course, the other possibility was that Frank had been set up in an ingenious plot that, properly executed, could remove two thorns in the flesh—Eric *and* Frank. Actually, three men, if Marty were being set up as well. But Randy wasn't in their league. Why Randy? My mind was reeling, by the time I reached the edge of town.

I decided it wouldn't hurt to get more information on Guy Strothers. Hoping to find articles about the commission's meetings, I headed over to the library to see if it kept past issues of the newspaper. Janine, the librarian, was familiar with the controversy. "My husband's on that commission, too," she said. Janine was married to Russell Cloud, an Ojibwe businessman. She tucked a bookmark into a mystery she was reading and leaned across her desk and lowered her voice. "I went to some of those meetings, Cassandra. Listening to the way the land-development people proceeded, you would think they were offering the county a gold mine. The project was sprung on the commission last fall and worked its way through the system, until it was approved in March." She chewed on the inside of her cheek. "The Bridgewater Company knew exactly how to play to the commissioners," she said. "Strothers knew they were hungry for development money."

Even though I'd never seen Strothers, I knew the type. Personable, energetic, even charismatic. I could see him mesmerizing the commission members with glowing descriptions of his project.

Janine was on a roll. She probably thought she was a key character in a local murder mystery and needed to use all her acquired knowledge of how to proceed. After confirming Frank's take on what had happened regarding Strothers and his retinue of strategists and attorneys and their four-color Power Point graphs and charts, she continued. "They showed videos of citizens testifying to the success of his concept in other areas of the country. Boy, was he ever slick," she said. "Even so, Russ thought the project didn't have a prayer of succeeding. But he was wrong. Because of their selling skills, or their persistence—or who-knows-what might have changed hands behind the scenes—the commissioners voted in favor of the project. Only my husband and Marty voted against it." She scratched her head and then patted her hair into place. "Later, when Marty came up with that EIS proposal, they couldn't ignore it. They *had* to vote for the Impact Statement, even though they knew it could shut down the development for good."

"Do you know how Strothers and the Bridgewater Land Company have performed in other projects?"

"Hmm, I don't know anything more, Cassandra. Sorry. Personally, I haven't been interested enough to look into it."

I photocopied several news stories to read later, thanked Janine for her help, and left the library wondering how and if all this political brouhaha could be connected to Eric and Randy's murders.

Reluctantly, I felt I had to add Frank to my list of suspects. No doubt some of Frank's tactics were suspect, as he pushed his own political agenda. I had to admit, though, that if he were guilty of some of the things he was accused of in his trial—bribery, fraud, forgery, tax evasion, even embezzlement—none of the court challenges over the years had ever held up. In the late nineties, he was elected chairman again. To the average reservation member, Frank Kyopa was a hero, bringing economic prosperity to a region that had never experienced it. In a few short years, he had expanded the tribe's tiny floundering casino and made it highly profitable. He had developed other new businesses, too. And he had attracted more outside subsidies than his predecessors had done in all their decades of leadership. But . . . he still jealously guarded the tribe's "cultural traditions," a stand Eric had labeled as "ludicrous." He still resisted any encroachment of outside development, a stand that got him crosswise of Strothers and his flunkies.

Strothers wasn't Frank's only enemy, of course. The political battlefield was riddled with them, from tribal leaders he had supplanted, to county and state bureaucrats he had ignored. I wasn't naïve enough to think he'd survived all these challenges by turning the other cheek.

Back at home, after my day of sleuthing, I stretched out on my recliner and booted up my laptop to see what I could learn about Strothers. First, I Googled BRIDGEWATER LAND DEVELOPMENT COMPANY and waited to see what would come up. As I expected, dozens of marketing information sites about "land development companies" filled the screen. I scrolled down until I found Bridgewater. It was a typical promotional site, wrapped in snazzy graphics and photos of successful developments. Not what I was looking for.

Back to Google for another try. I scrolled through several screens and got more of the same. I needed another approach. I tried LAND-DEVELOPMENT COMPANY EVALUATIONS. Nothing. Maybe LAND-DEVELOPMENT COMPANY NEWS STORIES. Bingo.

This one had possibilities. Thinking there might be something under *Chicago Tribune* real estate stories, I opened the site and typed "Bridgewater" into the search box. I hit pay dirt. Several articles had been written about the Bridgewater Land Development Company. But the most interesting was a column written by the one of the paper's business columnists the previous summer.

In a nutshell, the columnist wrote that Bridgewater, although it looked good on paper, was a very shaky company. The company's strategy had been to buy up property forfeited for taxes or other nonpayment, and then develop it. The strategy had worked for several years, but like a pyramid scheme, it was beginning to catch up with them. Bridgewater had taken on a lot of debt in its last deal, building a fifty-acre office park in a Chicago suburb, and the offices were only about fifty-five percent leased.

I was willing to bet they had a huge stake in the Minnesota deal going through to completion.

Chapter 13

Tuesday—Week Two

If such a thing as a perfect morning for a funeral existed, this morning didn't meet the criteria. I had awakened to the sound of pelting rain against my windows. From the looks of the charcoal-gray sky outside, I guessed we were in for a full day of the wet stuff. I dreaded the idea of going to Randy's funeral, yet I had to do it.

As I drove down the driveway and onto the county road taking me to the church, my wipers worked hard, but were losing the battle to keep the windshield clear. I hunched over the steering wheel, mentally willing them to work faster and harder. Over the sound of the rain pounding on the roof overhead, I listened to people sharing their weather stories with the morning radio-news host. A segment of the Colton Mills population was more dependent on the whims of Mother Nature than I was, and most were far more grateful for the unrelenting downpour.

"This has been the hottest June I can remember," a farmer said. "I was beginning to worry that my corn wouldn't reach knee high by the Fourth of July, but this rain could make the difference."

Even as a disgruntled gardener praised the rain for displacing the dust in her rain gauge, I cursed her godsend for creating the low visibility. My Jeep's ten-year-old ventilation system couldn't keep the windows from fogging up. I steered with one hand and used the other to swipe at the window, trying to keep a section of the windshield clear. It was only five miles into town, but when I passed the crumbling old gas station landmark, I saw that I'd only traveled a mile or so. At that rate, it would take me an hour to reach my destination. Because of the foggy conditions, though, I was afraid to push it any faster.

Concentrating on my multiple driving tasks, I barely felt the slight bump against the rear side of my vehicle. "Damn, someone's trying to pass me." I fought with the steering wheel to keep my car on the road.

The second bump got my attention. Something loomed out of the mist on my left and jolted my vehicle again, forcing me to move further to the right. Out of the corner of my eye, I could see the shadow of a larger vehicle keeping pace with mine. It wasn't trying to pass me. It was edging closer. He was probably having the same trouble seeing through the fog that I was. *No! He's doing it on purpose!* With that thought barreling into my head, I heard the sickening sound of metal against metal. *I'm being squeezed off the road.* My Jeep tilted dangerously, as its right-side wheels left the pavement and slid onto the shoulder. I fought with the steering wheel and felt my heart leap into my throat. If I hadn't been driving slowly, I would be plummeting down the embankment and into the river.

Because of the weather conditions, there was no way for me to identify the driver of the mystery vehicle. I couldn't take my gaze off the road. As the vehicle veered toward mine for what I feared would be the final shove, I slammed on my brakes. The other vehicle accelerated down the road. Through the fog, I watched my tormenter's taillights disappear around the curve ahead. Shaking, I pulled my vehicle back onto the pavement and drove the remaining miles into town, breathing rapidly and breaking into an unwanted sweat.

I pulled into the parking lot of the First Baptist Church and tried to get a hold of myself. I rested my head on the steering wheel and steeled myself to breathe deeply. *Who's trying to run me off the road? And why?* I cursed the weather for the umpteenth time. If it hadn't been so foggy, if conditions hadn't required I keep my eyes on the road, I could have identified the vehicle *and* the person behind the wheel. Or at least have memorized the license number. I wasn't stupid. The person had to be the same one who'd broken into the carriage house. The individual didn't want me to do anymore snooping around . . . or to take anymore photos.

Once more in control of my faculties, I cast a quick glance at the parking lot. It looked as if the whole town had turned out, regardless of the weather. I saw a horde of umbrellas spilling out of cars as their owners made their way into the church through the rain. I popped my own umbrella and joined them. Luckily, I spotted a vacancy in the last pew. After I had stashed my umbrella on the floor at my feet and settled back to listen to the organ music, I let my eyes roam over the backs of heads to see if I recognized anyone.

Willis Lansing slid onto the pew next to me, grinned and patted my arm. We sat, unspeaking, through the heartbreaking service. Then, as attendees followed the coffin down the aisle to the strains of "Amazing Grace," I self-consciously bowed my head and focused on my folded hands, fearing I would attract stares as I had at the wedding.

Willis interrupted my self-absorption. "Are you going to the cemetery?"

"No, I'm not. Are you?"

"No. But if you have the time, I'd like to buy you a cup of coffee."

"I'd like that," I said. "Grizzly's in fifteen minutes?"

Minutes later, I was removing my drenched raincoat and sliding into a booth. "What an incredibly sad occasion," Willis said, as he set two mugs of coffee on the table. "I heard that you were the one who found Randy. What unfortunate timing."

"Well, yes." I hated to relive that dreadful night. "Unfortunate for me. Doubly unfortunate for poor Randy. How did you come to know him?"

Willis carefully measured a teaspoon of sugar and stirred it into his coffee. "He did some work for me in the past. A fine young man. I hope they solve the crime soon."

Imitating Willis, I slowly stirred my coffee, although I hadn't added anything to it. "What kind of work did he do for you?"

"Randy was a talented leather craftsman. I enlisted his help on several projects over the past few months." He fastidiously dabbed at his mouth with a napkin. "Switching to another unfortunate subject . . . has the sheriff made any progress on his investigation of the Rendezvous murder?"

"Not that I know," I said, dipping one of Roxie's chocolate biscottis into my coffee. "But if they don't find the killer soon, I think I'm going to be the next victim."

Willis' gray eyebrows shot up in alarm. "What on earth does that mean?"

I told him about my darkroom break-in and my close call on the way to the funeral this morning. He shook his head and scowled. "I wish there were something I could do for you, Cassandra. If there is, please let me know."

"The most you can do is keep an ear to the ground," I said, standing and tidying up the table. "If you hear anything that might help, I'd appreciate your letting me know."

"Most assuredly," he said, rising to help me with my raincoat.

As I bused our coffee mugs, another customer stomped into the cafe and loudly ordered a tall house blend before he ever approached the counter. I wasn't as fast as Willis, who pushed ahead of me and plunged into the rain outside. As I started to pass the new customer, he turned toward me. I recognized his face from news articles I'd recently Googled. *Guy Strothers.* Talk about the devil!

He was a hulking six-foot-three at least. I felt puny and unsubstantial next to him. His presence was so commanding, it seemed to take up the whole room in the little coffee shop. His yellow Eddie Bauer-type raincoat was shedding water like a seal and he pulled out a cloth handkerchief to wipe his face, running it over his carefully styled and blow-dried hair. "You're Cassandra Cassidy, aren't you?" His voice was loud to the point of almost shouting.

How does he know who I am? My heart was hammering, but I sputtered out a reply. "Yes, I'm . . . uh-huh . . . I mean, yes, I am she. That person. Cassandra." Something to that effect.

"I'm Guy Strothers," he said, his voice still booming. "Bridgewater Land Development Company."

"Nice to meet you," I said, sticking out my hand. He ignored it. I jammed it into the pocket of my black funereal dress slacks.

"I want to talk to you." Without waiting for a reply, he took my elbow and guided me to the back of the coffee shop. He pulled out a chair for me and practically pushed me onto it. Seating himself across from me, he folded his arms on the table and leaned toward me. "I've seen some of your photographs. You must be pretty close to those people, to get so many pictures of them."

"Those people? What are you talking about?" I tried to keep my voice from shaking. His loud voice unnerved me.

"You know damn well what I'm talking about." He almost spit out the words. "Your Indian friends."

"I've gotten to know some of the local Indians," I said, curious about where he was heading.

"They're nice pictures. Very nice." He leaned back in the booth, his long legs stretched out into the room. He contemplated his well-manicured fingernails for such a long time, I started to get up to leave. He placed his hand on my arm, pinning me in place. His lips were tight and his eyes blazed. "And you live out by Madigan?"

I glanced fleetingly around the coffee shop for allies, in case I needed help. We were the only customers. "What does one of these things have to do with the other?" I rubbed my arm where he had gripped it.

"Somebody fed Madigan information that is hurting my business. I'd just like to know who it was." He had dropped his belligerent tone.

"I guess I still don't understand what you're talking about."

"I think you do know." He paused, peering at me over tented fingers. "And I could make it worth your while to discuss it sometime." He flashed a toothy smile and tossed a business card on the table. "If you want to talk about it further, call me." He rose without even looking at me and stalked out of Grizzly's and back into the rain.

I remained in the booth for another ten minutes racking my brain. Indians. Marty. Something connecting them with me to Strothers. What on earth? All I could muster up was that maybe Strothers believed I had gotten information from an Indian friend and told Marty about the illegally dumped materials on the reservation. It was farfetched and a stretch of the imagination, but with all the publicity in the papers about my finding both Eric and Randy, I couldn't fault Strothers for thinking I was an important instigator of doom.

I watched through the window as Strothers climbed into a dark-colored SUV, backed out of his parking space, and sped away. Then I had a more sinister thought. Was he the one who had tried to run me off the road, or was it just a coincidence that he showed up at Grizzly's when he did? Not for the first time, I rued the day I'd accepted the Rendezvous job. Attending that one event had initiated a series of others: I had found two murder victims and, within the week following, my darkroom had been trashed, my photographs stolen, and my vehicle had been purposely pushed off the road. Now, Strothers' comments had the effect of a punch in the stomach. Instead of speaking up for myself, I'd acted like I was a wilting, week-old greenhouse rose. It was difficult enough for me to stand up to this kind of pressure from Shaw, but now Strothers, too?

As I climbed back into my Jeep, I conducted a pity-party of one. I'd gotten into this situation simply by taking pictures and befriending a few local Indians. I wanted my life back. I drove straight to Anna's.

Stephanie, Anna's summer sales clerk, was at the counter. Pert, petite Stephanie fit into Anna's tiny originals, and she always wore one of them to show off the merchandise. Today, her Barbie-like figure was decked out in the lacy bustier Anna had tried to interest me in buying, paired with a pair of tight blue jeans. Whenever I saw Stephanie, I felt I was hopelessly sliding into middle age.

"Hi, Cassandra," she chirped, fussing with a garment she was arranging on a hanger. "If you're looking for Anna, she's back in her office." She gestured with her head toward the back of the store.

Anna saw me coming through her glass office door and motioned me inside. She peered at me over her half glasses. "You're looking uncharacteristically overwhelmed, Cassandra. Is this investigation getting to you?"

"Nope." I sank into an easy chair. "This is how I look when someone is trying to kill me."

"*Kill* you?" She stared at me, her eyes wide. "My dear, what are you talking about?" After I had described my early-morning encounter on the road and my conversation with Guy Strothers, her tone of voice changed. "I know Strothers. He's a dangerous man."

I sat straighter. "How do you know about Strothers?"

"I heard about him when I lived in Chicago."

"If he lives in Chicago, what's he doing around here?"

Anna shuffled through some papers of her desk and leaned closer to me. "Things weren't going well for him there. His wife left him in a very messy divorce that was played out in the Chicago papers." She tapped a pen on the desk and her voice rose. "But, he deserved to be divorced. He brutalized her both physically and psychologically. She was lucky to be rid of him." She crossed the room to her bookcase, straightened a couple volumes, and then turned to lean her back against the shelves. "He moved to Colton Mills to work on the Minnesota land development."

I pushed forward to the edge of my chair. "He lives *here*?" I asked, stunned by the revelation. "I could be running into this character on a *daily* basis?"

Anna rushed over to me and knelt in front of my chair. "I don't want to scare you, dear, but he has a reputation of being very nasty to people who get in his way."

"But . . . I didn't do anything!" I pounded the arm of the upholstered chair. "I didn't *say* anything to anyone about him either." I threw up my hands. "Where on earth did he get the idea that I said something to Marty that put his company in hot water? Anna, this is crazy!"

"Did you go to the police about the road incident?"

I shook my head. "I don't want the police involved in anything else where I am concerned. I have no proof that someone tried to run me off the road, and, unfortunately, my old Jeep has so many scratches and dents already, they probably couldn't tell if any of them were caused today. And, I certainly don't want to report anything about my conversation with Strothers. You can't arrest a guy for an imagined threat."

Anna returned to her desk and started to thumb through her calendar. "It may look dismal now, Cassandra, but this will all play out for the best. You'll see." She jabbed her finger on the calendar. "You've got some breathing room. Strothers will be in Chicago for next week's land-developer's conference. He's the keynote speaker. I would think he'd be there for at least a few days."

"Small comfort," I said. "But I'll take any relief I can get."

Chapter 14

Wednesday—Week Two

Whenever my cell phone rang, it was a good chance Shaw was on the line. He was still playing the odds that the one who found the body was quite likely the one who committed the crime. Whenever he called—which was often—I always referred him to Lawton Sanders. Today, I wanted him to call.

He didn't disappoint me. At 9:00 sharp, the phone rang. "Miss Cassidy," Shaw said, "I've been going over my notes and would like you to clarify something for me."

I cradled the phone on my shoulder while I pulled on my boots. "I'm listening."

"When you approached the sweat lodge, a week ago Sunday, was the flap of the tent totally closed or hanging partly open?"

"You know I won't comment on that, sir," I said. "You'll have to call my attorney."

"It would be so much easier if you would just answer my questions."

"Deputy, you know I'd be foolish to do that."

"If you have nothing to hide, it shouldn't be a problem."

I sighed, exasperated that we had to keep having these no-win conversations over and over again. "Would you like to know what happened to me yesterday?"

"Is it something that's relevant to this investigation?"

"It could be," I said. I paused for more dramatic effect. "Someone tried to run me off the road on my way to Randy's funeral, Deputy."

"Is that right? What happened?" He listened while I described the incident. "Did you report the incident to the police?"

"No, sir," I said, shrugging into my shirt and trying to button it one-handed. "But I hope you'll take it into consideration while investigating Eric's murder. A break-in at my house. Someone trying to run me off the road. They've got to be connected somehow. Don't you think?"

"Did anyone else witness this road incident?"

"I don't know. I doubt it, sir."

"I see," Shaw said.

I knew he was thinking his favorite suspect was making up incidents to get herself off the hook. To his warped way of thinking, it probably strengthened his case against me. "It happened, whether anyone else saw it or not." I know I sounded defensive, but I felt the urge to speak up for myself. "And remember, we had a fierce rainstorm that morning. There was thick fog and visibility was difficult. That's why I can't identify the driver of the dark car and why I couldn't get the license plate number."

When Shaw finally ended our conversation, my message light was blinking. It was Jack. I called him back and told him about the latest developments. He listened carefully, then ended the conversation. I didn't hear from him again until that afternoon.

"Meet me at the coffee shop in a half hour," he said. "I have some news that might cheer you up."

Jack's pickup was already in the parking lot when I pulled beside it. He had snagged a table in the rear of the coffee shop. I got a mug of my favorite brew and joined him. "This better be good." I shot him a stern look. "I need some good news this week."

"Okay, babe. How's this for openers?" He flipped open a notebook, circled something on the page, turned it toward me, and pointed to what he had circled.

"What's that?" I asked.

He grinned triumphantly. "I think Eric Hartfield was being paid off by Strothers." Wider grin.

I eyed him skeptically. "Where did you get an idea like that?"

"I have my ways."

"Your ways. C'mon, spit it out. What ways?"

He leaned closer and lowered his voice. "This is strictly between us, right?"

I hesitated before answering, folding and refolding my napkin. "Did you do something illegal? Could you be arrested?"

"If I got caught, maybe. Which I didn't. Now, do you want to hear?"

"Yes," I said, sighing. "I want to hear."

He took a sip of coffee, peering at me over his cup. "I paid Strothers a visit."

I nearly spit out my coffee. "Good grief," I sputtered. "On what grounds? What did he say?"

He was grinning again. Smugly, I might add. "He didn't say anything. Because . . . he didn't seem to be home." I dropped my head onto my chest, closed my eyes, and drummed my fingers on the table. After counting to ten, I raised my eyebrows. Jack continued. "His office was as clean and orderly as a dairy farm system, like he compulsively puts everything in place. I flipped through some of his file drawers. They held mostly financial folders. I couldn't understand the titles, so I kept looking."

"And . . . ?"

"Well, he had a lock on his desk drawers. Fortunately, I was able to trigger them open without much effort. That's where I hit the jackpot." He tapped his notebook.

Propping my elbows on the table, I massaged the scar on my neck. "What did you find?"

Jack motioned for me to lean closer to him so that he could whisper his response. "I found a ledger of some sort with figures written next to dates. Interesting, because it wasn't computer-generated like most of his financial stuff. And . . . I found some envelopes behind the ledger. Inside each one was a handwritten note, listing different amounts. Each amount and each address was different. It totaled more than $250,000 over a period of eighteen months, in amounts ranging from $10,000 to $40,000."

"Wow." I whistled and glanced hastily around the coffee shop. No one was sitting within hearing of us. "Was one of the envelopes addressed to Eric? Is that how you connected the dots?"

Jack sipped at his, by now, cold coffee and made a face. "Actually, that involved a little more sleuthing." He patted his notebook again. "The first thing I noticed was that the letters 'e.h.' signed every one of those notes. I went back to the ledger and found the same letters written alongside several figures and some addresses. In another drawer, Strothers had a folder containing a stack of newspaper articles separated via paper clips into two sets. Guess who had written every single one of them, Cass? *Eric Hartfield.* I skimmed through them and found that one set with earlier dates was very critical of Strothers and his business dealings."

Jack paused to sip at his cold coffee again. I knew he was doing it purposely, but I wasn't going to give him the pleasure of seeing me squirm. "In the second set of articles, which were dated about a year and a half ago to recently, Hartfield changed his tune and began singing Bridgewater Development's praises."

I let the information sink in and stew a bit. I wanted to believe it was something important that would get me off the list of murder suspects, but I didn't want to have my hopes raised needlessly. "So, you're saying the evidence indicates that Eric was accepting bribe money from Strothers to write favorable articles about his development company. That doesn't prove anything, Jack."

He closed the notebook and tucked it under his arm. "Maybe it's not a perfect smoking gun, Cass, but it sure smells like Strothers was paying Hartfield to print good things about him."

"Maybe," I conceded. "You're thinking Strothers was getting tired of paying him off . . . or maybe couldn't afford the bribery game anymore. Eric may have threatened to expose him and Strothers killed him."

"Right. Now you're starting to think like a detective. Makes more sense than it does to think you killed anyone, when you had absolutely no motive."

"Unfortunately, my dear Jack, because of the way you gathered the information, I can't share it with the deputy sheriff. And . . . how would Strothers have gotten a hold of Marty's 'hawk? And . . . how would he know about the sweat lodge? It's not like he's lived here all his life." I'd have to find another way.

* * *

Jack's research about Strothers, whether true or not, added one more arrow to my growing quiver of suspects. However, I was more excited by a call from Willis Lansing when I got back to the carriage house. "I'll be at Marty's house this afternoon," he said on my answering machine. "Maybe you'd like to find a way to be there, too?"

I'd been trying to finagle a way to get into Marty's house for weeks, and now I had additional reasons to show up on his property. One, to see if his vehicle had any red paint on it. Two, to find out if Strothers had ever threatened him, after he'd tried to vote down his development plan. Three, to find out exactly how much he hated Eric for his role in writing about the development issues he adamantly opposed. Four, to find out what he thought of Randy. My ruse, for my landlord's benefit, was to deliver my rent in person. I hadn't seen or talked with him since the Rendezvous. Even though the aspect of finally meeting with him was exciting, my palms were already sweating. In the back of my mind was the thought I could very well be walking into the enemy's camp.

Once again, the presence of Mrs. A on my shoulder offset my jitters. I could hear her whispering in my ear, "You go, girl," prompting me to stand tall and be bold. Mrs. A had guided me directly for four years—right up to the day when the social workers pulled me out of my eleventh-grade American History class. Mrs. A had been rushed, too late, to the hospital, after suffering a massive heart attack. It was one of the worst days of my life. After the funeral, I had packed up my belongings and driven away in the little Saturn Mrs. A had bought for me. I was not about to let the foster-care system get its claws into me for the few remaining months before my eighteenth birthday. I was leaving the only real home I had even known.

When I had stopped for gas in Ridge Spring, Minnesota, population 1250, I read a notice on the bulletin board asking for help at Evening Star Stables. I got the job and stayed in Ridge

Spring for two years, before moving on to Minneapolis. Now, the Mrs. A-instilled boldness urged me on to Marty's house.

Marty's SUV was in the driveway. Elated, I made my surreptitious examination of it. No red paint. Mission number-one accomplished. I knocked on the front door, several times. No answer. No surprise there. I headed for the back yard, reprising the walk I'd made on my first visit to the place. Hearing voices, I let myself through the gate. Marty and Willis Lansing were hunched over some objects on his patio table. Marty saw me and waved me in. As I drew closer, I saw that the objects were open toolboxes with screwdrivers, nose pliers, and other tools littering the tabletop. "Thought I'd deliver the rent in person," I said, in my best nonchalant voice, waving the check in the air.

Marty gestured toward Willis. "Cassandra, this is—"

"We've met," I said. "A couple times." I handed him the check. He folded it in half, and placed it in his shirt pocket. "Hello, Mr. Lansing." I glanced at the paraphernalia on the table.

Willis nodded at me. "Please, call me Willis, Cassandra." He followed the direction of my eyes. "Marty and I are about to do some black-powder shooting," he said. "He thinks he is a better shot than I am, so we agreed to a little friendly competition." He cast a quick glance at Marty. "I am certain Marty would not care if you watched. That is, if you are interested in seeing two old codgers have a little fun." I applauded his finesse in finding a reason for me to stay longer to complete my mission. He hadn't forgotten our discussion after the funeral.

"Well, sure," Marty said. "You're more than welcome to see me beat the ass off this bugger, Cassandra . . . although it surprises me that someone with such a sense of personal pride is willing to let anyone see him come up second." He chuckled and smacked Willis on the back.

Before I could formulate any questions that might introduce Strothers into our conversation, Marty was giving me a quick primer as they prepared their muzzle loaders. "I've got a cap-and-ball pistol single shot." He held up a firearm that looked like something out of a museum. "And Willis has several pieces, but today he's using his cap-and-ball revolver." He pointed to it on the work table. "It takes awhile to get ready to shoot, as you can see. What we've been doing so far is making sure the bore is clean and dry." He pointed his firearm at the ground and snapped off a few percussion caps. I jumped. "Did you see that? The grass moved. That means all is well and the gun shouldn't misfire."

Marty lifted a flask off the table and poured out some black powder. "First, I measure out the powder and pour it into the barrel. Then I take this soft lead ball wrapped in some cloth wadding and ram it into the barrel, on top the powder. Lastly, I fit a percussion cap on the nipple, right here, and we're ready to go." He placed it on the table.

Willis was loading his revolver at the same time, charging each chamber with powder, wad, and ball. He fit percussion caps onto the nipples and his gun was ready to fire, too. A bullseye paper target had been tacked to the same tree I'd seen Marty use on our first meeting.

Marty eyed the target. "I'll go first, as I have to reload more often than you do, Willis." He stepped up to the firing line that had been marked with a spray paint streak on the ground, lifted his weapon, drew a bead on the target, and fired. I had missed the black-powder contest at the Rendezvous so was unprepared for the incredible noise, the flash, and the smoke. I instinctively flinched and covered my ears. For obvious reasons, this was not a hobby to practice in a populated suburb.

With glowing eyes, Marty kicked his foot in the air. A pink flush had spread to his cheeks, just visible above his beard. "Now, this is shooting! Isn't it great?" He lifted his gun above his head and gave a war whoop. "The first time I shot one of these pistols, it was like nothing I'd ever experienced."

I nodded and grinned. "I can see you're enjoying this."

On a roll now, Marty described the variables involved in the use of old-time firearms. "It all depends on how accurately you measure the powder, how round the ball is, how well-centered the patch, and how tightly the whole thing is packed into the barrel, Cassandra. When you shoot a modern gun, your success depends on how good the quality control is in some factory." He jerked his thumb as if the factory were in the next block. "But with this kind of gun, you have to be really, really good to hit the target." When the smoke cleared, Marty checked on the target. He had hit it, dead center, every time.

I'd seen enough. "I'm impressed," I said. "Clearly, you have a knack for this sort of thing." I turned to Willis, who had been waiting his turn in relative silence. "Sorry I can't stay to watch your marksmanship, but I have to run." Despite their protests, I left their rivalry.

I worked a couple hours in my darkroom while thinking, thinking, thinking. I weighed what I had learned from my foray into Marty territory. What did I have to show for my trouble? Not much. Marty was a crack shot, sure. But how would that translate to being a crack tomahawk killer? And I didn't get to ask him any questions. At least I'd learned that Marty wasn't the one who had tried to run me off the road.

The gods smiled on me about 4:15 p.m., when Marty rang my doorbell. "I just wanted to tell you, in case you hadn't noticed, that the trim for the door finally came in and Chet nailed it up yesterday," he said. "Looks a lot better than my temporary repair job." He tapped at the trim in a few places.

"Thanks," I said, making a show of admiring the job. "You're right. I hadn't noticed and I apologize, Marty. Since I'm usually driving into the garage using the overhead door, I don't pay much attention to this side door." I stroked the new wood. "Looks nice. Even the paint matches."

"Chet's a good carpenter and handyman. I call on him at least once a month to help me around here. Well, I won't bother you. I just wanted to check it out and see that you feel safe here." He turned to go.

"Wait, Marty. I've just put on a fresh pot of coffee," I said. "Could I offer you a cup?"

"Well, I've just—"

"Marty, we've never talked about the Rendezvous." I gave his arm a little tug. "Now that you're here and we're alone, I'd like to run a couple of things by you."

He eyed me and cocked an eyebrow. "Sure you want to talk about it, gal?"

"Yes, I need to talk. As you can imagine, I'm going a little crazy. It's been a tough week for me." I held the door open for him and led the way through my living room and into the kitchen.

"You know I'm at the top of the sheriff's list of suspects," he said, as he accepted the steaming cup of coffee I handed to him. Without asking permission, he seated himself at my kitchen table. "I've gotten paranoid about discussing anything without my attorney present."

"I know what you mean." I tinkered with cups and spoons, avoiding eye contact. "I'm on that list, too, and had to hire an attorney. Lawton Sanders has been a godsend. He's fielded questions from the press, and I think, because he exists, Deputy Shaw hasn't dragged me down to the police station for more questions . . . although he still calls me on a regular basis." I seated myself across from my guest.

"Have you found out who broke into your darkroom?"

I shook my head. "But whoever it was wanted the Rendezvous pictures I had developed."

His eyebrows shot up. "What the hell. What do you suppose that's all about?"

The microwave dinged and I excused myself to retrieve some blueberry muffins and bring them to the table. "I have to assume that whoever killed Eric thought there was something incriminating in the photos and took them to find out."

"Any idea what it was?" Marty peeled the paper from the muffin and took a huge bite.

"Nope. No idea." I broke off a piece of my muffin with my fingers. "I don't have copies of the photos that were taken," I said, hating myself for lying to him. I might invite him in for coffee, but I hadn't crossed him off my list of suspects who may have stolen the photos. If he *was* the one who had stolen them—or who had ordered someone else to steal them—I wanted him to think he had them all in his possession. I shifted on the hard chair and crossed my legs. "If you don't mind, Marty, I'd like to ask you about something that's unrelated to the Rendezvous murder. At least I think it is."

He tilted his head and peered at me with open curiosity. "Go ahead. Ask away."

I dampened my index finger and used it to gather up the crumbs of my muffin. Then taking a deep breath, I plunged into the purpose of my interrogation. "I know you and Guy Strothers don't see eye to eye—"

"That's an understatement, gal." Marty slurped coffee from his mug.

"Has he ever . . . threatened you, because of your position against his development plans?"

"Hell, yeah, he's threatened me. He's threatened almost everybody in this town. Why, he's probably even threatened you." He chuckled and reached for a second muffin.

"He has . . . in a way," I said.

Marty's chuckle died and he slopped coffee onto the table. "How'd you get on that scumbag's bad side?" His eyes flashed and a scowl line deepened over the bridge of his nose.

"Well . . . actually, it has to do with you," I said, wiping up the coffee spill with a couple napkins. "He thinks he's put two and two together and come up with me as the bearer of some sort of information between the Indians and you . . . information that affects his business plans."

"That's nuts!" Marty's face had grown visibly red. He pushed back his chair with a loud screech, rising as though to leave. He was clearly angry.

"Wait. There's more," I said, easing him back down in his chair. I told him about my confrontation with Strothers in Grizzly's, and how Strothers had voiced his certainty that I had told Marty about the old paint factory on the reservation.

"That bastard! I'll—"

"There's more." I told him about someone's attempt to run me off the road, only a couple hours before I had the altercation with Strothers.

"He's a hothead," Marty allowed. His frown relaxed somewhat, and he settled back into his chair. "But no matter what I think of the man personally, I can't see him trying to run you off the road, then confronting you in the coffee shop right afterward. That doesn't make sense, even for him. I have to concede that I'm known as a hothead, too."

"If he didn't do it, who did?" I shot back. "And why?"

Marty picked up a third muffin and devoured it in three bites. "What does Shaw think?"

I shrugged. "There are no witnesses. I get the feeling he doesn't believe it ever happened. Anyway, he said the incident is in the police's jurisdiction, not the sheriff's. And the break-in is being investigated by the police department, too, so Shaw's not directly involved with that either."

"These damn jurisdiction fights!" Marty said, his voice rising again. "If those folks weren't so involved in their petty jealousies and shared their investigative information, they'd solve more crimes!"

"Yes, well—"

Marty was on his feet again. He strode to the window and turned. "Do you know where the sheriff is in the murder investigations?" he interrupted. "It still boggles my mind that two of them have taken place in one week. That's two more than I've seen in my lifetime."

"I haven't heard anything." I paused, stirring my coffee. "Have you?"

"I know some things and others I can guess at from working closely with law enforcement over the years."

I peered at him more closely. "Apparently, whatever they've found doesn't exonerate either you or me, or I wouldn't be hearing from Shaw on a regular basis."

"If you factor in only the one crime scene that took place in the sweat lodge, we would be the main suspects. Your footprints were at the scene and my 'hawk was imbedded in Hartfield's head."

"Everyone knows why I was at the sweat lodge. I'm a photographer. I take pictures of everything that takes place at such an event as the Rendezvous." I rose and put our empty mugs in the sink. "Do you have any idea how the killer got your tomahawk?"

Marty headed for the living room to reach the entry door. He stopped to examine a couple framed photographs on the wall and then straightened one perfectly straight picture. His gaze scanned the rest of the room. "I've thought and thought about that, Cassandra. A lot of people have been to my house over the years, and just about everyone knows where I keep my 'hawks. But I can't see that anyone I know well would have taken it or killed Eric. I keep thinking someone stole it, though. It wouldn't have been hard to do. I never locked them away."

I thought about that, but worked at keeping a straight face. It sounded like a convenient excuse. "How about fingerprints at the scene?"

"It's hard to get fingerprints off materials in a place like the sweat lodge, and I doubt they have the technology for it anyway. But . . . I'm sure they're trying."

"What about fingerprints on the tomahawk?" *More information. I need more information.*

My landlord winced and lowered his voice. "The handle was splattered with blood. And there was a lot of that, as you know from being at the scene."

"Actually, I don't know," I said and shuddered. "I was in shock. I don't remember any details, Marty."

He scratched his head, massaging his forehead. "Wouldn't you think, when the perpetrator left that scene, that he'd be covered in blood and that someone would have seen him?"

"You'd think so." I fingered my scar and chewed on my lower lip.

"The deputy said there was no sign of a skirmish or any indication that Eric tried to defend himself." Marty wagged his index finger at me. "He's trying to figure out just how the crime took place. Was someone waiting inside for him? Or outside? Was Eric there to meet someone? Was he killed outside or at some other scene and then carried into the lodge? For such a violent crime, the crime scene doesn't have very many clues."

I handed Marty his hat, which he had tossed onto a chair by the entry. "I'm hoping something breaks in the case pretty soon so I can get my life back."

"You and me both."

Through the living room window, I watched Marty cross the driveway and stride toward his house. Then, I danced all the way back to the kitchen. *Yes! I did it!* For the first time in days, I felt a surge of hope. "Way to go, Cassandra!" I said aloud.

Then I quickly folded. I learned the police had no fingerprints, the tomahawk was covered with only Eric's blood, and there was no sign of a skirmish at the lodge. The only physical evidence they had was my footprints at the scene . . . and a possible hair Shaw kept taunting me about. People had been convicted on less evidence.

I hadn't asked Marty a thing about how well he knew Randy or if he had ever visited his home or if he knew anything about that weapon. Of course, I still held two pieces of information. Strothers had threatened Marty . . . enough to be a motive for getting rid of him. And Eric had probably been blackmailing Strothers . . . a reason for Strothers to kill Eric. That last piece I had not shared with Marty. But . . . what could I do with the information? And what did any of it have to do with Randy?

Chapter 15

Wednesday, 5:35 p.m.

Knowing I needed even more information, I decided to make another trip to the stables to visit Jack. I hoped he would agree to elicit a few more answers from his touted friends in the sheriff's department. After parking, I headed for the horse barn. Jack was busy mucking out one of the stalls. "A little light on stable hands today?" I said, teasing him.

"Damn unreliable kids!" He tossed a forkful of damp wood chips into a cart, then leaned on the fork, appraising me. "What brings you here so soon after our luncheon tête-à-tête, sweet lady?"

"Since our meeting, I've had two interesting ones with Willis Lansing and my landlord." I told him what Marty had learned about the crime.

"How'd Marty know all that?" He pulled the stall door closed.

I walked with him as he wheeled the cart through the barn. "He said he found out some of it and guessed the rest of it. Jack . .

. do you think your friends in the sheriff's department would have some inside information they'd be willing to share with you?"

He threw me a look from the sides of his eyes. "I've already made plans to head that way this weekend. I'll see what a few friendly beers can pry loose."

We'd almost reached the end of the barn. A teenage boy appeared at the doorway, out of breath from running. "Sorry I'm late," he said. Jack thrust the fork in his hand.

We walked towards my Jeep. "By the way," I said, "How's the black gelding? Is his leg healed?"

"Midnight's coming along great. Matter of fact, the owner said he'd like to see the horse ridden and exercised on a regular basis."

"Good idea." I leaned on the wooden fence, spotting Midnight among the horses in the paddock. "Looks like he'd be a great ride. What's he like anyway?"

"Don't rightly know." Jack shrugged. "Unfortunately, I've been too busy to throw a saddle on him. He's turned out and hooked up to the walker every day, which is helping some, but he really needs to be ridden."

I patted the head of a dainty buckskin who'd come looking for a treat. "Why doesn't the owner sell him, if he doesn't ride him?"

Jack rewarded her with a nugget he pulled from out of his pocket. She took it and turned away. "I've suggested it to him, and all I get is a 'definitely not,' so I've quit pestering him. I've been looking for another rider who's capable of handling him and who has the time to do it on a regular basis. The owner is willing to pay someone to do that."

I headed for my car. "Of all the boarders here, there's no one who can or wants to do that?"

Jack snorted. "You've seen the horses in this stable, Cass. They're mostly Quarter Horses, and most everyone is interested in western-style riding. The riders want to learn how to cut cows and barrel race. That's why they hired me. Midnight, on the other hand, is a Tennessee Walker who direct reins, English-style, and wouldn't know a cow from an elephant."

I chuckled as I opened my car door and slid behind the wheel. "And he certainly wouldn't know the moves these Quarter Horses make."

Jack propped his arm across the hood of my vehicle. "You should know, Cass. You learned how to ride in a Tennessee Walker stable and . . ." He slapped the palm of his hand against his forehead. "Why didn't I think of it before? *You* can ride him!"

"Oh, no," I said, inserting the key into the ignition. "My riding skills are too rusty to handle a horse that hasn't been ridden in more than a year. Besides, I've got enough on my mind, without adding Midnight to my troubles."

"Riding a horse is like riding a bicycle. You don't forget how to do it." Jack reached into my car and switched off the ignition. As he pulled me out, he grinned. "You were a damn good rider. I know. I taught you myself. What better way to get your mind off your problems than to ride." He took hold of my arm. "C'mon, let's go see him."

I let him lead me back to the paddock. He grabbed a halter hanging on the fence, opened the gate, singled Midnight out from the horses, and led him out onto the grass. "There, look at him," he said, stroking the horse's neck. "Isn't he a sweetheart?"

Midnight had one white star on his forehead, the only white in his otherwise all-black coat. He regarded us through a set of intelligent brown eyes. I reached out and patted his nose. He didn't move away, but stood as I scratched behind his ears. In spite of myself, I was softening.

"Let's take a closer look at him," Jack said. He led the horse to the arena and hooked him up to a long lunge line. As he let out the line, Midnight walked slowly in a circle. Jack clucked to him and picked up the pace, settling into the smooth walk that defines the Walker breed.

More than a decade had passed since I'd ridden regularly. As I watched Jack skillfully perform his routine, I pictured myself on the horse's back and was hooked. "Okay," I said, throwing up my hands. "I'll see how it goes."

Jack grinned. "All his stuff is still in the tack room. I'll get it for you, along with a waiver you'll have to sign. Then you're good to go."

I took Midnight's halter and led him back to the paddock. Working with the horse turned out to be the diversion I needed. After only a couple sessions of ground work and some riding in the arena, I took him outside. He danced around and swung his head back and forth a few times, but I soon had him under control and headed for the trails that wound through the woods around the stables. Only minutes before, I couldn't understand how I could or why I'd even try to fit an animal into my life. Now, I couldn't imagine life without him. I was blown away by his elegance and beauty and charmed by his happy whinny. I had, quite simply, fallen in love with the creature.

* * *

On the way home from the stables, I called Janine. Fortunately, the library kept evening hours. I asked her to gather all the newspaper articles she could find on the political turmoil resulting from the environmental impact study. If she had the newspapers themselves, I would make photocopies. Ditto for those on microfilm.

After eating a late supper, I spent the rest of the evening poring over the material. The drama played itself out in almost daily articles for a couple months. The commission got a good taste of Strothers makeup. The initial EIS strategy had backfired, big time. When the EIS was filed, instead of backing down and leaving town, Strothers adroitly took the offensive and turned the tables. He sued the Indians, because they hadn't advised him of the hazardous material at the site, which essentially put the onus on the Indians, making them responsible for the problem, instead of Strothers himself.

"I came to Colton Mills in good faith, to build something of value for the Indian community. I feel I was double-crossed," he crowed to a TV reporter. "Frank Kyopa and his team knew of the hazardous waste on the property and should have made it public knowledge. I never would have pursued my project, if I had known the situation existed. Kyopa allowed me to get sucked into the development plans, knowing all along that he intended to provide the commission with the shocking information too late for me to do anything about it."

I stopped reading and thought about Strothers' comment. Was he implying that Marty was used as Frank's pawn? With every interview and article, Strothers proved himself a master manipulator. His star brightened with every letter that appeared in the newspaper.

"I think it's appalling the way Strothers was treated. The man came all the way up here from Chicago with a plan to help the Indians with affordable housing, only to be bushwhacked by the tribe when he had already spent considerable time and money on the project," wrote one letter writer. "The Indians are getting greedy now that they have the casino. They don't want anyone else to participate in their good fortune."

Strothers seemed to have several people in his back pocket. Jack and I already knew about his connection with Eric, although I still hadn't figured out how to use the information. He seemed to be skillfully leveraging all of his contacts to sway public opinion in advance of the impending lawsuit. Dennis Overland, commission chairman, was one of his biggest supporters. Janine had filled me in on his background. He'd made a career out of attaching himself to the coattails of others, using his football-star charm to carry him when his actual business talent failed. He had dropped out of college, after a second-season injury made him ineligible to play, and returned to Colton Mills. He made his first "career move" by marrying the daughter of the town's oldest milling family. The family moved into insurance, when milling went downhill, and had a well-established business in town when Overland joined them as a broker. His engaging personality and glad-handing ways served him well in the insurance game, and he had made a good name for himself by the time he was appointed to the commission. But Dennis had bigger fish to fry. Janine had said getting on the commission was his first step toward state office. And on that path, he allied himself with whomever he thought could help him most.

Big-city, rich, and powerful Guy Strothers was just that kind of man. Overland made the commitment to support him and was contributing to Strothers' public-opinion campaign in spades. The two were often photographed together, socializing at the Friday-night fish fry, contributing time at the town's county fair, presenting a check to the local women's shelter, or fielding questions about the development and upcoming decision on his lawsuit. The naïve local reporters fell prey to his magnetism, and the savvy Strothers turned them on to his planted Chicago contacts, who provided only positive input. As a result, articles appeared, touting how he'd helped local communities through his building and charitable involvement.

In article after article, however, my landlord was getting the short end of the stick. He was continuously identified as being opposed to progress and working against the wishes of the townspeople and, especially, the Indian tribes. In the most recent articles, he was not even subtly connected to the Rendezvous murder. Clearly, he was outclassed by the master of spin.

The articles also mentioned Frank Kyopa and his efforts to counter Strothers' allies, but he, too, was losing the battle. Frank's direct, confrontational manner did not play well in the media. The more he said to defend himself, the deeper the hole he dug.

Even though the EIS research was proceeding, its status was swept off the pages by the impending lawsuit. In the final analysis, it didn't really matter if it eventually stopped the development or not. If Strothers' strategy were successful—and it looked more and more as though it would be—he stood to gain as much in a financial settlement from the now-flush tribe as he would have gotten from a successful development.

After I had dumped all the articles into a trashcan, I went to bed. There was no good reason for me to keep them. I had learned all I needed to know about Strothers and Frank and Marty and their opposing viewpoints about the proposed housing development, and I was no further along in pinpointing any of them as Eric and Randy's killer. Now I knew why it was taking Shaw and the police so long to arrest someone. Sir Walter Scott said it all, when he wrote, "Oh what a tangled web we weave, when first we practice to deceive!"

Chapter 16

Thursday—Week Two

After an early-morning ride with Midnight and a couple errands, Anna called. "I'm attending a meeting of the Rendezvous Society this afternoon," she said. "I thought you'd find it interesting. Want to tag along?"

"Sure," I said. "The subject is currently an interest of mine."

"I'll pick you up at 1:15 sharp."

The Rendezvous Society met in a Civil War-era building that was the county courthouse until about 1899. Abandoned by the county in favor of a new courthouse built a hundred years later, the brick building housed the Odd Fellows hall for decades, until the group could no longer maintain it. Pigeons, bats, and rats inhabited it for a quarter century, until the town's Historical Preservation Society raised enough funds to restore it. It was now used as the meeting place of several Colton Mills social groups.

About a dozen people—all men—were already seated in chairs fronting a foot-high stage that ran the length of the room. A heavy maroon-velvet curtain served as a backdrop for the occasional community-theater drama, if it didn't require a professional-lighting setup. Some of the men were dressed as Rendezvous characters. Others were in street clothes. Marty and Willis sat next to each other the first row.

Anna and I took seats in the back, just as a buckskin-clad man jumped up onto the stage. From what I'd seen at the June Rendezvous, he was a mountain man. He had a rifle in his hand, which Anna told me was a Flintlock. His fringed hunting pouch, slung over his right shoulder and attached by an inch-wide leather strap, fell to his waist on the left side. A powder flask, also attached by a leather strap, crisscrossed the pouch's strap in front, falling to his waist on the left side. A sheathed knife was stuck into the waistband of his buckskin leggings. He wore no hat. His brown hair, pulled back into a ponytail, revealed a silver earring loop in his left ear.

"Welcome Ronnyvooers," he said in the hoarse voice of a habitual smoker. "I'm Muskrat, jest back from three months of trappin' out in the Rockies." He smiled broadly, revealing several missing teeth. It wasn't clearly apparent if the missing choppers were part of the authentic costume or if the person behind the Muskrat disguise was actually missing teeth. He shaded his eyes and squinted into the audience. "Is Jeff here?" he asked. "Jeff, git your sorry butt up here."

A man, not dressed for Rendezvous success, sauntered onto stage. "Thanks, Muskrat," he said in a Chamber of Commerce voice. "And thanks for coming, members and guests." In the next few minutes, he took care of several items of old business, finances, and new business. "We especially want to thank Five Paws," he said, nodding toward Willis Lansing, "for last month's demonstration on sewing leather. Next month, we'll hear from Leaping Turtle, who'll discuss quill writing and paper making. It promises to be an informative evening. But right now, we're happy to have Muskrat with us. He's going to discuss authenticity in clothing. Muskrat has been attending and studying our Rendezvous event for two decades."

Before Muskrat could begin, a hand shot up in the audience and a man rose to speak. "A coupla' weeks ago, a man was kilt at our Ronnyvous. One of our own is suspected in that death. Are we gonna jes bury our heads in the sand and pretend it don't happen?"

"Hear! Hear!" chorused the audience.

Jeff, apparently from the press-release school of managing conflict, responded in a more business-like manner. "The investigation into this incident is having a negative effect on all reenactor groups, Wild Boar. As soon as this is resolved—which I'm confident will be soon—we will get some positive articles to the local press and reverse any damage that's been caused."

Wild Boar jumped to his feet again. "Negative effect? Damage control? Shee-it! If that don't beat all. We otta face this thing square in the eye . . . like real men!"

Most of the group applauded, hooted, and shot their fists in the air. A second man joined Wild Boar. "The question is . . . could the murderer act'lly be one of us? Maybe right in this room?" He pointed his finger, scanning the entire audience. The voices hushed.

Wild Boar leaped onto stage to take control of the discussion. "What do we know fer sure about the crime, folks? One, that he was killed with a 'hawk. Two, that 'hawk belonged to Tomahawk Pete. No question about that." He stared straight at Marty.

"No. No question 'bout that," Marty said, shaking his head. "The 'hawk was definitely mine. Every one of you has seen it a dozen times. You know it by the brass nails."

"Not to mention yore initials on the blade." Wild Boar's eyes sparkled and he grinned, satisfied with the way things were going.

"Yeah, that, too," Marty said, in a softer voice. He lowered his head.

"We all knows the victim and you had no love fer each other. That's right, too, ain't it?" The self-appointed moderator wiggled his chin whiskers, like a character from an old Gabby Hayes movie. It seemed that he was about to judge Marty guilty.

Marty wasn't going to take that sitting down. He popped up in his seat and raised his voice. "I didn't kill Eric Hartfield, but if anybody deserved killing, it was that man. He was the kind that gave vermin a bad name."

"Those're fightin' words, Tomahawk Pete," Wild Boar said.

"I've never been one to mince words." Marty peered at the audience, not afraid to meet anyone's eyes.

"The sheriff is workin' on two premises," the speaker said, regardless if anyone was listening to him or not. "Either you planned the hit and set out to do him in. Or, you met him, got in a rip-roarin' argument, and 'hawked him."

Marty took two long strides toward the stage and, for a second, I thought he was going to attack the speaker. But he threw up his arms, as if pleading to the group. "Would I have used my own 'hawk, if I had set out to kill Eric Hartfield? Would any of you?"

"Probl'y not," Wild Boar said, squinting more closely at Marty. "Maybe someone else stole yore 'hawk and used it. How easy would it be fer someone to do *that*?"

"Pretty easy," Marty said, running his hands through his hair. "I don't lock up my gear. Never had to. Didn't see a reason for it."

Another frontier-outfitted man stood up. "There ya go, men. Believable facts. In all my years comin' to gatherin's, I've never had nothin' stole from me. Ya can't lock a tent, y'know. I once left a long rifle outside after a night of imbibin' and when I got up, the rifle was lyin' on my table and someone had even dried her off. The folks in this community is honest."

Wild Boar nodded agreement. "From what I've heard, the line of fellers that hated the rat who was kilt would stretch from here to Wisconsin. We think yer off the hook, Tomahawk Pete." He and a couple others turned and gazed in my direction. Apparently, I wasn't an anonymous guest in this gathering. "Let's keep our eyes and ears open. Maybe we should choose someone to help us keep track of any leads we get. Who'd like to be that person?"

"I nominate Five Paws," shouted a mountain man in the third row.

"Any other nominations?" Wild Boar said, taking charge. When none were forthcoming, he pointed at Willis. "You willin'?"

"If that's what you'd like," Willis said, standing and nodding around to the attendees. "Whatever I can do to help."

"Okay, Five Paws it is." Wild Boar banged the butt of his 'hawk on the lectern. "Whatever you folks can think of that can help our police solve these two crimes and get Ronnyvooers off the hook—and Tomahawk Pete in pa'ticular—get in touch with Five Paws. But now, since Muskrat has prepared a program, let's hear what he's got to say." He turned to Muskrat, who had faded into the background. "Some of you have worn outfits that you want Muskrat to critique. If you'd like to come up on stage, we'll proceed with the regular meetin'."

Three men obliged.

Then Muskrat took center stage.

"Now, most of you know one of the most important things about bein' a Ronnyvooer is pickin' a character. And the second most important is dressin' that character in the correct garb." His gaze took in the three guinea pigs. "Looks like we got us a trapper, a buckskinner, and a tradesman. Buckskinner here has done a good job. Nice possibles bag. Knife is appropriate to the 1830s. But a buckskinner prob'ly wouldn't wear Nike hikin' shoes."

The hiking shoe comment drew a laugh from the audience.

"When yore completin' the outfit, look for moccasins, the kind you can lace up to your knee, or boots of the period. Havin' the wrong footwear is the mistake that most people make. When you're pickin' a pair of boots, remember that 1830s boots didn't have right or left feet. Trapper, yore lookin' good, too. You might make it more authentic by carryin' a trap and some skins. And, fer God's sake, be sure you know how to set those traps without losin' a finger." Muskrat chuckled at his own little joke.

"See this here tradesman," he said, gesturing toward the last man on the stage. "Y'all know you can tell a lot about a man by lookin' at his garb. Like his occupation, his wealth, and social standin'. You see he's wearin' a natural-color linen shirt. Pure white cloth was the most expensive you could buy in the 1830s. Fancy prints are a little cheaper. Next down the line is stripes, then solid colors, and the cheapest is the natural color. That's 'cause they didn't have no Clorox bleach, only lye, so dyin' fabrics was cheaper. That's why colors cost less than white and that's why our tradesman has chosen natural linen." He thumped one of the men on the back. "So, what's yore name . . . Bad Eye? We can guess yore jest startin' out in yore tradin' career. Is that a fact?"

Bad Eye nodded. "Yessir, I'm jes startin' to bring goods to Rendezvous gatherin's."

By now, I was bored and lost in my own thoughts. I was proud of how Marty had stood up to his accusers, although it remained to be seen if pugnacity was the best strategy in light of the serious trouble he was in. One of the most interesting events of the evening was that my friend Willis had been appointed the "go to" person for any information that would help solve the crime. I made a note to keep in close touch with him.

Chapter 17

It was close to 3:40 p.m., when we emerged from the meeting and began the fifteen-minute drive to my house. I relaxed against the car cushion, happy to be the passenger for once. "Marty and Willis seem to have struck up a friendship," Anna said, maneuvering out of the parking lot. "Did you notice they chatted through much of the presentation?"

"Yes, I noticed," I said, hoping that Willis was gathering information from Marty that would help my own cause. I let my gaze drift lazily along the pine trees lining the two-lane road, enjoying the scenic ride I sometimes took for granted as I rushed from one assignment to another.

On a short stretch of straight road, a vehicle accelerated to pass us. I tensed and jerked to a straighter position. Anna shot me a quick glance. "Every time a car passes us, you relive that scary incident you had in the rain, don't you?" Her eyes followed the vehicle increasing speed ahead of us. "Speaking of that incident, Cass, look at the SUV's license plate." She sped up to make the letters more readable. It was a vanity plate made up of seven capital letters: STRTHRS. Anna and I looked at each other, our mouths agape. "Are you thinking what I'm thinking," she said.

"Strothers," I muttered. "Speaking of the devil. I wish I'd noticed if he had any scratch marks on the passenger side of his vehicle."

"Let's see where he's going, Cass. Maybe we'll get lucky." Anna increased her speed just enough to keep a safe distance behind the vehicle still in easy sight. Instead of turning toward my house, we continued on the winding two-lane highway that passed through a wooded area abutting the river. Ten miles later, the road veered away from the river and trees and straightened into a narrow ribbon flanking fields of corn on both sides. The vehicle ahead picked up speed in response to the straight road.

Anna raised her penciled brows at me. "What should I do? Keep following him?"

"If he doesn't go too much further, let's just see how this plays out. Okay?"

Anna speeded up again and we drove another twelve miles or so. Suddenly, the driver ahead applied his brakes. He made a screeching right turn onto an unpaved country road, churning up dust and gravel as he barreled along. We followed the dust trail for about ten minutes, when it abruptly ended. "Where did he go?" Anna brought her vehicle to a stop and peered about for signs of Strothers' car.

"He must have turned again," I said, craning my neck over my shoulder to see. "He was kicking up so much dust, we couldn't see five feet in front of us. There . . . there he is." I pointed to Anna's left. The outline of an SUV was barely discernable, before it vanished over the rise of a hill.

Following more carefully now, we finally came to another stop by a narrow driveway marked by a dilapidated mailbox perched precariously on a rotting wooden post. "Guess there's a house out here somewhere," I said, "but it's anyone's guess. No numbers or name on the box."

"We'd be fools to go up that driveway, Cassandra. No telling what we'd find. If we're chasing a killer, I don't want to put either of us at risk. What should I do?"

I kept my eyes glued to the long driveway, wondering what was at the other end and why Strothers was out in Timbuktu. For a big city guy, that seemed peculiar, to say the least. "I think you should turn around and head for home, Anna. We'd be crazy to purposely put ourselves at risk. At the very least, we'd embarrass ourselves, if it turns out Strothers is simply having supper with friends."

Anna made a U-turn and headed the car in the direction we'd come. "I'm surprised you're giving in without arguing about it first, Cass. Your common sense is in charge."

After she dropped me off at the carriage house, I went into a funk. I microwaved myself a frozen Lean Cuisine supper, visited the bathroom, shuffled through the mail, and continuously watched the clock. I put a load of dirty towels in the washing machine, cleaned up the laundry room and could not shake the feeling that Strothers was not dining with friends.

More than three hours passed. It was daylight saving time, so dusk was definitely delayed. At 9:20 p.m., my adrenaline was still pumping and I knew I wouldn't be able to get to sleep. I had to do something. Anna and I had been mere minutes away from learning whether or not the elusive Strothers had used his vehicle to shove me off the highway in a storm.

Without thinking any further and possibly discouraging myself from taking action, I grabbed my small digital camera and clipped it onto a strap around my neck. I buttoned one of my red shirts over my tank top, dashed down the stairs to the garage, and climbed into my Jeep. "This is simply too good an opportunity to pass up," I told myself. Checking out the SUV would either confirm or eliminate it as the car that had tried to feed me to the Oxbow fishes.

Not even the fleeting thought that Strothers may be long gone squelched my determination to investigate. I refused to listen to warnings that he could very well meet me on that deserted country road. I knew I didn't have much time to find the right turnoffs before it was completely dark. I glanced at the dashboard clock. It was already 9:45 and the sun was slipping behind the horizon. I followed the route Anna and I had taken earlier, congratulating myself for having a photographic memory. I slowed when I neared the well hidden driveway. Since the road was not visible from what I assumed would be a farm, I saw no need to cut my headlights, but I put them on low beam. About a quarter mile past the driveway, I found a bumpy farm road heading into a field. I parked the Jeep behind a row of bushes that had long ago been planted as a windbreak and trekked back to where the driveway loomed out of the now-complete darkness. It was now 10:25.

Nervousness prickled continuously at the back of my neck, competing with the adrenaline still coursing full speed through my veins to keep my on edge. Skulking around at night was not my style, and the usual angel on my shoulder seemed to have deserted me. I didn't care. I'd been robbed in a break-in, purposely pushed off the road, and verbally threatened. I was snatching at what might be my only chance to get something solid on Strothers that I could take to Deputy Shaw.

I shined the woefully inadequate laser light from my keychain on the driveway and then swept the area round me. Ditches on both sides were filled with grassy weeds about waist high, but other than these grasses, there was precious little cover. I inched up the driveway, praying that whoever lived at the end didn't have guard dogs. I hoped, too, that the exercise wasn't in vain . . . that the vehicle had not left in the time it took me to drive home and back again.

Topping the knoll where I'd seen the SUV disappear, I thought I saw the outline of a house. While covering another ten yards, I peered through the moonlit darkness surrounding it, searching for the object of my mission. Bingo! There it was, as big as life, parked directly in front of the dilapidated porch. My heart leaped to my throat. Was anyone outside? Was anyone watching me? My camera bumped against my chest with every step I took. A beam of light from a window illuminated a few feet of the yard. If not for the darkness surrounding me, I would be in plain sight of anyone from the house. What should I do? Run directly for the SUV, take my pictures, and head back to my Jeep? Be more cautious. Take a risk? Check out who was in the house with Strothers?

I took a quick survey of the property. The house was dominated by the sizeable barn a hundred feet or so to the left. I could barely make out a pickup truck and assorted machinery that littered the yard surrounding it. Although the driveway had no cover, trees and shrubs of various sizes peppered the farm yard. To reach that sparse cover, I'd have to negotiate a no-man's land of empty space. I squatted on my heels. I needed a clear head. The good news was that, so far, no patrolling dogs had announced my presence.

I could make out a figure repeatedly passing in front of the window. I surmised there were at least two people in the house. Who was the other person? Did I need to know? I had come to check out the SUV and to photograph any potential damage. It was a powerful magnet, teasing me to proceed in spite of my reluctance. What to do. *What to do!*

Without another thought, I sprinted toward the yard, gasping as I skidded behind an ungroomed bush. On my knees and as still as a stone, I collected my thoughts and listened. The front door was open. Angry voices carried through the night air to the outside. I crept closer and found refuge behind a lilac bush next to the porch. I moved a branch just far enough to peek through the leaves at the doorway. A man was seated at a table. I could only make out his outline. There. Another man. He seemed familiar, but I couldn't place where I'd seen him. He was older and dressed in farmer jeans held up by red suspenders . . . considerably overweight.

I peered through the leaves, wishing I dared to take a few pictures. Suddenly, another man appeared, pacing back and forth in front of the table. He smacked the palm of his hand for emphasis and raised his voice. I clutched my throat. I'd know that voice anywhere. *Strothers.*

What was he saying? He'd been in the house for several hours. What was going down? It didn't seem like a friendly meeting.

Once more, I scouted the area around me. Did I dare creep onto the porch to hear the conversation? What would the men do to me, if they learned of my presence? The SUV was fully exposed, but the side that may have come into contact with my Jeep was on the far side of the house. If Strothers' vehicle had rammed me off the road, there should be some evidence of it—red paint or, at the very least, scratches. I'd have to wipe off the door first. It would be covered in dust from the road. It would be challenging to photograph the side of the car in the extremely low-light conditions. As close as I'd be to the car door, even if I used a flash at all, all I'd end up with would be an overexposed blob.

Once more, I weighed my options. Creep onto the porch and listen to the conversation. Creep to the SUV, take my photos, and leave. Common sense ruled again. I unbuttoned my red shirt, slowly removed it, and wadded it into a ball. I'd have to use it as the rag to clean off the car door. I shivered, even though it was in the sixties . . . a not untypical late June evening in Minnesota. Using my laser light, I set my camera for low-light, close-up shooting. Then, checking to ensure no one was about to come into the yard, I tiptoed toward the vehicle. With every careful step, gravel crunched under my shoes, bringing me to the brink of a heart attack. I knelt next to the passenger side door and rubbed my wadded-up shirt across the door panel as hard as I could. It was too dark to tell if there were any scratches or red paint. I'd have to take the photos and hope it showed up on film. I dropped the filthy shirt to the ground, lifted the camera into position, aimed it, and pushed the shutter. To my edgy sense of sound, the click seemed unnaturally loud. I held my breath and waited several seconds. When nothing happened, I clicked off three more shots.

Then, without warning, I lost my balance and tumbled backward onto the driveway. My arm shot out to break the fall and, somehow, my finger hit a button that activated the flash. An instantaneous flash of light burst forth from the camera. Immediately, the voices inside stopped. Someone shouted from the front door. "Turn on the damn yard light!"

I skittered behind the vehicle. Light flooded the yard.

"I tell you, I saw a light out here," Strothers said. I could hear him clomp down the few porch steps and start cross the yard. I moved cautiously to the rear of the SUV, praying that he was making too much noise to hear me. I couldn't make it to the barn shadows undetected. I had to stay close to the vehicle.

"Bring me a flashlight," Strothers ordered. He stood in the yard waiting for the light. A minute later, he shined it around the yard, finally turning the light toward his SUV. The beam lit up the area around the driver's side and moved to the back. I willed myself to blend into the side of the vehicle. I cringed, terrified, as gravel crunched beneath his boots. Three more steps. That's all I had. He'd be on my side of the vehicle.

BOOM! *Pop. Pop. Pop.* Just as the light swung in my direction, fireworks rocketed into the sky over the tree line. "Aw, hell," one of the men said. "It's close to July 4th. Someone's just shooting off a few rockets. That's the light you saw. Come on back to the house."

I could hear Strothers spin around and knew he was watching the last remaining sparks in the sky. The sound of his footsteps heading back toward the house was a welcome one. I took my first breath in minutes.

"I'm all through for tonight," he said. "Follow up on what we talked about, and let me know what's going on by the end of the week. Don't disappoint me." The porch door banged shut and, before I could take one step toward freedom, I could hear Strothers stride toward the front of his vehicle. I scooted to the rear. Once inside his vehicle, he started the engine. He put the car in gear and started to back up to make a U-turn. Feeling desperate, I grabbed the spare-tire frame mounted on the back of the door, and fly-like, planted my feet on the back bumper. As the vehicle rumbled down the driveway, I held on tightly, praying all the while—*God, don't let me be visible to the men on the porch.*

Fortunately, they had other things on their minds. We were less than fifteen feet from the house, when the yard light was turned off. We were plunged into darkness again. When the SUV slowed to go up an incline, I let go and fell back onto the end of the driveway, landing on my left side. The gravel bit into my bare skin. Quickly, I rolled into the ditch. A full minute later, I dared to sit up and access the damage. Nothing, including my camera, appeared to be broken.

Not until I was halfway home did I remember that my wadded-up shirt was lying in the dirt of the farm house yard. My mouth went dry. What were the odds they'd find the shirt? More to the point, what were the chances they'd hand it over to Strothers and he'd recognize it as mine? The chances were good, on all counts. For the first time, I regretted that my red-shirt uniform was so easily identifiable.

As exhausted as I was, I couldn't wait until morning to see the results of my escapade. I had to spend time in the darkroom immediately. An hour later, I examined the first photo. All I saw was an indistinct blob. Ditto for photos two through four. "Damn!" I had wasted my entire evening and lost a few patches of skin for a dangerous stunt that yielded nothing. Worse, I had left incriminating evidence behind.

Chapter 18

Friday—Week Two

I awoke by 6:15 a.m., determined to tease something out of the dismal digital images I'd downloaded the night before. Again, three indistinct splotches filled the thumbprint squares. Not good. Not completely disheartened, I turned to my computer software for assistance. It had performed miracles before. I saved the photos and clicked on Photoshop.

For several minutes, I manipulated the first image for brightness and contrast, hoping to work some magic on the dark smudge that filled my screen. As I viewed the black blob, I relived my nighttime adventure. In my mind's eye, I saw my shirt lying in the driveway waiting to be discovered. A cold chill ran through my body. I'd acted on impulse, something I'd been prone to do most of my life. But this time, spying on a possibly dangerous man, in the middle of the night and at a remote farmhouse, was far more foolhardy than anything I'd ever done. There *would* be a consequence to pay. What kind, I couldn't imagine.

Forcing myself to keep working, I saved the changes to a hopelessly indistinct "Photo #1" and opened "Photo #2." I reduced the brightness by ten percent and increased the contrast.

A lifetime of acting impetuously hadn't turned out so badly, I decided, while attempting to console myself. A string of impulses several years ago had factored in putting me where I was—in front of my computer, trying to bring some resolution to the damnably indistinct images. My mind drifted back to the Insignia Club, a tiny bar-restaurant outside Minneapolis. I'd landed there as a waitress after a couple of years at the stables in Ridge Spring. Scott had landed there, too, snagging a solo guitar-playing gig on Friday and Saturday nights. The guy had mesmerized me from the get-go and the attraction was mutual. One thing led to another, and when Scott left town for New York, I followed him on a Greyhound bus a week later.

Life in New York was exciting. I found another waitressing job and, on the weekends, I basked in the reflection of Scott's growing popularity as he played to ever-increasing rave reviews. After six months, it seemed like a good idea to get married. So we did.

I loved being Mrs. Scott LeCaro. I loved the friends we made, who were mostly other musicians and waiter-types hoping to make it big in something besides waiting tables. Life was good. Life was fun. After a year, my Scott—who was now dubbed by music writers as a "steel-string master of beguiling chords and fast progressions,"—decided to take his show on the road. I stayed in New York, at least at first, and waited for him to come back.

Bored, I saw an ad to study photography with master photographer and teacher Jules Antoine and remembered how important taking pictures had been for me in high school. I scraped together my waitressing tips and enrolled in one of Jules' one-on-one classes. That was when my picture-taking took on a new dimension and photography became a passion. I prowled the streets of New York taking black and white photos with an old-fashioned Rolleiflex 6 x 6 that I'd picked up cheap in a secondhand store. Although I'd moved up to more high-tech cameras, I still relied on my old Rollei to get special black and white effects.

Jules was a master photographer of people. He made amazing art out of men and women going about their daily business, translating his emotions into visual form. He taught that a curious, caring approach allows one to open up to the camera. I applied his principles, not only in my "artsy" photographs, but in my wedding ones as well. I'd always wanted to turn Jules loose at one of my Minnesota weddings, to see how he would turn trite, posed pictures into interesting, alive art. The fact that my wedding business increased every year, while featuring unstaged pictures, suggested I'd been reasonably successful. At any rate, some of my more incautious actions had put me on a pretty good track. If I hadn't acted on impulse, I'd probably still be waiting tables.

Photoshop was teasing me as insistently as Strothers' SUV had tempted me in the driveway of the farmhouse. I couldn't hope for perfection, given the circumstances, but maybe I'd find something I could use. Photo #2 was dark, as expected. I manipulated it as much as I could, pulling out every trick for brightness, contrast, and balance. No luck. I couldn't bring up any image at all. When I added brightness to the third photo, however, a few lines began to take shape. Unable to figure out what I was seeing, I added some contrast, zooming in as far as I could go without losing the focus. A series of lines emerged, but I couldn't tell if the lines were scratches or something else. I printed the enlarged image to get a better look. Taking the paper off the printer, I pinned it to the wall and stepped back. I was looking at vertical lines that could or could not be scratches.

Great. I had risked life and limb, and this was all I had to show for it. So much for my midnight caper. My detective skills had a long way to go. *Better not quit your day job, Cassandra,* I thought, while toting my empty coffee cup back into the kitchen.

It was only 8:20 a.m., but I set about spending the next hour industriously dusting and pushing the vacuum over the floors and carpeting. Whomever my parents were, they hadn't passed down a cleaning gene to their daughter. I cranked up the CD player, hoping to drown out depressing thoughts with music from the Chicago soundtrack, stuffed another load into the washer, and plodded over to the closet for my meager housecleaning supplies. I worked in tempo to "When You're Good to Mama," and, at least temporarily, shelved images of myself decked out in prison orange.

As I transferred my first load of wash to the dryer and threw my jeans into the washer, something clinked against the bottom of the washer. I felt around for the errant quarter or dime I must have missed when going through the pockets. It wasn't a coin or even a big button. To my utter surprise, it was a hundred-dollar CF memory card from my digital camera. I stared at it, bringing the palm of my hand closer to my face. What was on the chip? I couldn't remember misplacing any wedding pictures. I stuffed the card into the pocket of my shirt and packed the rest of my jeans into the washer. Then, curiosity outstripping my need to do any more cleaning, I took the card to my office.

Once I had fired up my Mac, I fed the errant card into the card reader. I punched "Import Photos" on my computer and dozens of thumbnail images filled the screen. Pictures of buckskin- and calico-clad characters emerged. Ah, a card I'd shot up at the Rendezvous. I vaguely remembered slipping it into the watch pocket of my jeans and replacing it with a new one when I returned to my vehicle while waiting for the tomahawk competition to start. I'd taken so many photos at the Rendezvous, I hadn't missed the shots on this wayward card.

The photos made me smile despite the Rendezvous turn of events. Hundreds of local citizens had earnestly tried to turn back the clock for one weekend out of their busy twenty-first century lives. I went to work creating files for separate categories. Tradespeople—silversmiths, leather workers, blacksmiths—went into one file. The tomahawk-throwing competition got its own. Children went into another. I created files for women, gear, campsites, and goods.

With most of the photos categorized, I looked more closely at the dozen left over. I had snapped several to simply fill up the disc on the way to the parking lot for new batteries. I zoomed in on them, one by one, to see if they would fit into one of the other categories, or if they even deserved to be saved. Pictures of vehicles in a parking lot left me cold, creatively speaking.

After reviewing a half dozen mind-numbing photos, I was ready to tuck the rest, unviewed, into a catchall category, when a few marks on a pickup door caught my eye. Zooming in on the vehicle's door, I saw why they seemed familiar. They were the same lines I had photographed in the farmyard! In this photo, however, the lines were clearly part of a company logo . . . Bridgewater Land Development Company.

My heart was playing a drum solo as a startling thought reached my consciousness. A Bridgewater truck in the Rendezvous parking lot could place Strothers at the event! The photo might be enough to convince Shaw of the value in investigating him and dropping his focus on me. My hand trembled as I reached for the phone and punched in Jack's number. No one answered at the stables. I punched in his cell phone number. He answered on the first ring. "Jack, where are you?" I practically shouted into the phone. "I tried calling you at the stables."

"I'm just coming in from the pasture," he said, audibly breathless. "I'm about to ride out to look for Jim Tuttle, Frank Kyopa's nephew."

"What do you mean?"

"He's been missing for several days."

"Is . . . is that unusual?"

"He's sometimes gone for a couple of days to tend a trap line, but he didn't show up for his job as county dispatcher and that's not like him. I'm worried."

"I have something I need to talk to you about, Jack. If you saddle Midnight for me, I'll ride with you. Please wait for me." A half hour later, I was seated on Midnight's back. I suggested we search in a direction where I hadn't ridden before.

"It's kind of wild in there, Cass," Jack said, eying the heavy brush. "I don't think we should . . ."

But Midnight had committed himself. We followed the faint trace of a path that led to somewhere in the middle of the island. Sometimes the trail was so narrow, branches threatened to pull me out of the saddle. I filled Jack in on finding Strothers' truck in the photos.

"That's intriguing, Cass, but merely because you see his company truck doesn't mean he was there himself. An employee could have been using the vehicle. You'll need a photo of Strothers at the event." Jack pushed a branch from his face.

"I've got tons of photos to go through," I said. "I'll keep looking."

Jack was feeling apprehensive and wanted to get off the trail. "I can't believe Jim would be out here, Cass. Let's turn around."

"Even if we wanted to, we couldn't," I said, moving forward. "There's no room to maneuver. Midnight is skitterish enough. I can see the glimmer of a pond up ahead. Let's at least go there, let the horses refresh themselves, and then turn back."

"I don't think that's wise," Jack insisted. "We'll get bogged down in the muck." He had no more than said that than the trail opened to an expanse of tall, reedy green plants. A narrow shelf of ground looked as if it would allow us to skirt the area. "See . . . I told you, Cass. We can't get through that mess. Don't even try." He reined his horse around.

"Okay," I conceded. "I'll just ride along the edge a couple feet and find a better place to turn." As Midnight stepped into the clearing, I saw an old oak tree dominating the tiny patch of land on a slight knoll. "We're not the only ones who have been here, Jack," I said, pointing to a ring of rocks. "Someone has built a fire out here." Midnight kicked a muddy Budweiser can out of the way. "Drinking, I might add."

Jack drew abreast of me and we listened to the sounds of swamp insects and the occasional croak of a frog, while peering more closely around us. "Whatever they were cooking out here doesn't smell very appetizing," Jack said, wrinkling his nose.

"It smells more like something died." I covered my nose with my hand. "Maybe a coyote brought down a deer. Come on, Midnight, let's go home." I lay the reins on his neck and was about to turn him around when something caught my eye. "Jack, look over there. What's that?" I pointed. "Over there by the tree."

Both of us inched forward. When we were about ten yards from the tree, Jack stopped. "Oh, shit!" he said. He put out his hand to stop my progress. "Cass, go for help. I'll wait here."

* * *

Friday Evening

The corpse was that of Frank Kyopa's nephew, Jim Tuttle. He had been hanging from the century-old oak tree for three days. His hands were bound behind him with a length of the same rope found around his neck—a hand-braided rawhide rope. Jim was thirty years old and left a wife and two young children.

Law enforcement was not amused that I had turned up at the scene of the third body to be found in Clayton County in less than two weeks. By now, the sheriff's interrogation was so familiar that, with Lawton Sanders by my side, I anticipated most of the questions and answered them automatically. As I left the station and headed for home, I was surprised to see the sun still shining. For too long, I had felt I was walking under a dark cloud and that cloud had stubbornly followed me since I'd found Eric Hartfield's body. Even my "Cassandra" mantra had failed to drive it away.

I'd always reveled in my name, telling myself I was special and destined to be more than ordinary. If not, wouldn't my mother have given me a common name? Mary, maybe, but surely not Cassandra. Since childhood, I've chanted it to myself over and over whenever I was feeling stressed, like an affirmation that I'd get through my predicament. "Ca-SAN-dra, Ca-SAN-dra, Ca-SAN-dra," I'd chant, to the rhythm of my bike tires. The mantra usually relaxed me, but, today, it taunted me. After finding three bodies, I was beginning to think the Greeks had the more correct interpretation of my name. Cassandra: prophet of doom.

The seemingly senseless killing of Jim Tuttle didn't sit well with the citizens of Colton Mills. While Randy's murder had finally driven them to lock their doors, stock up on ammunition, and stay inside, this third murder seemed to drive them into pressuring law enforcement to work harder. At least the press was indicating this change in attitude. It was clear to anyone with half a brain that a serial killer was in their midst. As I listened to updates of the murder on TV, it appeared the police didn't have a clue or motive for any of the three murders. Thankfully, few citizens knew that I was on Shaw's list of suspects. Otherwise, they'd probably be pounding on my door.

The only way to keep from dwelling on that fact was to concentrate on what I could do to help myself. My mind drifted to the paltry evidence I had that put Strothers near the scene of the Rendezvous murder. I had found a digital photo of his vehicle on a CF card the sheriff didn't know I had. I was reluctant to turn it over to him. Two weeks had passed between the time of Eric's murder and my discovering the photo card in my pants pocket. Shaw would surely make something of it, like charging me with withholding evidence . . . or something worse.

It probably wasn't the smartest decision I'd ever made, but I hadn't even mentioned finding the digital photos to my attorney. Fearing what Shaw would do with the information outweighed the fact that I should share it with Sanders, even though I'd had the opportunity to do so at the station. I hated the feeling that, along with everything else this case was doing to me, I was growing mistrustful of almost everyone.

I was determined not to become a powerless victim, though. No one cared more about clearing my name than I did. But . . . I was a professional photographer and not a detective. I was a long way from being a candidate for the Detective Hall of Fame. Instead of digging myself out of a hole, my lame detection attempts had proven fruitless. I was digging a deeper hole. I'd stepped out of character, photographing car doors in the middle of the night. And what did I have to show for it? Nada. Not only had I failed to acquire any overpowering evidence, I had left evidence behind. Feeling somewhat encouraged that I hadn't received a visit or call from Strothers about the shirt, I found myself wanting to believe I had lucked out. Perhaps he couldn't link it to me, because he had never paid enough attention to me to know I was usually dressed in red.

As I parked my Jeep in the garage of the carriage house, I wondered for the hundredth time what evidence Shaw had on me, or if he was only bluffing, as Sanders seemed to think. When would the other shoe drop and when would I become an official suspect in Randy's and Jim's murders?

Chapter 19

Saturday—Week Two

My feet hadn't touched the floor of my bedroom, before I was dreading what the day would bring. Should I spend it indoors poring over the Rendezvous pictures on the digital card? What I needed was to get out of the house and clear my head. The weather report on the late night news had predicted a sunny day in the low eighties. It would be a perfect day to try one of my favorite places—Tall Pines National Park, where an Orienteering meet was being held. I could get off the beaten track and do some hiking, and yet be in the midst of people having fun. I laced up my red Lands End hiking boots, looking forward to what I hoped would be a mind-clearing walk.

Despite my determination to enjoy the day, I spent almost as much time peering in my rear view mirror as I did driving down the county road to the park. No one seemed to be following me, so I focused, instead, on the towering trees lining the winding driveway up to the park's main building. They soothed me. I found a spot in the crowded parking lot, slid out from under the wheel, and did a runner's stretch against my car. I grabbed the camera on my car seat (I have to have at least one camera or I feel undressed), pulled the strap over my head, and started out by the trail signage arrow. It was a good ten degrees cooler under the majestic Big Woods canopy.

The trail I selected wound upward and circled through the woods. Between the trees, I caught glimpses of brightly clad orienteering participants jogging to one of the orange nylon control boxes that dangled from a branch. Their presence reassured me, and I trekked on resolutely, willing myself to forget the events of the past month.

A woman in a blue and orange skin-tight suit jogged by, topographical map in hand, and veered off into the woods, seeking the next box. I knew a little about orienteering. The participant who best combined reading the topographic map with compass reading, and worked out the shortest route through the woods from start to finish was the winner. Participants negotiated the route from "control" to "control," punching their cards at each box. Finishers had their cards completely punched.

I liked the way the structure combined running with a kind of treasure hunt, and the fact that it had little to do with teamwork, a principle that seemed to challenge my compatibility. I decided I might join a local "O" club, as soon as the mess I was in blew over. The way my life was going now, however, I'd probably get lost in the woods and never find my way out. Picturing myself all suited up in a red and black jogging suit, it suddenly dawned on me that I no longer saw any orienteering runners. I had slogged beyond the boundaries of the course.

Damn. Better reverse. I turned to retrace my steps. That's when I saw him. The man was coming—make that trudging—up the trail toward me. He was still too far away to identify his

164

features, but I immediately spotted the farmer-style jeans and red suspenders. I stopped dead in my tracks. Where should I go? Did I have to stay on the path? Did he recognize me, too?

The man in question stopped to mop his brow. Then he plodded up the hill, head down. My eyes never left him and my imagination went wild. Hundreds of old men wore overalls and suspenders. At least dozens of them liked the color red. Maybe the suspenders had been a Christmas gift. Maybe the old gentleman was on a picnic with the family and simply getting away from the grandchildren for a few minutes.

At that moment, he lifted his head and saw me staring at him. He stopped with a jolt and stared back at me. *He's not just another hiker in the woods. He's the man at the farmhouse with Strothers. I think. Isn't he?* He stood perfectly still, straddling the trail so I'd have to either walk through or around him to get past. Winded as he appeared to be, he didn't look like he'd be much of an obstacle. Except for his size. He had a good hundred pounds on me. As we held eye contact, his right hand inched slowly toward his pocket.

Now, a man can reach for several things in his pocket—a hanky to wipe his brow, a stick of gum, a pack of cigarettes, a cell phone. But my already uneasy brain registered, *"He's going for a gun!"* I reacted the only way I knew how to react in such a situation. I drew my own weapon. I lifted my Canon and adjusted the telescopic lens to bring him into focus. Just as I pressed the shutter, he abandoned the trip to his pocket and whirled, hiding his face behind his uplifted arm. In a flash that belied his age and physical condition, he stepped off the trail and lumbered into the woods. Happily, not quickly enough. I had a perfect photograph of the red suspenders holding up his dungarees.

Feeling full of myself for my quick thinking, I was tempted to keep going in his direction, but once again, common sense prevailed. I jogged the remaining four miles of the trail, confident that, unless he had a four-wheeler stashed somewhere, I was out of his reach. When I returned to the parking lot, I photographed the vehicles and their license plates, just in case he had left his vehicle in the public parking lot and I could match it to those in other photos.

Back home and behind locked doors, I thought about him again. *What in hell was that all about?* I wondered. *Am I such an easy quarry that someone sent an aging, out-of-shape farmer to follow me? Or, am I only being foolish and imaginative and spooked about anyone and everyone without a name I know and trust?*

* * *

Sunday Morning—Week Two

Knowing it had been exactly two weeks to the day since I'd found Eric's body in the sweat lodge, I couldn't spend the day alone. A trip to Grizzly's for coffee and cinnamon toast was better than wrestling with my thoughts. While sipping latte, I read about the Colton Mills murders in the Sunday edition of the *Minneapolis-Tribune*. It reported no progress and an increasingly nervous population. "We are following up on some promising leads," the police chief was quoted as saying, although he acknowledged there were precious few clues at the scenes of the crimes.

Someone pulled out a chair and slid onto it at my table. I peered over the newspaper. "Jack, what are you doing here?"

"I knew I'd find you here," he said, propping his elbows on the table. "I found out some interesting stuff this weekend."

I folded the newspaper and placed in on the table. "How interesting?"

"You know I went up north, right? A couple of my buddies from the sheriff's department were there. They dropped a couple hints about the Rendezvous murder investigation."

"And . . . ?"

"They're thinking there could be a connection between the Rendezvous murder and those of Randy and Jim." He tipped his Stetson to the back of his head and grinned. "You gonna buy me coffee for that? And something to go with it?"

"Not sure," I said. "It didn't take a rocket scientist to figure that out. The cops made that connection as soon as I turned up at the scene of all three murders." I paused. "Did my name come up?"

He nodded. "I heard your name a few times. But more interesting is the other name came up."

I set my cup down, giving him my full attention. "Whose would that be?"

"Buy me coffee and I'll tell you."

"Go get it and be quick! And get me a glazed donut . . . two of them. I'm still famished."

After Jack placed his mug on the table and shoved a plate of several donuts toward me, he ruffled the hair on the top of my head. "Seems that your landlord, Marty Madigan, knew all three of the victims. Quite well, in fact." He reached for one of the donuts.

"We already know that Marty knew Eric and Randy. Colton Mills is a small town. It's no surprise that he'd know Jim, too. After all, Marty works closely with the Indians and Jim is Frank's nephew."

"You're right, it's not a surprise he'd know them." Jack removed his hat and scratched his head. "What *is* a surprise is that Marty has had run-ins with all of them." He shoved the rest of the donut into his mouth.

"Was the incident Randy told me about one of them?"

"Yep." Jack gulped down a swig of the hot coffee. "I think Randy downplayed to you what happened that day. He told the deputies about it over a beer afterward. They told me Randy could have filed harassment charges."

I used a napkin to wipe the donut sugar from my chin. "Randy thought Marty had a weird reaction to the injured woman from the accident, but I don't think he felt assaulted. If he did, it would have made more sense for Randy to kill Marty than the other way around."

Jack gazed at me intently. "Maybe you're right. I'm just reporting what I heard from the guys. They pretty much forgot about Randy's connection to Marty, until one of them remembered the bad feelings between Marty and Jim Tuttle."

"Bad feelings with Jim Tuttle?" I bolted up straight. "Tell me about that!"

"Marty has some conflicting ideas about the accepted way of life around here." Jack held up his hand. "On the one hand, he takes part in these old-time Rendezvous, where they use animal skins and roast the meat over open fires." He lifted his other hand. "Yet he's almost violently opposed to trapping."

"And Jim was a trapper."

"Not only a trapper, Cass. He was an outspoken trapper. Marty's been trying for years to outlaw trapping in the county, but every time he thought he was getting somewhere, Jim rallied enough support to ensure no bill ever got passed."

I spun my spoon in a circle on the table and glanced fleetingly at a couple passing our table. "How did somebody like Jim manage that?"

Jack shrugged. "Here's another interesting tidbit." He lowered his voice. "Jim got help from his uncle, Frank Kyopa—your friend and president of the Prairie River Band. The Indians don't want to see trapping go the way of hunting, so whenever it comes up, Frank sends his legal team to fight the fight."

I chewed on my bottom lip. "Hmm. Either of those issues could make someone like Marty mad and frustrated enough to resort to murder."

"Maybe, maybe not, on the face of it, Cass, but there may be more to it than we know."

I pushed back my chair and reached for my purse. "I'll keep nosing around."

Jack took my elbow and guided me outside. "Meanwhile, I'll keep in touch with the deputies and see if I can pry anything more out of them." He walked me to my car. "Is everything else okay?"

I nodded "Fine today, so far, but I think someone followed me while I was jogging yesterday." I told him about the incident in the park.

"Are you out of your mind? What were you doing in that park by yourself? You're leaving yourself wide open."

"I suppose I could just stay in my house and drive myself mad, like my landlord."

"Cass, you've got to watch out for yourself." He took hold of my shoulder and gave it a little shake. "Is there anyone you could stay with until this blows over? You're isolated out there in the carriage house."

I nodded again. "Don't tell me I haven't thought of that. Marty's out of town right now. So is Anna. And, no, I don't have anyone I can stay with."

"I've got an extra—"

"Don't even think about it." I wasn't desperate enough to avail myself of Jack's hospitality.

"Suit yourself, Cass. Thought I'd make the offer anyway." I climbed into my Jeep while Jack held the door open. "A lot of manpower in both the sheriff and police departments has been diverted to the Colton Mills murders, because they're afraid whoever committed them may strike again. Do you have any kind of weapon? Just in case you should need one?"

I squinted up at him. "If by weapon, you mean gun, then no, I have no weapon. I've never been into guns."

"Think about it," he said. "I'll loan you one of my firearms."

I laughed. "The only thing I've ever aimed and shot is a camera," I said. "And isn't there something illegal about borrowing somebody's firearm?"

"I'll take you to a range where you can get up to speed in no time. As for any legalities, we can worry about that later."

"I'll think about it." I glanced at the dashboard clock. "I have to go, Jack. I have an appointment at 11:00 and I'm late already."

Even though it was a Sunday, I had made a call to Heather, back from her honeymoon, and arranged to show her the black and white proofs of her wedding. While we poured over them, she served me a sandwich for lunch and by the time I returned home, it was pushing 2:00. I had three hours of work to do in the darkroom to print the pictures she wanted. I still had plenty of time to put the project to bed.

It was closer to 6:30 before I tucked the final folder into my briefcase for the next morning's meeting. I made myself a boring scrambled egg sandwich and washed it down with root beer. After staring at the television for a couple hours, I decided to head for bed and read a novel. Just as I put my foot on the first stair step leading to the upstairs bedroom, a muffled blast came from directly outside the carriage house. I ran up the rest of stairs and opened the door at the top. Light flickered just outside my bedroom window. Fire. *It was fire.*

I froze. *Fire.* Slumping onto the top step, I held my head and rocked back and forth as my mind played tapes of the fire that had plagued my dreams every night of my life. God only knew how long I'd have sat there, paralyzed with fear, if the piercing sound of sirens hadn't snapped me out of it. I wobbled my way down to the garage, opened the overhead door, and stumbled outside.

"Were you the one who called us?" a suited-up firefighter asked. "Someone called us on the cell phone, saying they had passed a fire."

"No. No . . . it wasn't me. I-I live here, but . . ." I could feel my bottom lip tremble.

"Don't worry, ma'am. I can see you're a little shaken. The fire is almost out and it didn't do much damage. It did wipe out the deck, but it'd take more than a fire to get through those stone walls." He tapped the wall for emphasis.

I wrapped my arms around myself to stop the incessant trembling. "I . . . I heard a loud sound . . . like a . . . like a bomb or firecracker or something. Do you know what c-caused it?"

"I'll leave that to the police to explain, ma'am." He motioned toward a police officer who materialized out of the dark. "Glad you're all right."

"The fire captain called me after they responded to the fire," the uniformed officer said, whipping out a notebook and a pen. "Know anyone who might want to do you harm?"

I pressed a hand to my forehead. What was he saying? "Why . . . why did you ask me that?" I said.

"It looks like someone lobbed an explosive at your house, ma'am."

"To . . . to blow it up?" My voice sounded small and frightened. I bit my lip.

"To start a fire," the officer said matter-of-factly, making notes on his pad. "But they didn't count on the fortress you live in." He peered down at me, pen poised. "Any idea who might be behind it?"

"I-I don't," I lied. He'd think I was a nut case if I gave him my list of possibilities.

He finished writing up his report. "We'll be in touch," he said. "There's nothing much we can do tonight, except scout the area for cars or people who shouldn't be anywhere near this property. We've taped the area off and one of our techs will be out in the morning to gather evidence. Meanwhile, if you think of anything more that will help, call me at this number." He handed me a business card with his name on it.

I stumbled up the stairs and called Jack regarding his offer to help me arm myself.

Sleep was elusive. As the fire in my dream threatened to envelop me, it intersected with the image of flames climbing the walls of my carriage house. I thrashed about, kicking the sheets away. I awoke coughing, in response to the real smoke still permeating my apartment. I pushed into my slippers and padded outside to see how much damage had been done from the fire bombing. Within the crime-scene tape, scorch marks climbed up the stone wall nearly to my second-story window. The fire had burned away the cedar deck and fried my deck furniture. But the firefighters were right about one thing: it would take a much more serious explosive to dent the two-foot-thick carriage house walls. I did, indeed, live in a fortress.

Chapter 20

Monday—Week Three

Finally showered and dressed, I paced my living room, ending up at the window facing the driveway. Who would go to the lengths of firebombing my house? Was it someone who knew that fire terrified me? *I'm dealing with a maniac*, I thought, shivering with the notion. *When is this nightmare going to end?*

Once more, I checked my watch. It was only 8:30 a.m. I had agreed to meet Jack at eleven. That gave me plenty of time to deliver the finished wedding photos to Heather. As brides go, she had been easy to work with and I didn't anticipate any problems. There weren't any. By 10:45, I was on my way to Jerry's, Colton Mills' only sporting goods store, on the edge of town. Jack was leaning against the counter, arms folded over his chest. He arched his eyebrows when I strode resolutely up to the counter and eyeballed the selection of pistols and revolvers in the display case.

"Here's one I sell to a lot of women looking for a self-defense handgun," Jerry said, holding out a palm-sized revolver to me. "It's a compact .38 caliber, only five and a half inches long and weighing twenty-four ounces. It's highly concealable and easy to carry."

"Carrying it is one thing," I said, as I turned the gun over in my hands. "Pointing it at someone and pulling the trigger is the hard part."

"Looks like a good one," Jack said, taking the gun from me. He asked for a couple of boxes of ammunition and we headed out to the range. The area was enclosed by a cyclone fence. Some beaten-up metal targets rose out of the ground at what looked to be a long distance away. We stopped next to a table and Jack explained the fine points of shooting to me. "You grip it like so," he said, demonstrating how to wrap my right hand around the handle, "and place your index finger lightly on the trigger."

The gun, although a lightweight model, was heavier than it looked. I grasped it and put my thumbs in position to hold it steady, as Jack had instructed. Then I held it straight out in front of me and pointed the barrel toward a target.

"I'll bet you're a natural Annie Oakley," Jack said, reaching around me to fine-tune my grip. "You're already strong from toting cameras and you know how to point and shoot."

"Yeah, but my tool of choice is held close to my eye, not at the full extension of my arm."

We moved to within about thirty yards of one of the targets and stuffed plugs into our ears. Jack loaded the cylinder, assumed a shooting stance, took aim, and pulled the trigger. The resulting blast wasn't as loud as Marty's booming black-powder pistol, but I jumped anyhow. By the time Jack had fired off all five rounds, I could handle the report without flinching. Pulling the trigger myself was another matter altogether. Jack stood behind me holding my shoulders as I gripped the revolver, extended my arms, and pointed the barrel.

"Now, cock the hammer with your left thumb," he said into my left ear.

Hammer cocked, I braced myself, gritted my teeth, and pulled the trigger. The gun exploded at the end of my hand, pushing me back against Jack and jerking my hand up in the air. "My target would have been laughing uproariously with that shot," I said, watching the splatter of sand that flew up when the bullet hit the earthen backdrop.

"It'll get better, Cass." Jack smothered his laugh. "Before you know it, holding a .38 will be as automatic as holding your thirty-five mm."

"That, I seriously doubt." I felt as if I were on a runaway bus, driving, but completely out of control. This latest step—arming myself—might help relieve some of my fears, but I was skeptical of how I'd handle myself in a situation that required a gun. Being a realist, however, I knew I had to take steps to defend myself and not remain a sitting duck. I was turning some undefined corner in my life. Where, I wondered, would it take me?

"Let's try again," Jack said, showing me how to plant my feet and point at the target. By keeping at it for the next hour, I managed to ding the target with at least one out of five bullets. It increased my confidence, but not much.

Back in the parking lot, Jack bumped me with his shoulder as we strolled towards his truck. "You were bearing down on that target like your life depended on it," he said. "Were you seeing any face in particular?"

"Maybe. Maybe not." Then I dropped the news I'd so far neglected to share with him. "The carriage house was fire-bombed last night."

He stopped, grabbed my arm, and spun me around. "Damn it, Cassandra!" he said. "I told you to get out of that place until this is all over. Now maybe you'll listen to me. The only good thing is you don't live in that firetrap where you used to live." We resumed our trip across the parking lot. "Did it do much damage?"

"Some. The deck was destroyed." I kicked a stone out of the way. "But more to the point, I'd like to know who is doing this to me, Jack."

"I talked with one of your top suspects today," he said, pausing. "A Mr. Guy Strothers."

My head spun around so fast I almost got a whiplash. "What did you just say? What kind of conversation?"

"Strothers stopped at the stable today. He pounded me with all kinds of questions about one of our boarders. Virgil Dewitt."

"Midnight's owner?"

"Right."

"Is he interested in buying Midnight?" The thought of not having him in my life hurt.

Jack shot me a worried look. "He asked a lot of questions about the horse, but they weren't questions an experienced horse person would ask. I think he was more interested in Virgil."

I relaxed a bit. "What did you tell him?"

"I didn't even tell him his name," Jack said. "We just talked about 'the owner.' But he kept bringing the conversation back to the owner so often, it bothered me."

"Like . . . how?"

"Like whether the owner comes to the stables to ride him and, if so, when he comes. Like how far away the owner lives. He came right out and asked me where he lives, on the pretense that he'd like to see him to talk about the horse."

\   "Did you tell him?"

"Of course not. Anyway, I couldn't, even if I'd wanted to. I don't know where he lives. He always pays Midnight's board in cash."

"How often does he come?"

"Once a month. And on those visits, he rarely checks on Midnight. He just peels off a couple of bills and he's out of there."

I stroked my forehead and felt the worry wrinkles. "I'd sure like to know what drove Strothers to drive all the way out to the stables to ask those questions. Anna knows a lot about him and she's due back in town tomorrow. I'm going to ask her if she knows of any connection between . . . what's his name?"

"Virgil Dewitt."

"Right. Between Strothers and Virgil Dewitt."

On the way home, I reiterated where I stood. Law enforcement held most of the cards and most of the tools needed to solve the three crimes. What did I have that the police and sheriff might not have? Marty had bad feelings toward all three of the victims. Eric had been blackmailing Strothers. I had a flimsy photo of Strothers' truck at the Rendezvous, but I couldn't very well tell them how I got the picture. I had seen Strothers drive to a farmhouse outside the city and hold a several-hours meeting with a man in overalls and red suspenders. I had seen that suspendered man on a hiking trail and taken his picture. Strothers had questioned Jack about the owner of a horse.

Back in my darkroom, I knew I had two tools that might give me an edge—my camera and my computer. And, I had some hazy images on a disc the sheriff didn't know I possessed. Putting away all my concerns about who was out to "get" me, I carefully examined the dozen parking lot photos, to see if I could put Strothers or any of my other suspects at the scene. I went over them again with the Mac equivalent of a fine-tooth comb. Trying all the tricks my Photoshop program could provide, I clicked on the magnifying zoom tool and pointed it in the corner of the first image. A click of the mouse doubled the portion of the image.

I proceeded through the first photo—across, down, across, down—until I'd explored every inch of it. All I had to show for the tedious exercise was close-up shots of vehicle doors, windows, an occasional face or arm, and a few stretches of empty parking lot. The next two photos revealed as little as the first one. I remembered that when I'd returned to the parking lot on the day of the Rendezvous, it was still fairly early in the day, so most attendees of the event had already vacated the parking lot.

The next two photos showed a couple of stragglers strolling toward the Rendezvous grounds. The first one in my zoom search was a woman. The second had possibilities. It showed a man walking toward me as I snapped his picture. Unfortunately, he had turned his head at that very instant, resulting in a blurred image. I printed out the photo for further examination anyway and moved on to the next one, hoping I had taken another shot with the man facing me. But the next one was more of the same—vehicles and the stomped-on grass parking lot.

I switched my focus on the as yet unexamined group of six hoping they would be more revealing. The first photo revealed nothing more than trees and more parking lot. The second showed a shape of what looked to be a person in the periphery of the shot. I opened the next image, hoping to see more details. For once, I had turned the camera in the right direction. A man was approaching the parked vehicles from the edge of the lot, which was bordered by trees. Was it a man? Hard to tell. The person was wearing a long coat that extended to the top of his/her footwear. The good news was that I had a full shot. The bad news was that the face was hidden by the morning shadows and a fur hat was pulled over the eyes. I printed the picture and moved on to the next two. They caught a portion of the person again, just at the edge of the photo. The last two photos showed more parking lot and trees.

I returned to the those revealing a person and zoomed in again, studying the image inch by inch. A beard was peeking out from the turned-up collar of the coat. I could now assume the mystery person was a man. I printed out a stack of close-ups to examine side by side. The man's outfit suggested he was a Rendezvous participant. I tried to recall if I'd seen the man in the dozens of photos I'd taken at the event. My memory was defective, so I brought up the entire portfolio of computer images and ran through them to see if he appeared again. No luck.

With my brain fried, I decided to take a break, lift some weights, and put a few miles on my treadmill. After my workout, I showered and changed. As I was pulling on my shirt, the image of the man crossing the parking lot popped into my head. Something about that picture bothered me. The thought sat just beyond my consciousness and wouldn't come forth. I put in a call to Anna and she invited me to meet her for a couple drinks. "Bring the photos with you," she said. "Maybe I can help. And let's hold our repast at Red's Roadhouse."

Red's Roadhouse was a new supper club that had opened up a couple of months ago. Anna had stopped in one night and pronounced it "just fine," which I took to mean "fine by Colton Mills standards." With my head feeling as if it were in overdrive, I looked forward to an evening of alcohol-inspired downshifting. The roadhouse still retained the shake-shingled outside wall that had defined the former establishment. Now, however, the door had been painted a bright red. Inside, chrome and stainless steel had replaced the heavy dark wood and the reds favored by seventies supper-club designers—red booths, red drapes, red carpet. There must be a supper-club designer bible somewhere, for I'd seen the same look in many towns. Red's was a decided improvement. Maybe in twenty years, critics would scoff, but I was impressed. Mrs. A would have pronounced it "ritzy."

The dining room was on the right. I turned left into the bar. It was dark. Across the room, a dim light illuminated a guitarist who was perched on a stool and strumming in an unfocused style, as if he were looking for chords he'd lost. At first, I couldn't see much of anything, after coming in from the lighted room. I shaded my eyes, to find Anna. As my eyes adjusted to the lack of light, a raised arm waved me to a booth against the wall and midway across the room. "Hi, Anna," I said, as I leaned in for a hug. The startled face of another person swam into my field of vision. "Willis! I'm so sorry. I thought . . ." I was without words to explain my faux pas. My familiar world wobbled on its axis. Anna grinned from her place beside him. "Nice to see both of you." I tossed my briefcase onto the bench before me and slid onto the padded seat across from them.

"Nice to see you too, Cass," Anna said, purring like a contented kitten. No explanation about Willis, but what did I expect from someone with Anna's aplomb? I ordered a Sam Adams.

Anna filled me in on her recent buying trip. Willis told Anna about our black-powder-shooting afternoon. I sipped my beer, relaxing. The guitar player had found his groove. A very nice one, I thought dreamily. Original stuff with riffs that could make Eric Clapton take notice.

Anna was giggling. "Cassandra, you are much too immersed in the 1840s." She leaned toward Willis, who fondly took her hand in his own. The tableau unnerved me. What was Anna drinking?

"Speaking of the 1840s, I've got something to show you," I said, pulling out my briefcase. Just as I reached for the photos, Jack's .38 clattered onto the table.

"Why, what on earth, Cassandra?" Anna threw me an alarmed look. "When did you start carrying a firearm?"

I hastily replaced the .38 into my briefcase and pulled out the folder of photos. "I had a couple of scary incidents while you were away." I filled her in on the man in the woods and the fire-bomb incident. "Of course, that's in addition to my darkroom being trashed."

"That's awful, just awful!" She clasped her hand over her mouth. "Who do you think is responsible?"

"If I knew that, the guy would be in jail. Could be anyone, I guess."

Anna reached across the table to squeeze my hand. "I've told you Strothers is a vindictive man, Cassandra."

"I think Strothers is after someone else in this area." I told her about his visit to the stables.

"Virgil Dewitt," she said and frowned. "That name doesn't ring a bell." She turned to Willis. "Do you know him, Willis?"

"No, I do not, Sorry," he said, sipping his glass of wine.

"I'd really like to know if Strothers has some connection to Dewitt," I said. "Do you think any of your Chicago friends could help?"

She nodded. "I'll call a friend there. She may know who he is."

"I'd appreciate that, Anna." I fanned the photos out on the table, facing Anna and Willis. "But, meanwhile, I have another mystery to solve. I took these in the Rendezvous parking lot the day of the murder," I said. "In fact, it could have been near the time of the murder. I had returned to my car to replace my battery packs and shot these on my digital. Do you find anything unusual about them?"

Anna studied them closely through her half glasses. "The man's dressed in frontier clothing," she said. "What was the temperature that day, do you remember?"

"It was really hot for June," I said. "In the eighties. I remember sweating up a storm."

She tilted her head, pursing her lips. "Isn't it rather strange that the person is dressed in a fur hat, long coat, and long, laced-up moccasin boots on such a hot day? People who dress for Rendezvous try to stay in character, not only for the period, but also for the weather. He must have been sweltering in that outfit."

I'd totally missed the significance of the winter clothing. Maybe that was what was so jarring about the photo. "Do you recognize any of the clothing, Anna?"

"That would be a difficult task, Cassandra. The clothing we wear for such events is pretty generic," Willis said, pointing at one of the pictures.

Anna peered again at the photo she was scrutinizing. "Here's another thing that's really strange," she said. "What do these boots look like to you?" She pushed the photos towards me.

The man's pants were tucked into the boots and the coat nearly covered them. In one of the photos, the boots were clearer as his coat fell open as he walked. I shrugged. "Everything the participants wear seems strange to me, so I'm not the one to ask. What do you see?"

"They have designs on them," she said. "I find that odd, because the rest of the outfit is pretty standard." She stroked an exquisite silver bracelet on her wrist.

"Does it look like the guy's trying to disguise himself?" I persisted with my questions. I had already learned more that I had known before entering Red's. "He's so covered up, Anna. From what you've said about the weather and choice of outfit, this guy doesn't seem to know much about authentic clothing. Maybe he pulled a fur hat over his eyes and donned a long coat so he'd pass for a Rendezvooer, if anyone saw him."

Anna glanced up in surprise. "I assume you've already searched through all the other photos of Rendezvous participants that you have?"

"Yes," I said, gazing at the top photo. "The guy in this outfit doesn't show up in any of them. And I can't remember seeing him there either."

"Well, it is an intriguing idea, Cassandra," Willis said, snapping his finger against the photo, "but you cannot make the jump to accuse anyone of being a murderer merely from this picture. You'd have to find the clothing in the person's possession and, even then, still not have proof that would stand up in a court of law."

I fiddled with my beer, making wet patterns on the table top. "If I can find a way to do that, I'll do it, Willis."

"Please be careful, Cassandra," Anna said, a frown etching her forehead. "I know you want to get to the bottom of this, but you're playing a dangerous game. I'll see what I can do on my end. For starters, I'll try to find out about Strothers' potential relationship to this Virgil Dewitt."

"Good," I said. "I've run out of places to look." My tone brightened. "But . . . I'm going to see what I can find out about those boots."

"Well, that's a safer course of action. Stop in and I'll loan you some books about frontier clothing."

I excused myself and headed to the ladies' room. There, I smiled at myself in the mirror. "Willis and Anna, who would have thought," I said to my reflection. "They make a nice couple."

Approaching our booth, upon my return, I saw a fourth person had been added to our threesome. Anna smiled. "Cassandra," she said, gesturing to a man seated across from her, "this is Nick Parker, a friend of mine who used to live in Colton Mills." It was the guitarist.

"Nice to meet you," I said, shaking hands with him. My eyes burned into Anna's, but she strategically shifted hers to her new best friend, who was now taking up half of my side of the booth.

He quickly scooted out of the booth, ran his fingers through his longish salt and pepper hair, and mumbled, "Nice to meet you, too." He gestured for me to enter the booth and then slid in after me.

Even with a couple of Sam Adams beers under my belt, my instincts told me I was being set up. This meeting had all the earmarks of Anna's perennial orchestrations. A gremlin on my shoulder told me not to be so self-centered, that when I was under the influence of Sam Adams I can misjudge situations. Despite my misgivings, I reacted to his touch and felt my face warming. *Must be just because I haven't been with any interesting men lately,* I thought. But I was getting wa-a-y ahead of myself. "Nice playing," I said, hugging the wall. "But why haven't I heard of you before now?"

"He just came into town this week," Anna chirped, her hands fluttering.

I focused on removing the label from my bottle of beer. "Oh, you're a traveling musician," I said, my voice flat.

"Nope, afraid not," he said. He chuckled and turned toward me. "Red's is the only place you'll have the privilege of hearing me. Playing is strictly a hobby."

"Nick is planning to resume his career as an EMT," Willis said. "He will be managing emergency services for three counties."

With that, the miniscule stage lights went up and Nick headed for the stage. I couldn't wait to take up Anna's matchmaking when Willis wasn't around. Matter of fact, I'd also take up the "Willis" matter. We chatted on about the weather, Anna's business, and Willis' hobbies, completely avoiding the Rendezvous investigation.

As soon as I felt I could leave Red's, I headed for the door, surprised that I felt a little tipsy. How much beer did I have anyway? As I was about to push open the door, it opened for me. Preoccupied, I didn't notice who had performed the courtesy until a hand clamped on my upper arm and the instigator had pulled me outside.

"I thought I recognized your Jeep," Strothers said, propelling me across the parking lot. He flipped a cigarette onto the pavement. "C'mon. I've got something to talk to you about."

My stomach churned as he half-pulled, half-carried me. I felt weak and scared and reproached myself for letting down my guard. I knew I should shout, scream, do something, but I couldn't penetrate the Sam Adams fog.

Strothers' fingers pinched my arm. My boots dragged on the asphalt, making a rasping sound in the night. Everything moved in slow motion. I saw the ordinariness of the parking lot lights sending their diffused light onto the parked cars. Insects drifted like snow through their amber glow. A slight breeze sent a Dairy Queen napkin skittering along the ground. At the edge of the lot, a girl laughed aloud and, in the periphery of my vision, I saw a knot of teens perched on the concrete abutment, passing a bottle among them. They ignored the two of us.

We had reached the shadows and I could see his vehicle. What would he do, if he got me into his vehicle? Gathering all the strength I could, I twisted away from him, dropping to the ground as I did so. It was just enough to make him relax his grip. I tried to run, but stumbled, the stones of the parking lot biting into my knee.

Strothers was on me like a hawk on a mouse. "Get up, bitch," he growled, sticking his face near mine. I smelled his beery breath. He had me by my hair, but he had been thrown off balance when I tried to get away. He hesitated just long enough for me to pick up my foot and kick him in the crotch. He gave an explosive grunt and dropped to his knees, letting go of me. I ran, drunkenly zigzagging toward the patch of light that was the Roadhouse. I collapsed against the door.

My next memory is of someone was stroking my forehead, holding my hand. "You're going to be okay," he said, his face so close that a lock of salt-and-pepper hair brushed against my face. "We'll take care of you." I closed my eyes. The last thing I heard was the sound of sirens, coming closer and closer.

Chapter 21

Tuesday—Week Three

I awoke the next morning by 6:16, feeling decidedly groggy. I remembered staying in the Emergency Room just long enough to have my scratches treated and pull myself together. By the time Anna dropped me at home, I had been primed for sleep. With a dozen things on my mind, now, I was eager to get into my darkroom again. An hour later, I was pulling photo paper out of its last chemical bath, when the doorbell rang. "Who is it?" I said, shouting.

Marty's gruff voice was equally loud. "It's me. Marty."

For a heavily bearded, robustly built guy, Marty always looked good—clean, well-pressed, and physically fit. But not today. Even the hat pulled over his hair could not disguise his uncombed mane. His bushy beard needed a trim. Bleary-eyed, his clothes looked and smelled as if he had slept in them for several days. He stood in front of the door, feet apart, hands on hips. He not only looked like a wild man, he looked like an angry wild man.

"What the hell is going on here?" he asked, by way of greeting. "I got a call from the sheriff that I might want to get my ass home, because somebody fire-bombed my house!"

"It's obviously true," I said, gesturing toward the scorched wall and taking in the temporary walkway the fire department had laid down across the ruined deck.

We stood side by side, surveying the damage to the deck and the sturdy wall. Although the wall was unscathed, flames had charred the stones all the way to the roof. My deck chair—what was left of it—lay in a pool of debris-littered water generated by the firefighters. The acrid smell of fire still hung in the air.

"Damn it," Marty said, slapping his hat against his thigh. "Do you have any idea who did this? Or why?"

"I've got my suspicions, but nothing I can prove."

He eyed me with interest reflected in his face. "I must say, I'm mighty confused. Just can't understand why you've ended up in the middle of this."

"Do you think you should have been the target instead?"

He gave me a piercing look. "I was a target, but not with a fire bomb."

I scowled. "What are you talking about?"

"Somebody nailed a shirt, of all things, to my gate."

"What kind of shirt?" I experienced a sinking feeling, knowing what the answer would be.

"It was covered with dirt, so I couldn't tell much about the shirt itself." Marty held up what was formerly a white shirt. *Not red.* I felt a tingle along my forearm. Not my shirt, but the message it sent was clear anyway. Marty was still talking. "What bothered me most about this thing was the note tacked to it."

"A note?" I asked, swallowing hard.

Marty nodded and looked genuinely puzzled. "With the envelope addressed to you." He passed the envelope to me.

I hoped my expression wouldn't give me away. I wasn't prepared to tell Marty how the shirt could be connected to me. I willed my voice not to quaver. "Did you . . . you know . . . tell the sheriff about the shirt?"

"I certainly did," he said, his jaw tightening. "They're picking it up later this morning."

"For the time being, Marty, would you do me a big favor and not mention this note to the sheriff?"

He didn't answer right away, considering. "Is everything okay with you, gal?" He pointed to the envelope. "Is that something that puts you in some sort of danger?"

"I'll know after I open it." My hands were visibly trembling, but I made no move to open the envelope in his presence.

"All right," he said. "I'll do that for you."

Again willing my face not to register my inner distress, I uttered a lame, "I-I hope they find the person responsible for the fire." I walked purposefully into my house and collapsed onto the sofa, dangling the note between my thumb and index finger as if it would burn my skin. After stalling for a full minute, I finally slit open the envelope. One note-size piece of paper fluttered out. On it, written in large capital letters, I read: MEET ME IN MY OFFICE TUESDAY, 10:00 A.M., OR THE RED SHIRT GOES TO THE SHERIFF.

It was signed by Guy Strothers.

I'd been waiting for the red shirt to jump up and bite me and, now, I was getting my comeuppance. My chest tightened with the thought of another face-to-face confrontation with Strothers. Apparently, this was what he had wanted to "discuss" with me at the Roadhouse parking lot. He certainly wasn't giving me any time to stew about his edict. To say that I was scared out of my mind was saying nothing at all. Even more terrifying, however, was the knowledge that I was on my own. I couldn't enlist anyone's help or advice, because I hadn't told anyone about my visit to Strothers at the farmyard, in the middle of the night.

* * *

I dressed in a gray pant suit, paired with an ivory-colored blouse—no red shirt for this meeting—and set out for Strothers' office in downtown Colton Mills. In the longest five miles I'd ever driven, I thought I knew how a prisoner felt as he took his final walk to the executioner.

"Come in!" Strothers barked, in response to my timid knock on his office door. He was seated behind a mammoth mahogany desk. "Pardon me if I don't get up," he said, in what I interpreted to be a murderous tone. His mammoth hands were twisted into fists on his desk. He nodded towards a leather chair in front of his desk. When I was seated, he asked, "Why do you think I asked you to come here today, Miss Cassidy?"

"I'm not sure," I answered, my stomach in knots. "Something about a red shirt." I tried to maintain steady eye contact, to show him I was not intimidated. It took all the energy I could summon.

He reached into his desk drawer and whipped out my dirty shirt. There was no mistaking that it was mine. Holding it up in front of him, he said, "I believe this is yours. You left it behind after following me to a farm house out in the country a couple nights ago." His eyes blazed with anger.

"What makes you think that's my red shirt," I asked, willing myself to speak evenly.

"You're well known for wearing red shirts, Miss Cassidy. Several people have told me that. It was found in the driveway of a farmhouse where my truck had been parked. It had been used to wipe dirt off the door of my vehicle."

I didn't trust myself to respond, so I remained quiet.

190

"I'm note interested in playing games with you." He threw the shirt aside and placed his palms flat on the desk. "I want to know what the hell you were doing at that farm in the middle of the night!"

If I had learned anything in the years since Mrs. A taught me the value of verbal bravado, it was that the best defense is a good offense. I followed my instincts and fought back. "You're making some strong assumptions, Mr. Strothers. Dozens of people in this township wear red shirts. I have a couple questions of my own, since you seem so determined to scare me with strong-man tactics." I scooted to the edge of my chair and glared at him with equal intensity. "Were you paying Eric Hartfield to write favorable things about you and your company?" The question spilled out of my mouth before I could stop myself. I wasn't sure what he expected me to ask him, but that wasn't it. It took a few seconds for the question to register in his mind. I thought he would erupt out of the chair and attack me for the second time, but he sat quietly gazing at me.

"That is a very serious, very loaded question, Miss Cassidy." Rubbing his hands together in front of him, he brought them to his face and tapped the fingers against his tightened lips. "Where on earth did you get that idea?"

"I noticed that Eric's articles abruptly changed from being quite adamantly critical about the Bridgewater Land Development Company to praising it, about a year ago."

"And from that observation you made a jump in logic to thinking there was a payoff involved? What a quaint conclusion." Strothers chuckled and shook his head. "You couldn't be more wrong." He pushed himself away from his desk and strode around it to stand beside me. I thought he was about to attack me again, but he reached out to cup my chin in his hand. "Once Eric Hartfield had done his homework, he saw that my company was a benefit to the area. That's when he started to support me." He had adopted corporate-speak. "It's that simple, my dear. There is no conspiracy here." He patted my cheek and returned to his desk chair.

I rubbed my cheek. "Then you and Eric were good friends?"

"We were never good friends. We were mutually respectful professionals."

I was in pretty deep already and decided to go for broke. "Did you go to the Rendezvous to meet with Eric?"

He opened his mouth and, at first, no sound emerged. Then he snapped, "What Rendezvous are you talking about?"

"The Rendezvous where Eric was killed. Two weeks ago."

"I've never gone to one of those hokey things in my life," he said, his voice icy. His eyes narrowed. "And I don't like the sound of what you're implying, Miss Cassidy."

"Your truck was parked at the Rendezvous on the day Eric was killed."

"And you, Miss Detective, are making another unbelievable insinuation to support your cockamamie speculations. Exactly how do you know my company truck was there? Did someone tell you that, or did you see it yourself?" His gaze bored into mine. "For the sake of argument, we'll assume the truck was there." He raised his voice and spoke slowly, emphasizing every word as though I were a dummy. "Did it never occur to you that my employees *also* drive my truck?"

I pressed on. "Do you know who was driving it that day?"

"If I did know—and I'm not saying I do—it's none of your damn business who was driving my truck!"

I willed my eyes not to waver. "It could become the sheriff's business, if he inquires about who left your truck in the Rendezvous parking lot the same day Eric was killed."

"And who's going to give the sheriff a reason to ask that question? You? Or have you already?"

"I'll keep that information to myself, Mr. Strothers," I said, lowering my voice.

"I'm beginning to get the picture here." Strothers studied his fingernails. "You followed me to the farmyard, because you have developed some outrageous theory that I'm connected to Eric Hartfield's murder, in order to save your own neck. Is that it?" His fist banged on the desk. "What the hell were you trying to prove?"

I flinched, but continued. "Did you try to run me off the road on the day of Randy Pearce's funeral?"

Strothers threw his hands into the air and stared at me, clearly dumbfounded. I could see him fight to keep his temper in check. His eyes were blazing. "You live a dangerous life for a small-town wedding photographer," he said. "You've made some amazing accusations that I take very seriously. Where your suppositions come from is beyond my comprehension."

"I'm not—"

"Not another word! Hear me out!" The jaw muscles worked behind his tanned cheeks. "Obviously, you have decided to remain mum about why your shirt ended up in my driveway." He reached for the red evidence. "That being the case, I have no choice but to deliver it to the sheriff. I doubt you will be sharing the contents of the note I sent you with him, as it will implicate you in whatever you were doing in that farmyard."

"But—"

"That's all! You can go now." He swiveled his chair away from me. "Close the door behind you."

I fled his office, breathing a sigh of relief to know I was still in one piece. If Strothers wasn't an enemy of mine before, he was certainly one after my performance. What was I thinking, to ask him such loaded questions? By tipping my hand, I had worsened my own position. I dreaded what would happen if and when the shirt ended up in Shaw's hands. How could I explain my stupidity in driving out to that farmhouse!

I went back into my darkroom, turned on the safe light, and cracked open a roll of exposed film. I pulled the strip out of its last chemical bath and hung it up to dry. Too nervous to stay and work, I headed toward my second office.

"Hey, Cassandra," Roxy said, pulling out a paper cup. "Tall or extra tall today?"

"Make it extra tall, iced, to go." I was still shaking. "Better make that decaf today."

She placed the coffee on the counter. "I hear you had some trouble out at your house."

"How did you hear that?"

"Well, we *do* live in a small town," she said with an impish smile.

"You're right about that."

She leaned her forearms on the counter. "How's Marty doing with all this?"

"Marty?" Lately, I seemed to be getting all the sympathy of chopped liver. "Marty's been out of town. It was *my* place that got hit."

"I meant to say, how was Marty's trip?"

"He didn't say anything about his trip." I sipped my coffee. "Should he have? I assumed he was taking or picking someone up with his helicopter." She swiped the already clean counter with a cloth. Her mouth opened to speak, but didn't. Curious, I prompted her. "Do you know where he went, Roxy?"

"I've gotten to know Marty pretty well in the last couple of years," she said, hedging and, apparently, debating whether to tell me more. "He's a regular here, like yourself."

I nodded and sipped at my coffee.

"Anyway," she said, seeming to make up her mind to go on. "Do you know the story about his wife and son leaving him while he was in Viet Nam?"

I nodded. "That had to be thirty-forty years ago."

"His boy would be middle-aged by now, but every so often Marty will get a lead about where his family members might be. If he can, he'll follow up."

I raised my eyebrows. "Is that what he was doing?"

"Someone told him about meeting a guy—a pilot—in Kansas City, who reminded him of Marty. Apparently, Marty thought there was enough about this sighting to investigate."

"He told me the sheriff called him to come home after the house was fire-bombed."

"That probably means it was another dead end." She sighed and turned away from me to wait on a new customer.

I returned to my Jeep. It was an interesting story. Or, possibly, an elaborate cover-up.

I stopped at the Burger Barn, picked up a hamburger to go with my coffee, and drove to the roadside park along the Oxbow. The river lapped gently against the bank and my mind drifted back to the conversation I'd just had with Roxy.

Marty was an enigma. He'd dodged Viet Cong bullets and, now, he piloted a helicopter stateside for medical trips. A rough, tough guy, he wasn't easily intimidated. It appeared, however, that Marty was still locked into his past, fixated on events that had occurred nearly forty years ago. What kind of person could not let go and move on? Had this tragic experience eaten at him so long that he'd lost perspective and finally taken his bitterness out on Eric? How about Randy and Jim? Or, did it have to do with the land development and hunting issues? I was no better at practicing psychology than at impersonating a detective.

One thing for sure, my experience with Strothers had convinced me it was time to take steps to protect myself. Luckily, I had a date with Jack at the gun range.

I noticed only one other shooter, who was stationed at the far end of the range when we arrived. I loaded my weapon as Jack had taught me, assumed the proper stance, and pulled the trigger.

"Not bad," Jack said, grinning. "You almost hit it that time!" I glared at him for pointing out my less-than-stellar attempts at drilling a human being in the head or chest. He took possession of the handgun to demonstrate what was wrong with my technique. Holding it with two hands, he showed me how to sight down the short barrel and slowly squeeze the trigger, not "pull" it as I had been doing. I followed his instructions, and after a half hour was hitting the target more often that I was missing it.

While getting ready to load another round, I saw the shooter out of the corner of my eye, apparently finished and coming our way to reach the exit. I waited for him to pass by and then a double take. He caught my eye and turned his face abruptly away, striding more briskly through the exit. Not quickly enough. Not before I saw the red suspenders holding up his farmer jeans.

"Cass, you're not paying attention," Jack complained.

I grabbed hold of his shirtfront and started to babble, feeling my excitement rise. "Jack, I swear the man who just left the range is the guy who followed me in the park on Sunday."

"Can't be," he said dismissively. "That's Ned Obregon. He's been a farmer around here forever."

"Where does he live?"

"Out in the country somewhere. He's a farmer, for cryin' out loud."

"But *where*?"

He threw up his hands. "I'll find out for you. Practice squeezing the trigger, and I'll be right back." He left to talk with someone inside the building. He wasn't gone long. "It's just as I thought. That was Ned, all right. He lives out on Coyote Road."

"Jack, Coyote Road isn't far from where I live."

"Living somewhere near you does not mean he's going to follow you into the woods."

I hadn't told Jack about my nocturnal visit to photograph Strothers' vehicle, so he had no way of knowing I had another frame of reference. I was sure the man who had just left the range was the same man who had not only followed me, but who was in the farmhouse with Strothers. I fixed my gaze on his and spoke with conviction. "I can't tell you how I know, Jack, but I'm confident that man works for Strothers. He *has* been following me, and he may be the one who threw the firebomb at my house."

"Cass, I think you're wrong on this one."

"Humor me, Jack. Let's follow him and see where he goes."

Jack sighed wearily, threw our shooting gear into his bag, and strode beside me out to his truck without further comment. Ned's pickup was leaving the parking lot as we exited the store. Once in Jack's truck, we followed it at a safe distance as it lumbered down the street and turned onto County Road 18. About a mile down the road, it turned into the parking lot of Leo's Bar.

"So much for that," Jack said, his first words since voicing his objection to my conjectures. "He could be in there for the night."

"I'm going in," I turned to him, my jaw set. "Are you coming with me?"

Jack rolled his eyes. "And miss a chance to pick you up off the floor? No, I'm in."

Ned was sitting at the bar with his back to us. A couple of tattooed twenty-somethings were playing pool, noisily egging each other on and slurping Coors between turns. A couple sat at a table, watching a baseball game playing on the TV suspended from the ceiling. We ambled up to the bar and took a couple stools at the opposite end from where Ned sat. He was tearing strips off pull tabs, trying to hit the house's jackpot. From his irritable expression, he wasn't doing well. We ordered a couple of Bud Lights and waited.

When Ned had finished going through his stack of pull tabs, he reached for his beer. When he lifted the bottle to his lips, his gaze fell on the two of us. He literally choked and began coughing, unable to catch his breath. When he finally got control of himself, he slammed the bottle onto the bar, threw the bartender a couple of bills, and bolted outside. The tires of his truck spun in the gravel, as he powered out of the parking lot.

"I think we accomplished something," I said, jumping off the bar stool.

"I agree," Jack said. "You've got yourself a confirmed enemy." He handed the bartender a $10 bill. "Keep the change," he said. As we returned to his truck, he added. "You must be proud of yourself."

"No, I think I've seen the last of Ned following me. When a guy's cover is blown, he's useless, isn't he? That's what I read in the detective novels."

"I hope you're right, Cass," he said, sliding under the steering wheel. "I hope you're right."

Chapter 22

Wednesday—Week Three

At 9:40 the next morning, I parked in the churchyard for another funeral service. Jim Tuttle's. I'd have given anything not to attend and be "on display" as one of the people who had found him hanging in the woods. Hoping to appear as incognito as possible, I ditched my usual outfit of bright colors for a more conservative navy pantsuit and slipped on an oversized pair of dark sunglasses. I found my favorite spot in the next to the last pew and settled in for another sad service. Thankfully, most attendees paid little attention to me.

As I left the church, I discovered my disguise hadn't been as successful as I'd hoped. A couple of reporters had positioned themselves outside. As I filed past them with a group of mourners, they pushed a microphone into my face. "Miss Cassidy, do you have any idea who killed Jim Tuttle? Did you have anything to do with it?"

I pushed them aside and escaped to my vehicle. Shoving the shift into gear, I had started to drive away, when someone rapped on my window. It was Deputy Shaw. He made a motion for me to open my car window. "I'm glad to see you were paying your respects to Jim," he said by way of greeting.

I waited, staring vacantly through the windshield over my steering wheel.

"It's very curious . . . you showing up at all these murder scenes," he said, leaning casually against my vehicle.

"Tell me about it," I said, being sarcastic. I finally looked at him. "And it's wearing me down."

"Is there anything you'd like to talk about regarding my investigation of these three murders?" He peered at me with beady eyes. I stared back at him with clamped lips.

He tried for a smile, but it resulted in something more like a grimace. "My records show you were with Jack Gardner when you discovered Tuttle's body. Is he a friend of yours?"

"A sort-of friend. From the stables." I slipped the shift stick into gear again and started to roll up the window.

Shaw took a step back, but held up his hand to stop me from leaving. "Has he discussed the connection he had with Eric Hartfield?" Despite my reluctance to let Shaw know he'd scored a hit, my head jerked up involuntarily and my mouth fell open. "By your reaction, I'm assuming that either you didn't know or you're surprised that I know."

Nothing . . . absolutely nothing Shaw could have said would have shocked me more. Not only shocked me. I felt like the proverbial three-legged stool that had one leg kicked away. I was thrown completely off balance. The deputy stood with his arms crossed over his chest, regarding me with a smug look on his face.

"In case you don't know, Gardner was the father of Eric's sister's child. Gardner skipped town before she had the baby and

Hartfield never forgave him for it. Then Gardner showed up in town a year or so ago and Eric went looking for him. Who knows what transpired between the two of them? Maybe something that would make Gardner want to eliminate Eric. Can you shed any light on that theory for me?"

My mind couldn't absorb what Shaw was saying. Jack not only knew Eric, but could have had the best of all motives for killing him. I could feel Shaw watch my facial reactions, as I processed the information. He leaned into the window again. "Want to talk about it?"

I finally found my voice. "I-I don't know anything about it."

"You have my number," he said, flipping his notepad closed and backing away.

Numb with shock, I drove out into the street with such care, I felt like a senior citizen who had just received a speeding ticket. How was I was going to handle this latest development? Why had Jack withheld such important information from me? I needed to talk with someone I could still trust.

"You look like you've lost your best friend," Anna said, as soon as I entered her shop.

"I was at Jim Tuttle's funeral," I said. "I hope I never have to attend another one under these circumstances."

She bustled over and draped her arm around my shoulders. "I do, too, Cass. No one should have to go through what you've experienced these past two weeks. I've got some news that could possibly brighten your day, though. I know more about Strothers and Virgil Dewitt."

"I could definitely use some news about Strothers."

"When I was flying home last week, I sat next to a real estate developer from Chicago. She gave me her business card. I thought since she was in that business, she'd probably followed Strothers' development activities. I called her." Anna steered me to the back of her shop and pushed me onto the antique sofa. "She said she'd look in her files and fax me what she found. Ten minutes ago, I got a fax from her."

"Anything useful?" Suddenly, I felt hopeful of a break.

Anna cocked one perfectly plucked eyebrow. "Something you'll at least find interesting. It turns out that Virgil invested in one of Strothers' office developments about five years ago. The project didn't go well and Virgil sued him for breach of contract. According to his lawsuit, materials and workmanship were substandard. Strothers refused to accept any liability, so it went to a civil jury trial."

I perked up. "What happened?"

"The court agreed with Virgil. It cost Strothers a ton of money, especially when he was found liable for breach of contract, among other things. One thing that didn't help Strothers in the trial was his temper. He actually threatened Virgil during the trial a couple times. No surprise that he lost his case."

"If he'd threaten me for an imagined act, I wouldn't be surprised if he'd like to kill Virgil." A shiver went through my body and I dropped my head into my hands.

"I thought you'd be thrilled to hear that news." Anna sounded hurt.

"I am, Anna, but I heard something today that's got me . . . upset." I told her about Jack's relationship to Eric.

"What can I say? I'm as stunned as you. That's not good news." We were both silent for awhile. A customer entered the store and I stood to go. "Watch who you talk to, Cassandra," she said, pecking me on the cheek.

Although Anna's information was intriguing, Shaw's had trumped it. I steeled myself not to over-react. Jack might not have told me about his knowing Eric, because he was embarrassed about it. He'd spent so much time cultivating his carefree-cowboy image, he didn't want to wreck it. But no matter how hard I tried to keep from making a molehill into a mountain, a little voice kept telling me, "you're a fool." What else had Jack lied to me about?

To help settle my mind, I found the books Anna had loaned me on frontier clothing. I pulled out the enlargement I'd made of the parking lot stranger's boots from my digital camera and compared them to photos of boots in all the books. No match. I remembered someone at the Rendezvous meeting saying that many pieces of clothing were custom made. If that were the case with the boots, how could I find out who may have made them? Marty came to mind, but he was the last person I'd ask for help.

Maybe Willis would know. I reached him on his cell phone and told him I needed information about how to find a custom boot maker. "It's about the photo I showed you at the supper club."

"I'll get a name and call you back," he said.

I'd no more than ended my call to Willis than my cell phone chirped. The number on the caller ID was unfamiliar. "Cassandra Cassidy," I said.

"This is Nick Parker. I've been wondering how you're doing after the incident Monday evening at the bar."

My heartbeat fluttered. "I'm okay," I said, reaching up to smooth my hair. "Thanks for your help."

"All in a day's work. Anna told me a little about your conflict with Guy Strothers. I don't know him personally, but I know him by reputation. Would it be too upsetting to talk about it?"

"No, I guess not."

"How about in a couple hours? I'd like to bring supper, if you're going to be home."

Supper. I had no food in the house and I was ravenous. "Sounds good."

"Great. Pizza and beer?"

"The idea of more beer gives me a headache," I laughed. "Make it pizza and Coke and it's a deal. Pepperoni."

"Pepperoni pizza and Coke it is. I'll see you at your place about 6:15."

Well. I had just agreed to a date. Or had I? Maybe Nick only wanted to tell me what he knew about Strothers. He could have told Anna, who could have told me, but . . . whatever. I could use a male presence in my life more intriguing than Willis, Marty, and Jack. At least for one evening, if nothing more. I went upstairs to shower and change my clothes.

Nick arrived on time. "Whew," he said, "I followed Anna's directions. You are certainly out here all by yourself."

"That's the truth," I said, taking the pizza box from him and lifting the lid. "Mmm, smells good enough to eat!"

"Sausage and green pepper," he said. "They were out of pepperoni and that's about as adventurous the pizza cuisine is in Colton Mills. Hope it's okay."

"It's perfect," I said, heading for the kitchen. "C'mon in and follow me."

I had already completed a furtive examination of my dinner guest. In the dim light of the Roadhouse, I hadn't notice a scar that ran from Nick's left eyebrow to the middle of his cheekbone. It gave him a rugged look. He was taller than I was by a few inches. And slim. His marine blue eyes danced beneath dark eyebrows, and they exactly matched the blue stripes of his short-sleeved shirt. I also noticed his well-developed biceps. He didn't get those by playing the guitar, I decided. His hair had been unsuccessfully tamed with a hair product. Wiry curls flopped around his ears.

Nick moved confidently to the kitchen and deposited the six-pack of Coke on the table. I had set the table ahead of time . . . if you call dropping a couple of forks, plates, and napkins in the middle of the table setting it. I'd decided against music, as it seemed too date-like. I still wasn't sure how to interpret his visit. I produced a platter for the pizza and added ice to the glasses. "Take a seat," I said. "I'm eager to stem my appetite."

We made small talk while we devoured the pizza. Where we came from. How we landed in Colton Mills. He, from a small dairy farm in Minnesota. Married young. Divorced young. No kids. Wife ran off with a man she met at McDonald's. Learned guitar and singing in church. Studied journalism at the university, worked on a newspaper in northern Minnesota, settled in Colton Mills after realizing he didn't like the city. Wrote an article on EMTs. Fascinated him. Pushing forty and wanted something new. As he talked, he moved his hand in the air, as if he had once smoked cigarettes and all that was left was the gesture. He grinned openly and often.

Before I knew what I was doing, I'd told him about my experience being married to a musician and described how I had gotten to Colton Mills. Flustered that I'd revealed so much about myself, I switched subjects. "Tell me what you know about Strothers." I busied myself taking plates to the sink.

He grinned at me sheepishly, peering down at his hands, then back up at me. "To tell you the truth, I used that as an opening to come and see you. I don't know anything about the guy."

I gasped aloud and placed my hands on my hips. "You can't trust anybody these days!" I said, teasing and feeling my face flushing. So it *was* a date.

At that very moment, the phone on his belt played the beginning of some unrecognizable song. He quickly took the call, spoke only a few words, and rose from the table. "The unpredictable world of an EMT," he said, pushing his chair under the table and turning to face me. He smiled crookedly. "It's an emergency. I have to go."

I walked him to the door. He took my hand and kissed me on the cheek. "I want to see you again." Already on his way down the stairs to the outside door, he turned to offer a little wave. That was that. I put my hand on my cheek, and, humming a little tune, went to finish cleaning up the kitchen.

Chapter 23

Thursday—Week Three

After a night of tossing and turning, I vowed to become more serious about clearing my name. I wanted my life back. There was no sense in even feigning an interest in guys like Nick, if Deputy Shaw were to decide to arrest me. I did not want to spend even a minute behind bars, and I certainly didn't want guys visiting me in jail.

I returned to my computer with renewed energy and again faced the grainy digital photo with the shadowy figure of a man in the corner. Who else could help me identify him? I'd asked almost everyone but Marty. I'd be taking a chance, if the man in the photo turned out to be Marty. I'd be tipping him off to the existence of the photo, and then I'd have no place to hide. But, at this point, I was willing to take the chance. Nothing ventured, nothing gained.

I enlarged the entire photo, then isolated separate portions of it and enlarged them, too. When I had finished, I had filled several folders with about a dozen exposures each. With strength of purpose, I headed over to Marty's with my briefcase by 11:10. He was in his backyard, as usual. I told him what I had and presented one of the folders to him. "Think you can shed any light on the person in this photo?" I pointed to the image.

Marty leafed through the pictures, taking his time with each one, turning them in different directions to catch the light. "I'm going inside to get a magnifying glass." He tromped off to the house. When he returned, he said, "The outfit is curious, Cassandra. The man is wearing unusually warm clothing for such a hot day. That's not in keeping with the Rendezvous."

"But, do you recognize who it is?"

"There's something familiar about the figure." He squinted. "I can't quite put my finger on it. If I could get a copy of the photos, I could study them later."

"Go ahead and take the folder, Marty," I said. "I have the photos in my computer and can print as many as I need."

He gathered the pictures up and slipped them under his arm. "Have you shown these to Shaw?"

"He doesn't know about them," I said. I explained how I had taken it with my digital camera, removed the card and stuffed it into my jeans pocket. "I completely forgot about it, until it fell out while I was doing my wash. When I—"

"Have you had lunch yet? I made some sandwiches and a salad and I'd just as soon not eat alone."

"Sure." I glanced at my watch. "Sounds better than the microwave dinner I was planning."

Plus, I'd finally get inside Marty's house!

We walked through an entranceway tacked onto the kitchen, typical of centuries-old houses. Coats, caps, and other kinds of men's outdoor clothing hung from pegs framed by dark wainscoting. Boots and shoes peeked out from under the coats.

When we continued through a door at the end of the passageway, an old-fashioned screen door sprang shut behind us. We emerged into a dimly lighted kitchen. I noticed that Marty still had the room-darkening shades pulled down to cover the two windows that looked over the back yard. He switched on a light. White floor-to-ceiling wood cabinets flanked one entire side of the kitchen. Another wall had been retrofitted with twentieth century appliances—a gas stove, refrigerator, and sink. The faded blue-flowered linoleum still bore the outline of appliances that had formerly stood there.

The scant counter space that divided the upper and lower cabinets was cluttered with an ancient bread box, a can of Maxwell House coffee, a pile of magazines and newspapers, and what looked like a day or two's mail. When I pulled out a chair to sit at the weathered wooden table, an orange tabby cat jumped down to the floor. It rubbed against Marty's legs as he puttered at the table, moving salt and pepper shakers, napkin holders, and various condiments to one side to make room for the salads and sandwiches. He had apparently been reading a military magazine, which he picked up and added to the pile of papers on the counter.

I'd been in rooms like this before, but this one was populated by a bachelor who cared nothing for decorating and updating. I peered around for anything personal. No magnetized photos of smiling grandchildren adorned the fridge. Aside from the counter clutter, the room was a study in minimalism. A door led to the next room, but with the draperies in that room pulled together, it was dark, too. If I'd been bolder, I would have visited the bathroom as a maneuver to see more of the house.

Marty and I made small talk about the weather. He busied himself setting the table and putting out the food. "Up for a beer?" He held out a can to me. "Nothing beats the heat better than a cold one." I opened the tab. He opened his and sat across from me. The weather seemed to be the only topic we could talk about. We kept discussing it. "The weather in Kansas City was even hotter than it is here, if you can believe that," he said, taking a bite of his sandwich.

I didn't let on I knew he had been in Kansas. "Oh, so that's where you were when the sheriff called you to come back home."

He cleared his throat. "I had some engine trouble with the helicopter and it was in the shop when the sheriff called. I had to wait overnight to get airborne."

"Were you in Kansas for business or pleasure?"

He took a sip of his beer and settled back in his chair, as if to ignore my question. "A little of both."

"I heard an accident victim was transported to a burn unit in Kansas City," I said, prompting him to continue his story.

"That's right," he said. "My schedule was open, and I was ready to get out of town for awhile." He took another sip of beer and another bite of his sandwich. "And besides that, I had some personal business. I've been trying to solve a puzzle for forty years." He carefully placed his half-eaten sandwich on the salad plate. "I've been chasing around the country following up whatever clue came my way. Sometimes, even out of the country. Mexico. Canada. Ireland, of all places. But after a couple of years, the trail got cold and I'd be lucky to get a lead a year."

"What are you looking for?" I asked, taking another bite out of the surprisingly good tuna sandwich.

He examined the ceiling, his eyes focused on a distant point. Finally he said, "I don't know much about you, Cassandra. Let me ask you a question, though. If your mother disappeared with your brother and you had no idea where they were or why they left, what would you do?"

If I had seen the dreaded "family" question coming, I could have deflected it. As it was, he had taken me by surprise and his question had the effect of a blow to the stomach. I struggled to keep from spitting out my sandwich.

"You don't have to answer that," he said gently. "I don't talk about my family much either."

"Does . . . does your family live close by?" I asked, relieved to be off the hook. "I don't think I've ever seen them visiting."

"As far as I know, they don't live nearby," he said. "That's what I've been trying to discover for forty years. If they just took off . . . or if something terrible happened to them, well, it's a living hell not knowing."

"Forty years is a long time."

"Sounds crazy," he said. "But when a part of you is taken away, without your knowing why, it leaves a scar."

My hand involuntarily flew up to stroke the scar on my neck. "I can only imagine."

* * *

After taking the plunge with Marty, I was convinced the best way to get information was simply to throw myself into the enemy camp. Since it was only 1:15, I decided to visit Jack, the newest on my "questionable friends" list. He didn't know I knew about Eric. I wanted to see his reaction to the person in the mysterious parking-lot photo. Glad I had made several copies while I was at it, I hopped into my Jeep and drove over to the stables.

Jack was astride a loping horse on the right side of the arena. When he reached the far end, he turned the horse toward the center. Orange construction-zone cones were positioned in a straight line at about ten-foot intervals. As I watched, Jack dropped the reins in front of him and urged the animal into a trot. Without any obvious guidance, the horse maintained its gait, weaving in and out of the cones until it came to a stop in front of the gate. The guy knew how to handle a horse. I applauded as he dismounted.

He came over and casually threw his arm across my shoulders. "Hey, Cass. Long time no see. What's our pretty detective turned up now?"

I shrank away from his touch and held out one of the folders of photos in front of me. "I'm trying to identify the person in this photo, Jack. Willis Lansing and Marty are looking at it, too." I handed him the folder.

"Where'd you take the photo?"

I described the circumstances to him. "The authorities don't know this photo exists, Jack, so be careful who sees it. Think you'll have time to look it over in the next couple days?"

"Sure, no problem." He tucked the folder under his arm. "By the way, Virgil came by this morning to pay Midnight's board."

"Did you talk to him?"

"For a few minutes. I thought he should know that Strothers was here asking about him the other day."

"Was he surprised?"

"He said he didn't know Strothers was in the area, that he thought he'd gotten beyond his reach. He thanked me profusely for letting him know."

I frowned. "Funny he hadn't read about Strothers in the newspaper."

"Guess he's not a newspaper reader. At least now that he's informed, he can watch his back."

"Good thing you talked to him. Maybe we can keep one person out of Strothers' clutches."

Jack eased down on his haunches to stroke a striped cat. "Virgil would be a sitting duck for someone like Strothers." He gazed up at me. "I'll do all I can to help you."

"Did you tell him I'd like to buy his horse?" I bit my lower lip.

"Yes, and he didn't give me a forceful 'no.' Just said he'd think about it. Maybe he's softening."

"I can only hope." With that, I pulled a handful of carrots out of my pocket and went to see Midnight. Anticipating treats, he trotted over. I led him into the barn, secured him across the aisle, brushed him, saddled up, and headed out on the trail. We rode quietly through the woods, and then he ran flat out on a straightaway quarter-mile stretch of field. It was invigorating. As I reached down to pat his mane, I realized I was thinking more and more of him as "my" Midnight. After only one short month, I couldn't imagine a future without him.

On my way back to the carriage house only thirty minutes later, I thought about the four people who had seen copies of the parking-lot photos—Anna, Willis, Marty and now Jack. One more person might be able to help me. Frank Kyopa. He was in town, attending a commission meeting. I made a U-turn and headed towards town, staking myself in a conspicuous spot outside the City Hall meeting room. Hopefully, the commission would take a break. I didn't have to wait long. Ten minutes later, they emerged, chatting among themselves. I caught Frank's eye and motioned him over. "Could I have a couple minutes of your time?" I asked, brandishing the last folder of photos. "I have something I'd like to run by you."

We went back into the meeting room and I spread the pictures out on the conference table. "I snapped these pictures when I left the Rendezvous to return to the parking lot for some new camera batteries," I explained. "As it happens, that was about the same time Eric was murdered. It probably means nothing, but I'd sure like to know who is emerging from the woods in this photo. Does anything look familiar to you?"

Frank selected one of the close-ups and then another, studying them one by one. "Very, very interesting, Cassandra. This could be the photograph of the murderer. Too bad the images aren't clearer."

"I know. I was snapping randomly, trying to fill up my CF card."

"I can't identify the person." He shook his head. "I've seen boots like that somewhere, though."

"I'm figuring they're one of a kind," I said. "Would someone on the rez make boots with that design?"

"Never. Those boots were made for people playing at being an Indian, not for Indians." "Like a reenactor?"

"Yes, most likely a reenactor."

"You're positive they're not n."

"I can say with confidence they're not made by anyone around here. You'll find the maker traveling the Rendezvous circuit." He handed the folder back to me, but I waved it away.

I spent the rest of the afternoon grocery shopping, picking up a few things at the cleaners, making a stop at the drugstore and watching some late-night television. Life goes on, even if that life is in danger of being incarcerated with a "lifetime" sentence of murder in the first degree.

Chapter 24

Friday—Week Three

Satisfied that I had taken several positive steps toward clearing my name, I put the photo riddle out of my mind and focused on my preparations for three upcoming weddings.

My first meeting was with a wedding party at the old flour mill that gave Colton Mills its name. I'd found the mill area difficult to light and set up, but it always produced some striking photos. Situated on the Oxbow River, its water wheel was once again operational, thanks to historical preservation efforts in the 1980s. The two-story, wooden structure was situated at the bottom of a steep hill that was accessed by a winding gravel road that allowed vehicles to descend gradually into the valley.

Tall pines flanked the road, lending an air of mystery to the descent, and they accentuated the dramatic sight when you emerged into the mill clearing. The city had taken advantage of the steep slope in front of the mill and built amphitheater seating, with about twenty rows marching up the hill in front of a stage that complemented the look of the old building. It had become a popular venue for musical groups, weddings, and other events.

I was winding up the nine o'clock meeting, when Shannon, the bride-to-be, remembered a key part of the ceremony that had slipped her mind in the bustle of activity. "How could I have forgotten," she said, pressing her hand to her chest. "We have to leave space for a portrait of my best friend. She was going to be my maid of honor, but she was killed in a car crash." I murmured something sympathetic in response. "I couldn't bear to go on with my wedding without having Kathleen in it somehow," she said. "Could you suggest an appropriate place for the picture . . . one that will ensure she is an integral part of the ceremony?"

I made a few suggestions. "What is your friend's name?" I asked. "I'd like to add it to my layout sheet."

"Kathleen Dewitt."

I started to write the name, when, without warning, it clicked on some other memory in my brain. "Was . . . was your friend in an accident a few miles outside Colton Mills last year?"

Shannon nodded. "Yes. Her boyfriend was driving and lost control of the car on the ice. I miss her so much."

My heart had leaped into my throat and I cleared it several times. "Did . . . do you know if Kathleen had a horse?"

"Why, yes," she said. "Midnight. She loved that horse."

As I did. "I don't suppose you know Kathleen's father?" I held my breath.

"Not really." Shannon stopped to think. "She didn't talk about him much. I do know his name is Virgil."

I tried to keep the excitement out of my voice as I asked, "Where did Kathleen live?"

"Right here in Colton Mills. She had an apartment on Eighth Street."

"She didn't live with her father?"

"Oh, no," Shannon said. "He lived somewhere in Wisconsin. Madison, I think That's why I didn't know him very well."

"Where did Kathleen live on Eighth Street? Do you—"

My question was cut off by one of her bridesmaids. "C'mon Shannon," she said, pulling the bride-to-be's arm. "Let's go. We're late, big time."

"Sorry, Cassandra. We'll talk again sometime."

Before I could utter another word, they dashed off to her car.

As I drove toward town, I couldn't get Shannon's conversation out of my mind. Virgil was an interesting mystery man. He had battled Strothers and won. At least for now. I wished I could locate him . . . to ask him questions about Strothers, but mostly to see if he would consider selling Midnight to me. Feeling more hopeful, I was eager to use what little information Shannon had given me about Kathleen. Maybe, if I were lucky, someone could lead me to her father

On an impulse, I turned off Main Street onto Eighth. A short street, only a couple of blocks long, it retained its postcard-perfect, small-town charm despite its proximity to the center of town. Most of the apartment buildings in Colton Mills were in newer sections of the city, but there were still a few apartments on Eighth that had been carved out of the old, larger homes. I parked my Jeep and started to walk. I estimated there were about six houses where Kathleen Dewitt may have lived. They were all well-kept, restored Victorian-era homes, set back from the street behind century-old trees and shrubs. The leafy oaks and elms cast cool shadows on the brick sidewalk.

I turned into the driveway of the first house and strode up to the entrance under a grand porte-cochere that had once sheltered guests leaving their carriages to enter the house. Ascending the six broad steps, I entered the foyer where tenants' mailboxes had been retrofitted into the woodwork. I skimmed the names, not really expecting to find Kathleen's name after all this time. I pressed the button labeled MANAGER.

A buzzer sounded and I opened the great oak door, which admitted me to the inside of the house. I faced a wide wooden staircase, winding its way to the second floor. A thin, stooped woman, who looked like she may have come with the original house, shuffled out from an office to the right. "May I help you?" she asked in a wavering voice, peering up at me through incredibly thick eyeglass lenses.

"Could you tell me if you had a tenant by the name of Kathleen Dewitt a year or so ago?"

"Well, I wouldn't know," she said. Then in a burst of authority that belied her frail appearance, she continued, "And I couldn't tell you, even if I did know. That is, unless you're law enforcement. You're not law enforcement, are you?"

For a wild moment, I considered handing her one of my ID cards. Maybe a Visa card would do, judging by her nearsightedness. But I thought better of it, thanked her, and left.

I didn't fare any better at the next two homes. Then, at the fourth, one of the names on the mailboxes caught my attention. K. DEWITT. It was a long shot that Kathleen's name would still be on the box after a year. Dewitt was not a particularly unusual name, and the "K" could stand for Kenneth, or Karen, or Kevin. I hung around the foyer, hoping a tenant would enter the building and shed some light on the occupant of Apartment 206. When no one came, after about fifteen minutes, I made a note of the address and left for Anna's shop.

Anna bustled happily toward me. "Cassandra, I didn't tell you, but I sent a picture of the boots to Hugo, my contact in New York. He thinks he can help you! He used his sophisticated equipment to enlarge the part of the photo showing the boots and said he was able to get a fair resolution, much better than you had. He agrees that they were custom made. He's never seen the type of beadwork down the side of the boot. And . . . " She clasped her beringed hands in front of her and leaned towards me. "And he's going to check around with his contacts to see if they can find the craftsman who made them." Disappointment must have shown in my face. "That's good news, isn't it?"

"Yes, that's great news, Anna," I said, although I'd have preferred to have a name attached to the owner of the boots. "Any idea how long it will take to hear from his contacts?"

She pursed her lips. "No, he didn't say. He won't dawdle, though. I stressed that the matter was extremely urgent. He owes me for some research I did for him last year, and I'm one of his best customers, so that will help, too."

"Anna, I really appreciate what you're doing." I hugged her. "Sorry that I want it done yesterday." Anna was one friend who didn't have any connection to Eric. I could trust her. She had my best interests at heart. Nevertheless, I left the shop with a feeling of dread, wondering when the next shoe would drop.

* * *

I had almost forgotten about the Prairie River Band Powwow, which is held every year. It was a small one, as far as powwows go, but important to the participants. As the official photographer, I had to attend, even though my interest and enthusiasm were at an all-time low.

I left Anna's shop around 12:30, famished and hoping to find something to eat at the powwow. I arrived at the fairgrounds, cameras in tow, in time to photograph the Women's Jingle Dance. The rhythmic noise created by rows of now mostly artificial, store-bought bird bones, deer hooves, or jingly metal pieces lifted my spirits, and I was soon positioning myself to photograph the dancers as they demonstrated their graceful use of fans and other ceremonial regalia.

At the end of the event, they swarmed around me, wanting to pose for individual photos. The rest of the day progressed much in the same pattern, as I took pictures of women gracefully performing in their colorful fancy shawls. The drums beat out rhythms for the men's grass and fancy dances and I snapped away, filling my camera bag with several CF cards full of images.

At about half-past seven, I finally pulled away from the fairgrounds. Reflecting on the status of dinner makings in my newly stocked refrigerator and my level of energy to make anything from them, I decided to indulge in fast food. I pulled into the local drive-in and ordered a cheeseburger and fries, making a mental note to balance the caloric overload with equivalent miles on my treadmill. I relaxed against the seat and drove through the takeout line.

As I turned the corner behind a line of about a half-dozen cars, the houses on Eighth Street came into view. Munching my burger, I drove slowly by the house to see if I could learn anything. After driving around the block a couple of times and down the alley in back of the house, I snagged a parking place in the next block. I wiped away the last remnants of french fry salt with a napkin, slurped the last of my Diet Coke, grabbed a clipboard from the back seat to use as a prop, and sauntered back to number 1310. It was still fairly early in the evening, and I hoped some tenants would be out and about.

I climbed the stairs and walked into the entry way. This time, I didn't have long to wait. A thirtyish man, just coming in from a run, huffed up the stairs and took out his house key. He glanced over at me, where I was leaning against the wall, my clipboard poised for action. "Are you taking a survey or something?"

"Kind of," I said. "I'm looking for a new apartment and don't want to make the same mistakes I've run into in other apartments." Darn, I was getting good at deception.

"Like what?"

"Oh, loud music, people arguing, that kind of thing."

"This is a pretty quiet building."

"Have you lived here long?"

"Only a couple of months."

"Do vacancies come up very often?"

"I haven't seen any vacancy since I moved in, and I waited for this one for about six months." He inserted a key into his mailbox.

"Do you know everyone in the building?"

"Almost everyone." He stuffed a number of envelopes into his shirt pocket.

"What would you say is the age range?" I pretended to make notes on my clipboard.

"Most are about my age."

"I noticed on the mailbox that there are some singles in the building," I said.

He glanced at the names on the mailboxes. "Out of ten apartments, I'd say eight are married couples. Well, I'm not sure about one of them, because I don't know who lives there."

Aha! "How could that be in a building with as few apartments as this?"

"Well …"

I peered at him questioningly.

"Well, I don't see anyone coming or going from one of the apartments, but, sometimes, late at night, I hear music."

"Yikes!" I said, feigning alarm. "You don't think the house is haunted, do you?"

He laughed. "I don't believe in ghosts." He was inserting his key in the door, when he turned to me again. "I'm probably reacting to the fact that the apartment was rented to a woman who died, and her name is still on the mailbox. Probably watching too many TV mysteries." He glanced at my notes. "This is a great building. Don't let that affect your opinion of the place."

Not at all, I thought, congratulating myself for my persistence.

When I left the house, streetlights were already lighting the block. I stood on the sidewalk, peering up at the second floor. No lights burned in number 206. I strolled to my vehicle, plotting the next move in my "save Cassandra" strategy.

Chapter 25

Monday—Week Four

Anna, the consummate Sherlock, had gotten into the spirit of tracking down the beadwork artist. Things were moving along, according to her latest message on my answering machine. "Just to give you an update on the boots, Cassandra. Hugo called and said he's narrowed the beadwork style down to two moccasin makers. One of them lives out East, not too far from him. He sent him the picture to see if it's his work, but he hasn't heard back from him yet. The other one is hard to reach. Evidently a free spirit who travels the reenactor circuit all year long. Hugo's checking to see if the guy has an e-mail or any other way of reaching him. I'll keep you posted."

Nick had called me late Friday and I agreed to meet him for a Saturday-night dinner and a movie. God! We were even dating small-town style. Sometimes I felt as if I were in a time warp.

Other than that quite pleasant break in my usual routine, the weekend passed with no progress on clearing my name. I didn't want to dwell on the fact that three entire weeks had passed with no progress on naming the killer of Eric.

On Monday morning, I was driving to my first appointment when my cell phone rang. It was my newest bridal client, Stacy.

"Cassandra," she said, "I'm running a little late. Would you be too upset if I met you at 9:30 instead of 9:00, same place?"

"No problem," I said, "see you there." With an extra half hour freed up on my schedule, I drove to the library. Janine was working. "Long, hot summer we're having, isn't it?" I groaned inwardly at my lame attempt at normalcy.

"I'll say," she said. "Especially hot for you, though, isn't it? How are you doing?"

"I'm doing one day at a time. Thanks for asking. Listen, do you have old Colton Mills telephone books . . . say a year old?"

"We sure do. C'mon and I'll show you where to find them." She led me to an area along the back wall. "Look through them to your heart's content, but you'll have to leave them in the library. They can't be checked out."

I thanked her and pulled the regional directory that contained Colton Mills off the shelf. I opened the book to the D's, and traced the names down to Dewitt. Kathleen's name was there and it matched the address on Eighth Street where K. Dewitt was currently listed. I still wasn't sure what significance to attach to the name and address match. Whoever was living there now may not have gotten around to changing the name on the mailbox. But if that were the case, why was the apartment still in Kathleen's name in the phone book? And why was music playing in the apartment late at night only on a rare occasion?

I returned to the counter. "Janine, do you remember a car crash last year? The one that killed a girl named Kathleen Dewitt?"

She tilted her head to one side and stared across the room. "Hmm . . . do you know when it happened, Cassandra?"

"The beginning of the year, I think. Maybe January or February."

She pursed her lips. "That's more than a year ago. A lot of news has pushed that one out of my mind. You know, winter car accidents in Minnesota aren't exactly earth-shattering news. I don't remember her name, but I'll tell you where to look, if you're interested."

I checked my watch. "I have about fifteen minutes."

"Okay, follow me." She led me to the computer room and pulled a couple of compact discs out of a cabinet. After delivering instructions, she left me to my own devices.

The first disc held local newspaper stories for January/February of the previous year. I clicked through the disc's directory searching for anything that said KATHLEEN DEWITT. Nothing. I tried ACCIDENT and was rewarded with about ten hits. But they weren't what I needed. Maybe CRASH. I entered the word and again received several hits. Scrolling down, I found the headline: "Young Woman Dies in County Crossroads Crash." Quickly opening the article, I scanned it until I found the name of the victim. It was Kathleen DeWitt! I pushed PRINT, snatched the article off the printer, folded it, and stuffed it into my back pocket. Tossing a dollar bill at Janine for the copy, I dashed to my Jeep and headed for my meeting with Stacy. I was late.

Driving through town a couple hours later, I thought about Kathleen's apartment and wondered what was behind her name still being on the mailbox. It probably wasn't important, but the diversion kept me from obsessing over my own worsening situation. Like the fact that I hadn't heard from Willis yet. Surely he'd been given plenty of time to look into the boots matter and the photo riddle. I reached for my cell phone and dialed the number he had given to me. I was also eager to find out if he'd learned anything that would help Marty, as the representative for the Rendezvous group.

"I'm sorry to disappoint you, Cassandra," he said, when I reached him, "but I have not found any useful information about those moccasin boots yet."

"That's all right. I'm sure you're a busy man. But Willis, while I have you on the phone, can you remember if you got to the Rendezvous before Marty that Saturday morning?"

"I believe that Marty camped out on the grounds overnight, so, no, I did not get there before him." Willis paused, as though thinking. "I did arrive quite early, however, as I followed that young man from the stables to the site and he left shortly after dawn."

"What guy from the stables?" I could hear my voice rise with dread and I turned down the sound on the car radio.

"You know, dear . . . the trainer there. Jack." He paused. "I don't know his last name."

"Gardner. Jack was at the Rendezvous?"

"He had to trailer a couple horses for two of the participants. I didn't know the way, and he said I could follow him."

I gulped a lungful of air and counted to ten to steady my voice. "Any idea how long Jack stayed?"

"No, I'm afraid I don't, Cassandra. I didn't even talk to him, as I had other things to do. He went one way, and I went the other after we arrived."

I thought I had been surprised when I learned Jack knew Eric. Now, he was at the Rendezvous? And with all our conversations about Eric, he never thought it pertinent to share that information with me? I had told Jack almost everything about my situation. He had looked through my photos. What if it weren't to help me, as much as to learn if I had a picture of him?

The fact that Jack didn't tell me about Eric or the Rendezvous could only mean one thing—he had something to hide. He had been helping me keep abreast of what I knew. With that thought, I smacked the steering wheel with my hand. Why had it taken so long for this piece of the puzzle to fall into place? Jack had not only set up my appointment with Randy the night I found him dead with a knife in his back, but Jack was with me when we found Jim. He had protested against our taking that trail through the woods. Quite pointedly.

Lost in my depressing thoughts, I nearly back-ended the car in front of me, which had slowed to let someone dash through a crosswalk. I slammed on my brakes and felt my heart lurch into my throat. The near accident completely snatched my breath away and I pulled over to the curb to settle down. My mind was whirling with so many thoughts, nothing was making sense. Clear thinking was necessary. My life could depend on it, especially if Jack was a murderer.

Finally, I felt I had control of myself enough to resume driving back to the carriage house. I resisted the impulse to call Jack and scream bloody murder at him. One, it would be blatantly stupid. If Jack had killed any or all three, of the men, he would do the same to me if I were no longer useful to him. Two, as long as he didn't know what I had learned, and if I were careful, I could use him at the same time he was using me. I had to take everything Jack had told me with a grain of salt. What could I believe? Had Eric really instigated a blackmail campaign against Strothers? Maybe Jack had made it up to throw suspicion on Strothers and away from himself. What had he told me about Marty? Oh, yes . . . he set me up to talk to Randy Pearce about Marty's violent behavior. Maybe he had coached Randy in advance so that I would believe Marty had a motive for killing him. I would have to tread very, very carefully where Jack Gardner was concerned.

Thinking about Jack made me think about Midnight and, unbidden, my mind returned to the Kathleen DeWitt mystery. I needed to get into what I was sure was her apartment. Maybe I could learn how to find her father and offer to buy her horse. The second my mind headed in that direction, I thought I knew how to pull it off. When I had driven through the alley the week before, I'd noticed a shallow faux balcony with a scrolled wrought-iron railing on the back of the building, just outside what must a bedroom window. At one time, the window had overlooked a substantial garden between the building and the alley. All that was left now were some overgrown foundation plantings centered around a full-grown tree that brushed against the building. I could climb the tree and enter the apartment through the second-floor window. There should be just enough room on the platform separating the building from the railing of the ornamental balcony.

I glanced at the dashboard clock and, although I was mentally weary, I determined now was the best time to tackle the break-in. I wouldn't be able to sleep with so many questions on my mind. Although I had time to drive all the way out to the Carriage House and back to town, I wasn't up for it. Fortunately, I was dressed in what I figured would be fairly decent tree-climbing clothes— Levi's, a long-sleeved red-plaid shirt, and my best pair of Land's End hiking boots. If my memory served me correctly, I had some old leather gloves in the truck, for tire-changing purposes. I also had a tire iron and a crowbar and a few other tools for emergencies on my photo shoots. My weight-lifting regimen would serve me in good stead to boost myself into the tree. The climb itself should be fairly easy. Once I had talked myself into the scheme, I felt more energized.

First, however, I had to get something to eat. My unexpected trip to the library, the meeting with Stacy, and my phone call with Willis had taken any thought of lunch away from me and my backbone was playing a version of *Dry Bones* on my stomach organ. I'd have to kill enough time to ensure it was dark and perfect my plan. Deputy Shaw would rub his hands together in glee, if I were brought in for one more questionable shenanigan.

I wasn't ready to discuss any of my new revelations with even Anna and I didn't want to run into anyone I knew, so I chose a neighborhood café that served Scandinavian-style cooking, instead of one of my usual haunts. While I dined on Swedish meatballs over egg noodles and a generous slice of cranberry-apple pie in total anonymity, I plotted exactly how I would proceed, once I had parked near Eighth Street. Getting through the window posed a problem, since I'd never broken into a building before. If I remembered correctly, it was a hinged window, opening onto the faux balcony, which was about ten-fifteen feet off the ground. As long as the window had not been updated with new safety glass and fasteners, I was counting on the crowbar to get me inside. Alarm systems were few and far between in Colton Mills, so I was confident I wouldn't face that challenge.

I spent the rest of the afternoon and early evening accomplishing several errands, spending over an hour in the photo shop buying the chemicals and paper I needed to replenish my darkroom supplies.

The sun had barely set when I parked on a dark side street two blocks away from Kathleen's building. Feeling slightly queasy, I remained in the car for several minutes while considering again what I was about to do. I would be hit with some serious criminal charges, if anyone caught me. Notwithstanding that possibility, my curiosity overcame my misgivings, and I gathered my gloves and tools and began the short walk to the apartment house. Not a leaf stirred on any tree. The sky was moonless and clouds covered most of the stars. Every footstep echoed in my ears as I picked my way carefully through the uneven gravel alley.

Right when I thought I should turn back, the building loomed in front of me. I peered through the darkness to identify the tree and to search for signs of the faux balcony outside my target window. It would take me only a few more steps to reach it. In five minutes, I could be up on the balcony ledge. I stood as still as a statue and pondered the right thing to do. It was now or never.

Listening for the sounds of anyone in the area, I finally felt comfortable that I was alone. I reached up and grabbed hold of the lowest-hanging branch. After a couple of tries, I succeeded in pulling myself up over the branch, until I was standing on it. Then reaching for the next branch, I hoisted myself even higher. I was decidedly rusty at tree-climbing, especially in the dark, but I eventually managed to climb until I was within a couple feet of the ornamental balcony. Carefully, I stretched out my arm, until my hand touched the top of the railing. Grasping it tightly and then letting loose my grip on the tree branch above me, I took hold of the railing with my left hand and pulled myself over the edge and onto the narrow balcony. It was covered with months of accumulated dirt and leaves. I silently instructed myself to dispose of my footwear as soon I left the premises, in case the boots left imprints.

Moving quietly toward the window, I pushed my face against it to see if I could detect any signs of light. I couldn't see a thing. Probably shades or heavy draperies covered the window. I placed my ear against the pane and listened. No noise came from inside the room.

I felt up and down the window casing to find the latch that held the two windows together. I slipped the crowbar between them in what I figured was an adequate breaking-and-entering procedure. After a few tries, the old wood splintered and I had access to the latch. I set the crowbar on the window sill, reached inside and pushed open the window wide enough to wriggle through the space. I parted the draperies, peeked inside the cave-dark room, and stepped inside.

The air smelled stale, like no one had refreshed it in months. Maybe my hunch was right and I was standing in Kathleen's apartment. As my eyes adjusted to the dimness, I defined the shapes of furniture in what I assumed was a bedroom. I pulled out my keychain and shined my small laser light on the bed and dresser, to see if there were signs of occupancy. Everything was well organized and neat, but every piece of furniture was covered with a thin layer of dust. Nothing in the wastebasket. Step by step, I inched my way through the room, into the hallway, and toward the kitchen. The countertops were devoid of any signs of fresh food. Their surfaces were also covered with a layer of dust. I pulled open the refrigerator door. A welcoming light illuminated the room. No food, but several bottles of white wine rested on their sides, chilling. How long had they been there? Was Kathleen the drinker, or someone else? The freezer was empty and the ice maker was turned to OFF.

I returned to the hallway and entered the windowless bathroom. Closing the door, I switched on the light. A bar of soap and a hand towel rested on the porcelain sink. I couldn't tell when they had last been used. The soap was dry and the sink was clean. The shower floor was dusty. I opened the top drawer of the vanity. It was filled with typical women's toiletries, including eye shadow, mascara, and lipstick. The next drawer held bottles of hairspray, hair gel, shampoo, brushes, barrettes, and assorted hair ornaments. I felt like the intruder I was.

Back in the hallway, I wandered into a second bedroom. I shined the laser light around the room and quickly identified it as

Kathleen's bedroom. The cast-iron bed was made up with a decidedly feminine spread, accented with colorful red and pink flowers and a ruffled binding. A stuffed white bear and brown horse rested against the foot of the bedstead. A collection of horse statues, along with some photos of a woman on a saddled black horse filled one shelf. An easy chair filled one corner, with a low bow-legged table next to it. A stereo took up half the table and the rest was covered with a half-dozen or so framed pictures of a girl at various ages. In front of the pictures were two wine glasses and a candle. The setup looked like a shrine.

I assumed the pictures were of Kathleen. I'd be able to tell for sure when I saw Kathleen's picture at Shannon's wedding. Just to make sure I wouldn't forget the face, I selected the smallest photo and slipped it into my shirt pocket. As long as I'd embarked on the slippery slope to criminality, I might as well add burglary to breaking and entering.

Just as that flippant thought passed through my mind, a click in the hall made my blood run cold. Someone had inserted a key into the apartment door lock. I stood ramrod still and listened, quickly snapping off my keychain light. A door opened. Someone entered the living room. Lamplight in the living room made a thin illuminated ribbon down the hallway floor. My knees grew weak and I feared I would fall to the floor. My clammy hands started to shake uncontrollably. My eyes stayed riveted on the stream of light. *What should I do? Where should I go? Will I be caught?*

Heavy footsteps headed for the kitchen. The footsteps of a man. Feeling desperate and in fear of my life, I searched with my eyes for a place to hide, afraid to move even an eyelash. Tiptoeing one careful step at a time, I headed for the closet door. Turning the knob with a sweaty hand, I opened the door far enough to slip inside, shutting the door completely behind me. Feeling about and praying nothing would fall to the floor, I settled behind the densely packed clothes and tried to still my pounding heart.

I couldn't hear a thing, but my imagination went wild. The man was probably opening the refrigerator and removing a bottle of wine. He'd open the bottle and head for the shrine to Kathleen. He'd be right outside my hiding place. *What's that?* Footsteps. He was passing the closet door. A cough. A sigh. More footsteps heading straight toward the easy chair. I fought my sudden dizziness and tried to quietly suck in a deep breath. This was no time to faint.

Abruptly, a thin line of light appeared almost beneath my feet. The door ended about a half-inch above the floor. Could he hear me breathing? I could hear his wine being poured into the glass. And what was that? *Music.* Classical music coming from the stereo. Debussy's *Claire de Lune.*

More footsteps. What was he doing? Where was he going? A door opened and then closed. He was in the bathroom! This was my time to move. I twisted the knob and slowly opened the closet door, pausing to listen for any activity in the bathroom. Over the sound of the toilet flushing, I crept out of hiding and dashed down the hallway toward the other bedroom and my escape window. Then, without warning, I tripped and fell.

"Who's there!"

The man's voice sounded alarmed. He was in the hallway. Numb with fright, I froze. *I can't be found. I'll spend the rest of the night behind bars. Maybe the rest of my life.* I scrambled to my feet and bolted for the window, as the man's footsteps raced down the hallway and into the living room. I fumbled with the heavy draperies, trying to find where they parted. *There. Good girl. Stay calm.* I crawled through the window and onto the narrow fake balcony. With only one foot touching freedom, I felt the viselike grip of a man's hand on my arm. My heart stopped. My breathing stopped. *It's over.*

No. The crowbar. I reached for it with my free hand and jammed the sharp end into the man's arm. Cursing, he let go just long enough for me to vault the balcony railing. I dropped two stories to the ground below and landed with a thud in an overgrown lilac bush. A pain seared my left ankle. Other than that, I seemed to be in one piece. I threw one hasty glance at the window above me. My assailant hadn't attempted to follow me. He was either on his way down the stairs to come after me or on the phone to alert the police. I wrestled my way out of the bush and hobbled as fast as I could through the dark alley.

As I reached the end of the alleyway and was about to turn toward the safety of the side street where I'd parked, I saw the lights of a vehicle enter the other end and stop under the balcony. I loped to my Jeep and within mere seconds was entering Main Street. Only then did I dare to switch on the headlights.

Chapter 26

Tuesday—Week Four

My first thoughts upon waking were, "No one followed me. No police cars pulled me over. I'm in my own bed. I'm not behind bars." I lay perfectly still and reviewed the most dim-witted thing I had ever done. What had I accomplished? Absolutely nothing. I had learned that apparently a grieving father had left his daughter's apartment as she had lived in it . . . sort of a living shrine to her where he could toast her with a glass of wine and think of the good times they'd enjoyed together and of the events they'd never share, like her wedding and her children—his never to love grandchildren.

Finally rising from the safety of my bed, I practically tripped over the heavy black trash bag filled with my get-away wardrobe. I had emptied my pockets into my catch-all basket on the counter as soon as I'd entered the carriage house apartment, and then peeled off my clothes and stuffed them into the bag. I planned to burn them, so there would be nothing to tie me to the apartment break-in. A long shower had calmed my nerves. I had wrapped my banged-up ankle in cold packs, treated the cuts from landing in the bush, and crept into my bed, trying to erase the image of being one crowbar jab away from time in the slammer.

Barely dressed, I heard my cell phone ringing and momentarily stiffened. I limped to the dresser to retrieve the phone and examine the LCD display screen. Anna's name and number appeared. "Morning, friend. What's up?" I said, sounding overly chipper to hide my guilt.

"Back atcha," she said. "We've hit a small glitch, Cassandra. The first craftsman I called says the beadwork on the boots is similar to his, but it's not his work. He's pretty sure the other guy did the beadwork, but he doesn't know how to reach him. If anyone can track him down, I know Hugo can do it."

I made small talk with Anna as best I could. My adrenalin was still too elevated from the night before to think clearly. "Thanks for your persistence. I appreciate it and will practice as much patience as I can, until you hear from him."

The cold packs, refreshed once during the night, had worked their magic on my ankle. I had very little to no swelling. I'd have to favor it for a few days, but wouldn't need medical intervention. I gathered a few newspapers and carried them with the trash bag of evidence to the burn barrel. In a few minutes, any evidence had gone up in flames. Then I spent the next ten minutes hosing down my Jeep, to erase any signs of alley dust. I felt home free from my near debacle of establishing a criminal record. I decided to keep the apartment escapade to myself. As long as no one else knew about it, there was little chance of it coming to light.

I spent most of the morning in my darkroom and at my computer pouring over the Rendezvous and wedding pictures, in order to put the least amount of stress on my ankle. When the phone rang again, I jumped involuntarily. No amount of fooling myself removed the fear lurking mere millimeters beneath the surface of my bravado. It was Deputy Shaw's assistant.

"Deputy Shaw would like to see you in his office at two o'clock this afternoon," she said curtly. "He wants you to bring a red shirt with you . . . like the ones you regularly wear."

"Do you know what this is about?" I asked, my chest tightening.

"No, I don't. Just bring the shirt and be here by two o'clock."

My throat went dry. Shaw had put two and two together. He knew I was at the farmhouse the night I photographed Strothers' vehicle door. Strothers must have filed a complaint after all. "I'll be there," I croaked. How would Shaw use the information? On the face of it, it didn't seem like a chargeable offense. I hadn't damaged anything. I hadn't hurt anyone. Maybe it was another fishing expedition. Maybe it was another building block in his case against me. I needed to talk to Sanders about it. Immediately.

Thirty minutes later, I was sitting across from him in his office. It wasn't easy for me to spill the whole story to my attorney, especially since he was Anna's brother. I had to go back to square one and tell him about Jack breaking into Strothers' office and finding information that suggested Eric was blackmailing Strothers. After what I had learned about Jack, I no longer felt the need to protect him. "We decided, after finding out about the blackmail payments and reviewing the articles proving a change Eric's attitude, that Strothers had a serious motive for killing Eric." Then I related how he had accosted me outside Grizzly's and accused me of telling Marty about the paint factory.

"All that occurred right after someone tried to run me off the road on the rainy day of Randy's funeral. I wanted to find out if Strothers was the one who wanted me in the ditch . . . or worse," I said, defensively. "When Anna and I saw his vehicle pass us, we followed him all the way to that farm somewhere in Timbuktu.

Anna thought it was too dangerous to go any further and we left. But you know me. I couldn't leave well enough alone. I returned on my own after dark with my camera. I photographed the passenger side door. First, I used my red shirt to wipe it clean of dust, and then stupidly tossed it onto the ground to free up both hands. Then, being the klutz I am, I fell over in the driveway. I made just enough noise to alert the men in the house. Strothers came running outside and almost spotted me. Fortunately, some kid in the area shot off a few fireworks and that diverted their attention. I hitched a ride on the back of Strothers' truck until we were out of the range of the yard light. Unfortunately, I left the shirt behind in the driveway."

Sanders had taken extensive notes. "After all that, did you find anything incriminating in the photos?" He gave me a hopeful look, while chewing on the pen.

I iterated how I had connected the dots, from identifying the logo on Strothers' vehicle to that on a truck parked in the Rendezvous parking lot. "It proved the truck was in the Rendezvous parking lot the day Eric was killed, Lawton. Because of that, I felt the farmhouse's escapade was worth it."

Sanders was silent for several seconds. He raised a bushy eyebrow and rocked in his high-backed office chair. "You've been busy, haven't you, Cassandra? A little unorthodox, but you've turned up some interesting tidbits of information."

"What kind of trouble am I in with Shaw?" I slumped in my chair and hid my face in a propped up hand, too worried to watch his reaction.

"No criminal charges that I can ascertain," Sanders said. "Possibly a trespassing charge, but that's nothing to worry about. I imagine Shaw is quite mystified as to why you were at the farmhouse, but, in reality, he has no proof you were there. Only Strothers' say-so. It all depends upon what line Strothers fed him when handing over your shirt. He probably suspects it has something to do with his investigations of the three murders, and he'll try to get it out of you. I'd expect a serious grilling, but we can handle that. And, although this isn't really legal advice . . . I'd try to find a red shirt that is either much too big or too small for you. One you haven't worn in quite a long time perhaps. And with a different label, of course, so that it is totally unlike the one in Shaw's possession."

The chirping of my cell phone jolted me out of my reverie as I drove back home, following my appointment with Sanders. I was stewing over my guilt for not telling him about my real break-in adventure the night before. It was Jack, not exactly the person I wanted to have a conversation with. "Hello, Jack. What's up?"

"Cass, we're trying to find Virgil and I'm looking for information." He sounded breathless, his voice coming in small bursts. "Is there anything you can think of that will help us? Anything at all?"

"Why the urgency in finding Virgil?"

"Guy Strothers was out at the stables again, asking questions. He talked to one of the employees here who blabbed everything he knew about Virgil. I'm concerned he'll do something to him. He seems to really have it in for the guy. We've gotta find him and warn him of trouble."

Warning bells went off. Could I trust Jack? Was he stringing me along with another set-up scheme? If he were telling the truth and Virgil were in some sort of danger from an enraged Strothers, would my guilt be magnified if I ignored his safety for my own? "Okay, Jack . . . I guess I can give you a little info, but I'm not sure it'll help much. I know where Virgil's daughter lived, before she was killed."

"Kathleen's been dead for more than a year, Cass."

"I know, but I happen to know that her apartment has been rented by her father all this time."

"How do you know that?"

"Don't ask me how, Jack. I just know it." I gave him the apartment address.

"I'll call Steve, a guy I ride with in the Mounted Patrol. He's working as a part-time deputy and owes me a favor." Thankfully Jack hung up and didn't quiz me about my recent activities.

As soon as I entered my kitchen, upon reaching home, I saw that the landline phone was blinking. Someone had left another message. I was from Anna. I dialed her right away.

"Cassandra, we've found the guy!" she said, as soon as we had connected.

"I needed some good news," I said wearily. "I had a session with your brother this morning and I have another interrogation by Deputy Shaw this afternoon. Tell me about the moccasin maker."

"He's an Ojibwe Indian," she said. "He grew up on the rez and goes by the name Standing Heart. When I called him, he was packing up to attend a Rendezvous near Pipestone."

"But Frank Kyopa told me the boots were not made by anyone from the reservation."

"Frank or no Frank, we've got our man," Anna said firmly. "I think I'll drive down there and meet him face to face. Hopefully, he can tell who purchased the boots from him. Any chance you can come along?"

"I can't. I've got a couple appointments set in stone. Are you sure you want to do this? It could turn out to be a wild goose chase."

"I'm going to go, no matter what. I've been wanting to see some clothing samples from a seamstress who lives near there anyway. I'll kill two birds with one stone. I'll take the pictures you gave me to confirm the boots. You take care, dear, and I'll call you as soon as I get any information."

Later, driving through town on my way to the police station, I passed Kathleen's apartment house. In front of the building, I wasn't surprised to see a posted sign: APARTMENT FOR RENT. I memorized the telephone number, drove around the corner, and pulled over to the curb. I punched the number into my cell phone. "Eighth Street Apartments, this is Myrtle speaking."

"Could you tell me which apartment is for rent in your building, please?"

"Certainly. It's number 206. A lovely apartment. Very clean. Two bedrooms. Are you interested in seeing it?"

"When will it be available?"

"In two weeks."

"Thanks for the information. I'll call you back." I sat for some time, simply staring out the windshield. Obviously, Kathleen's father was taking the next step in his life. I felt guilty for my part in pushing him into making the decision to move on. I had invaded his privacy. It was probably for the best, though.

Lawton Sanders met me at the entrance to the police station. "Follow my lead, Cassandra," he said. "As much as possible, limit your answers to yes or no. No details. Remember, he has no proof you were even on the farmhouse property. Let's play it by ear."

Fortunately, Sanders advice served me well. I was so noncommittal about every reply to every question that Shaw gave up. I was back in my Jeep with forty-five minutes, no worse for wear.

Jack heard from Steve later in the afternoon and called me back. "Your information might have helped," he told me. "Steve was in town, so he stopped by the apartment building. Talked to a Myrtle there."

"Yes, Myrtle's the manager."

"She said Virgil always came by about the same time every month and paid the apartment rent in cash. She never knew where he lived."

"Great. Sounds like another dead end."

"He did get a little snippet of information though." Jack cleared his throat. "Myrtle said whenever he was there, she sometimes noticed a vehicle with an out-of-state license number on it parked at the curb. She asked someone in the office about it and that person said she thought it was a Wisconsin plate."

"Kathleen's friend told me Mr. DeWitt lived in Wisconsin, so that would make perfect sense. It would explain why we don't ever see him around town. He must drive here from Madison, pay the rent and the board for Kathleen's horse Midnight, and then drive back home. It doesn't, however, explain his secrecy . . . unless he's trying to stay away from Strothers. I think I told you about the lawsuit over a property dispute. Strothers lost a ton of money and has felt a great animosity toward Virgil ever since."

My fears for Virgil outweighed my reluctance to spend any more time with Jack. I'd stay alert and keep my mouth shut concerning anything about my own investigations. "I think we should go to Ned Oberon's farm and ask him where Strothers is," I said. "If he finds Virgil first, God only knows what he'll do to him. I'd never forgive myself, if I could have helped him. The poor man is still grieving the loss of his only child."

"I'll finish my chores with the horses and pick you up."

On the way to Oberon's farm, we strategized as to how we should approach Ned. "Let's hope he's not armed," Jack said, accelerating to a scary seventy-five mph. I tried to ignore the speedometer by peering blankly out my side window. "If he pulls a weapon, we're out of there. If we can get him to talk to us, we'll play our next move by ear."

"Excellent plan," I said, rolling my eyes.

"You got a better one?" Jack didn't let up on the accelerator as we squealed around a forty mile-per-hour curve. Actually, it was as good a plan as I'd had in most of my capers. I held onto the door handle as we sped down the road. Finally, Jack pulled into the farm driveway and I relived the night I had photographed Strothers' truck in the farmyard. I drummed my fingers on the arm rest to expel my rising apprehension.

The first thing I noticed was a pickup in the yard. We got out of Jack's truck and walked briskly up to the kitchen door. The sound of a TV laugh-track filtered through the door to the porch. Jack knocked, then knocked louder. The TV sound stopped and footsteps marched towards us. Ned opened the door wide, but as soon as he saw it was us, he immediately moved to close it. Fortunately, Jack was quick enough to wedge his boot between the door and its frame. He pushed the door open and grabbed Ned by the collar.

"I didn't mean any harm to you, ma'am. Honest," he said to me. His rheumy eyes pleaded at me behind their thick glasses. "I quit workin' for him when I couldn't do what he wanted me to do anymore." He lifted a shaky hand to his bald head and shifted his gaze to the floor.

"Quit working for who?" Jack said.

"Strothers," he said. "I quit workin' for Strothers. You gonna hurt me?"

"Not as long as you answer my questions," Jack said, giving him a little shake. "What did he want you to do?"

"He had me build him a fire bomb. Said he wanted to use it to shoo some skunks outa his back yard. He was lyin' to me. He made me throw it at her house." He pointed at me. "That's when I said I couldn't work for him no more. I needed the money he was payin' me. Farmin' don't pay much. But when it comes to somethin' like that, well, I told him to find someone else. I ain't got the stomach for it."

I tried to catch his eye, but he kept his head down. "Did you follow me into the woods?"

"Yah, that was me," he said, chin on his chest. "I wasn't gonna hurt you none, jest keep an eye on you." He peered up at me. "That's all he asked me to do. Keep an eye on you."

"Know where Strothers is now?" Jack glared at him and raised his voice.

"No, sir. I ain't seen him since he come here to pick up the bottle with the stuff in it."

"Know anybody who might know where he is?"

Ned shook his head.

"Think!" Jack said, pushing him against the kitchen counter. "Somebody we know could get hurt real bad unless we find Strothers first."

"*Uff da*," Ned said, shaking his head, visibly upset and scared. "I shouldn't of let myself get talked into this. Money ain't worth it."

"You can redeem yourself, if you help us find him now," Jack said.

Ned shook him off and shuffled wearily over to the refrigerator and pulled down a scrap of paper held in place by a magnet. It advertised the local farm co-op. "Here," he said, handing it to Jack. "Might do you no good, but she might know where he is." The scrap of paper held a penciled telephone number.

"Who's this woman you're talking about?" Jack asked.

"Strothers' answerin' service."

"Ok, Ned, here's what I want you to do," Jack said, waving the piece of paper in front of Ned. "I want you to pick up the phone and call this number. Think about what you'll say, because

244

when you hang up, I want to know where to start looking for Strothers."

Ned stroked his chin as he paced the small kitchen. I could see the fear in his eyes. Coming to a decision, he finally picked up the phone receiver from a black table-model rotary-dial telephone, the likes of which I hadn't seen since I first lived at Mrs. A's. It was connected to its base by a curly cord. He dialed the number and waited. "This is Ned," he said, his voice cracking. "I hafta reach Guy quick-like. No, I tried his cell phone and he don't answer. I've got some information he wants. Know how I can get a hold of him? He still in Colton Mills?" He reached for an envelope on the counter beside the phone. "The Village Inn. Yah, I got the numbers. You betcha. Thanks."

He handed the envelope to Jack. "Looks like a Wisconsin number," he said. "My brother Eldon lives in Madison and I always use that area code. Guess Strothers' ain't in town."

"Poor bastard," Jack said as we drove back to the highway minutes later. "All he wanted to do was make a little money and he got sucked in by Strothers. You've got to give him credit for not going further than his conscience allowed."

"I don't care about Ned," I said. "Virgil lives in Madison. Strothers is from Chicago, so what's he doing in Wisconsin? If Strothers was plotting to warn me away from an investigation of Eric's murder by hiring Ned to fire bomb my apartment, who knows what he's capable of doing. Maybe Virgil is in serious danger."

Jack picked up his cell phone and punched in Steve's number. "Hey, buddy," he said, "you're not answering so I'll leave this info in your answering machine. I've got a hot lead on Strothers and I think it's important enough to alert the authorities in Madison, Wisconsin. Virgil's life could be on the line." He read

Steve the Village Inn's telephone number. "Call me as soon as you can."

Chapter 27

Wednesday—Week Four

Jack's warning was too late. When Steve returned his call, it was to report bad news. The Wisconsin authorities had already answered a neighbor's 911 call on a similar matter. Virgil's house was fully engulfed in flames by the time they got there. Although a vehicle was in the garage unharmed by the fire, when they extinguished the raging house fire, they discovered the badly burned body of an adult male in the ashes.

"That poor man," I said when Jack delivered the news.

"Steve told the police we may have a lead for them, if they determine the fire was caused by arson. Of course, we have no proof it was Strothers. He may simply have been on his way back to Chicago. He'd probably take the highway that skirts Madison."

"Strothers is too slippery," I said. "He'll have an airtight alibi. If only we had tipped off the authorities sooner, maybe Virgil would still be alive."

"Don't beat yourself up over it, Cass. It's not your fault. It's for the Wisconsin police to solve."

"But, if they—"

"We were simply too late, Cass. I regret it, but we tried."

My heart was not in my work the rest of the day. I stumbled through my appointments, trying not to think of how one more life had ended in tragedy, most likely at the hands of Guy Strothers, who didn't want a repeat of the Chicago property fiasco in his Colton Mills dealings. Marty stopped me later that day as I was driving into my garage. He, too, had heard about the Wisconsin fire.

"I seem to remember your saying there was a connection between that man Virgil Dewitt and Strothers," he said, frowning. "Was this fire good news or bad news?"

"Bad news for Virgil and possibly bad news for me, too," I said. "I think Strothers was so focused on getting to Virgil, he didn't have time to bother me in the past couple days. But now that he's dispatched Virgil, it's only a matter of time before I hear from him again. Deputy Shaw hasn't forgotten me either. This isn't Wisconsin, Marty. This is Minnesota and he's got three murders of his own to solve. I found all three bodies. Strothers or no Strothers, Cassandra Cassidy is his prime suspect."

"I'm still on that list, dear. Deputy Shaw is coming to pay me a visit tomorrow. He knows more than he's letting on. It was Abraham Lincoln who said, 'You can fool all the people some of the time, and some of the people all the time, but you cannot fool all the people all the time'."

Over and over again, I pondered those words, until I finally drifted off to sleep around two o'clock in the morning. I also wondered what would become of Midnight. Would some unknown relative claim ownership of him? Maybe I should get a dog. A dog was man's best friend. I needed a good friend.

Chapter 28

Thursday—Week Four

It was Thursday already. I placed an X over the past two dates on my wall calendar and thought about all that had occurred in Colton Mills during the month of June. Since I had no reason to drive into town, I brewed my own coffee. While sipping it at the counter, I reached into the basket where I'd deposited the contents of my pockets after visiting Kathleen's apartment. I pulled out the picture I'd taken from her bedroom. A young woman, comfortable with the camera, gazed confidently into it. "You must be Kathleen," I said to the picture.

But I wouldn't know for sure if it was Kathleen until I saw the picture at Shannon's wedding, still two weeks away. Yielding to a perverse need to tie up loose ends, I tried to think of how I could find another photo of her. The Internet. School yearbooks. Drive out to Shannon's house. The library. The library article! I had completely forgotten the clipping about Kathleen's accident I had copied at the library before meeting with Stacy! Perhaps a photo accompanied it.

I pulled off my Levi's from a hook in my closet where I had hung them. The article was in the back pocket. I unfolded it and brought it back to the kitchen. Just as I had hoped, the picture of a young women was a dead ringer for the one in the frame in front of me.

I poured myself a second cup of coffee, feeling relieved. Now I could put that mystery to rest. Virgil, grieving for his daughter, had kept the apartment and visited it each month to maintain his connection with Kathleen. Now the apartment was vacant, and Virgil was lying in the ashes of his home in Wisconsin.

I idly scanned the rest of the article as I sipped my coffee. It was a familiar story of too much speed on a too-slippery road, the driver losing control, and the passenger getting the worst of the accident. In the next paragraph, a name jumped out at me so unexpectedly, I spilt coffee across the counter. "The driver of the vehicle, Eric Hartfield, escaped with only minor injuries."

Eric Hartfield! There was more. According to the article, the accident was compounded by a series of errors, causing enough delay to prevent Kathleen's swift transport to the hospital. The dispatcher had sent the ambulance driver in the wrong direction. The ambulance driver had taken too long to call for a helicopter evacuation. Then the helicopter pilot was late in arriving. The article quoted the dispatcher: "We did the best we could, but our best wasn't good enough to save her." The dispatcher's name was Jim Tuttle.

So many terrible thoughts crowded my mind, I had difficulty separating them into something that made sense. I was willing to bet Randy Pearce was the ambulance driver and Marty the helicopter pilot. Before I could change my mind, I punched in Jack's number and got his voice mail. "Jack, I need to know if

Randy was the ambulance driver for the accident that killed Kathleen Dewitt last year. It's important."

Then I punched in Marty's number. Busy. I tried again. Still busy. I ran down the stairs and across the yard to his house, ignoring the sound of my ringing cell phone. The caller would leave a message. Marty's vehicle was in the driveway. Not surprisingly, he didn't respond to a knock on the door, so I headed around the house to the back yard. Dashing down the sidewalk, while ignoring the increasing pain in my ankle, I called out to him as soon as I spotted him. He was standing near the table where he always placed his tomahawks before throwing them. "Marty! *Marty!* I have to talk to you!" I shouted, while sprinting toward him.

"Go back! *Go back!*" he shouted at me.

I was already halfway across the yard. "Marty, I have to ask you something important." At that moment, I saw a movement under the house's second-floor balcony from the corner of my eye. Willis Lansing stepped out of the shadows. He held two black powder pistols. Both were pointed at me!

"Cassandra, dear, you certainly have a nose for trouble. Now I shall have to deal with you, too" He motioned with the pistols for me to move closer to Marty.

"What's going on?" I asked. "Is this one of your reenactments?"

He laughed. "Your coming here is a most unfortunate happenstance. I have grown quite fond of you."

I cast a quick glance at Marty. His face was white under his beard. I turned to face Willis again. "Unfortunate? This . . . this isn't a reenactment for another Rendezvous, is it? This isn't an . . . an act."

"You are an unusually bright young woman, Cassandra. Now I have no choice. There must be two victims to an accident."

"What do you mean . . . accident? What accident?" My head swiveled back and forth between Willis and Marty. Marty seemed incapable of speaking. I turned my questioning eyes to Willis.

"Before you dropped in, Marty and I were having an interesting discussion." He smiled at his friend. "Tell Cassandra the nature of our discussion, Marty."

I turned to Marty, but he didn't respond. His eyes seemed to be apologizing to me.

"Come, come, Madigan. Tell this young lady what we were talking about." Willis waved one of the pistols at him. "It would be most upsetting, if I have to discharge this weapon before I am ready."

Marty didn't move a muscle. His eyes never left Willis as he spoke to me. "He says his real name is Virgil Dewitt and not Willis Lansing, Cassandra. His daughter Kathleen was killed in a car accident last year. It appears he blames the driver of the car and the emergency crew for her death. He's set on revenge."

"But, Virgil is . . . " My mind was spinning. "I . . . I thought Virgil DeWitt was killed in a house fire on Tuesday. The police found his body." I turned to face Willis. "It was his . . . your house . . . in Wisconsin," I stammered.

He laughed, the sound harsh and hideous to hear. "As you can see, my dear, I am very much alive. The body they found among the ashes was the body of a nemesis of mine."

"*Strothers!*" I gasped, finally understanding.

"Ah, yes," Virgil said, poker-faced and showing no signs of remorse. "I anticipated the arrival of Guy Strothers and met him with a welcoming party he did not expect. I torched the house and drove away in his vehicle. Fortunately, the police believe I was the ill-fated victim of the fire." His voice was cold and I started to shiver uncontrollably. I had never met a serial killer face to face before. Is this what happens to a person who loses a loved one?

"How much of this did you know about?" Marty spoke to me, but his eyes never left Willis. *Virgil.* I was so confused.

"Part of it," I said, staring directly at the pistol pointed at me. "Did . . . did he kill Eric and try to pin his murder on you by using your tomahawk?"

"I applaud your detection skills, Cassandra," Virgil said. "Too bad you will not have the opportunity to share your findings with law enforcement."

Law enforcement. Marty had said Deputy Shaw was coming to his house today. A glimmer of hope stirred inside. Maybe, if I could keep Virgil talking, we would have a chance to . . .

Virgil was about ten feet from us. Neither Marty nor I would be able to reach him in time to relieve him of his pistols. "You were the man in the parking lot photograph, weren't you?"

"Indeed, I was. Thank you for tipping me off about its existence. It prompted me to speed up my plans."

"And Kathleen's apartment?" I continued, trying to stave off the inevitable. "Were you paying the rent in cash every month and visiting here?"

His frowned. "How you managed to put these pieces together, I don't know. But yes, you have figured out most of it."

"What are you going to do now?" I wanted to wrap my arms around Marty and weep for those who had lost their lives because of Virgil DeWitt's sorrow, but I stood frozen in place.

DeWitt took a step forward. "You and Marty are two remaining loose ends. You will walk toward the target and be killed when Marty accidentally discharges his black-powder pistol, Cassandra. Overcome by what he has done, he will turn the second weapon on himself." As if he could read my thoughts, he waved the pistols at us. "But before you go, please secure Marty for me. I don't trust him." He threw me a set of handcuffs and a roll of duct tape from a patio table next to him.

I cuffed Marty's hands to the arm of a cast-iron patio chair and covered his mouth with duct tape. "I'm so sorry," I murmured. "I should have figured this out sooner." I desperately tried to think of a way to stop Virgil. He only had two shots. One from each weapon. The possibility remained that I could somehow distract him—at least long enough for the deputy to arrive. But how?

Virgil continued his diatribe. "Once I have dispatched the two of you, I will take care of the other interloper." He gestured with his head toward a chair in the shadows of the patio roof.

Dear God! It was Deputy Shaw! He was bound hand and foot and duct tape was plastered across his mouth, too. My heart sank and acid rose in my throat. I had been counting on Shaw to rescue us. Now, with those hopes dashed, I steeled myself for what was to come, closing my eyes and breathing a prayer for help. I wanted to leave this earth standing tall and being the brave young women Mrs. A had loved.

Virgil was ready to begin his last murder spree. "Now," he said. "Walk slowly toward the target, Cassandra, and don't try any tricks. I'm not in the mood."

I took one last look at Marty and turned away to head for the target. My feet felt like lead. My ankle chose this moment to shoot sharp reminders of my past indiscretions. With only one shot, Virgil couldn't afford to miss. I already knew he was an ace shooter. A million thoughts raced through my memories. Mrs. A would be furious at me for putting myself in this predicament. All her training had been for naught. Would he shoot me in the back? On impulse, I whirled around and faced him. He had one of the pistols aimed directly at me.

Suddenly, a figure emerged on the balcony behind him.

I froze and kept my eyes focused on Virgil, who was visibly angry for my failure to follow orders. A lariat silently snaked through the air and settled over his chest. It was yanked taut. The pistol aimed at me discharged harmlessly into the air. The other one dropped to the ground. Virgil was jerked off his feet and dragged backward.

I dashed forward and snatched the weapon from the grass, aiming it at my assailant. My hand shook violently, and I used my other one to hold it steady. "Don't move a muscle," I said, my voice strong and filled with anger. "I won't hesitate to use this thing."

Jack dropped from the balcony in a flying leap and secured Virgil to a balcony support post. "There." He pushed the black Stetson off his forehead, wiped his brow with the back of a hand, and surveyed his handiwork. "You're not going anywhere until someone comes to take you away."

I rushed to his side. "How did you—"

"I picked up your message on my cell phone while I was at the feed store," he said. "Since your place was on the way, I decided to stop and see what was so important. You weren't home, but your vehicle was. I figured you might be at Marty's, so I went looking for you. When I saw what was happening, I called the sheriff on my cell phone."

"Did you hear the whole thing?"

"Most of it. Enough to know the sheriff wouldn't get here in time. I was afraid to distract Virgil, when I didn't have a gun to back me up. I went back for the only weapon I had in the truck. My rope."

Two deputies, guns drawn, rounded the corner of the house. Quickly sizing up the situation, they secured Virgil in cuffs, then untied the shaken Deputy Shaw. "DeWitt intercepted me when I arrived to question Mr. Madigan," he said, rubbing his wrists where the ropes had dug into his flesh. "He forced me to drive my squad car into the garage, where it would be hidden from view.

His vehicle is in there, too. Or, Guy Strothers' vehicle, according to his own confession."

Shaw turned to Marty and me. "I apologize for keeping the two of you on my short list. My deputies and I completely screwed up this investigation. We're not used to situations like this in Clayton County. We're regrettably rusty. I'll get back to you tomorrow for your testimonies. Again, you have my profound apologies."

I watched him march an exhausted and cheerless Virgil DeWitt across the lawn. It was at that precise moment reality hit me. They were hauling away the man who had taken out his unresolved suffering and need for revenge on three Colton Mills men. The same man who had been one lucky lasso toss away from the last of his murderous plans. Plans that would have ended my life, too.

Chapter 29

Friday—Week Four

Four weeks of my life had passed by in a blur. Four weeks, when I hadn't known from one day to the next whether I would be spending the rest of my life in prison. I owed Jack big time. But he owed me some answers. When I finally got through the telephone gauntlet of reporters calling him, I invited him to meet me at the only place I could think of where we could clear the air.

He rang my doorbell right on time. "Good news, Cass," he said by way of greeting. "Looks like you'll get your horse. Virgil requested that his attorney turn Midnight over to you. He knew you had been riding him on a regular basis."

"That's big of him. I'm surprised, aren't you? Especially since we're the ones who foiled his plans." I grinned. "That news is the only good thing to come out of this mess, as far as I'm concerned." I ushered him into the kitchen where I'd prepared one of my gourmet meals—a frozen pepperoni and sausage pizza heated in a 500-degree oven, accompanied by a cold six-pack of Coors.

"You turned into a pretty good detective," Jack said, grinning as he popped open a can.

"Better than you know," I said in a tense voice, between bites of pizza.

"What do you mean?"

"What I mean, Jack Gardner, is that all the while you were supposedly helping me, you were lying through your teeth."

"What the hell are you talking about?"

"For starters, you neglected to let me in on the not insubstantial fact that you knew Eric Hartfield." My gaze bored into his eyes.

"Where'd you get the idea that I knew Eric?" Jack looked sincerely baffled.

"Deputy Shaw told me you got Eric's sister pregnant years ago, when you were working at the Evening Star Stables, then skipped town. He said Eric was gunning for you when you showed up in Colton Mills."

"Never happened, Cass." He shook his head in stupefaction. "Never happened. None of it. Nada. It was a case of mistaken identity. The sheriff took my DNA, saying they were investigating whether or not a child was mine. They didn't say whose child they were talking about. I found out just last week they were talking about Hartfield's sister. I'd taken her out a few times, but the results of the tests last week cleared me of being a father of her child. It wasn't mine. Couldn't be mine."

"Are you telling me Shaw used information he didn't know was even true to—"

"Happens all the time. You know that."

"Okay," I said. "That's not all. Why didn't you tell me you were at the Rendezvous on the day of the murder?"

"At the Rendezvous?" His mouth dropped open. "I've never been at that Rendezvous in my life!"

"Are you telling me that you did *not* trailer some horses to the Rendezvous for the use of a couple participants?"

"Yeah, I'm saying I wasn't there. Where'd you hear that fabrication?"

"From Willis—Virgil—whatever his name is. He said you told him you were going to the Rendezvous and he could follow you up there, since he didn't know the way."

"Oh, that. I think I know what you're talking about now." Jack finished the beer in his can and reached for a second one. "Virgil asked me directions to the reservation *casino* and I told him I was heading up that way and he could follow me, if he wanted. Obviously, the man had an agenda and part of it was to bamboozle folks like you and me." He grabbed a napkin and wiped his fingers of pizza sauce. "Cass, if you believed that shit, does that mean you suspected me of being a mass murderer?"

"Well, it made sense, didn't it? I hear you were at the Rendezvous and you hadn't mentioned it. You told me to visit Randy at his house and then I find him murdered. You decide to ride out on the stables property to find Jim, protest about heading in the direction I suggest, and then we find him hanging from a tree."

Jack placed his hand over his heart. "I'm devastated that you would allow such a thing to even enter your mind. Shocked you'd actually believe it!" He reached for my hand across the table, but I was quicker. I might be grateful to him and I might have misjudged his connections to the three murdered men, but I wasn't about to show him my gratitude by getting any closer to him than I'd been in the past months.

Media outlets outdid themselves covering the story of how three murders were solved in one dramatic bust. Always hungry for heroes, they were lionizing the latest one. And he was in his element. When I turned on the late-night news, there was Jack, decked out in his full cowboy regalia. "Mr. Gardner, where did you develop your amazing roping skills?" asked one of the TV reporters.

He tipped his Stetson off his brow and assumed an "aw shucks" manner and tone of voice. "I wrangled steers and horses in west Texas for a few years," he drawled, flirtatiously eying the twenty-something interviewer. "It's a skill you gotta know, if you're gonna cowboy for a livin'."

"Mr. Gardner is going to demonstrate his skill with a rope," continued Ms. Interviewer.

The camera panned over to Jack, who was already astride his horse in one of the stable's corrals. From the other end of the enclosure, someone opened a gate and about half a dozen calves dashed in, bunched together and heading for nowhere in particular. Jack expertly roped a calf his horse cut from the group. The calf hit the end of the rope and flipped to the ground. Jack jumped off and tied up the calf's legs, while the horse held the roped calf taut. The camera pulled in for a close-up of the cowboy, who doffed his hat. His wide smile flooded my living room. It had taken him an impressive six seconds. Jack was on his way to a whole new career, and I predicted his newfound celebrity would project him far beyond the confines of Patriot Stables.

The interviewer was wrapping up her story. "Jack Gardner," she said. "Today's cowboy, made in the image of hundreds who went before him. With one important twist. His roping skills snagged the only serial killer Colton Mills has ever experienced . . . a killer who took the lives of three innocent citizens and would have added three more notches to his belt."

I groaned and changed the channel.

The sheriff was basking in the limelight during this broadcast. Even though he hadn't done a darned thing, three murders had been solved in his jurisdiction in one fell swoop. Tight-lipped about how it all occurred, he explained only Jack's role in the capture. "Virgil DeWitt has been arrested and charged for the murders of all three men. He is incarcerated and will await his trial

Epilogue

Saturday—Week Four

Colton Mills was breathing a collective sigh of relief. Anna had called me several times and I finally agreed to a celebration dinner at her house. Marty and Nick had also been invited. "Okay, who wants to begin?" she said, plopping into a comfy chair, after pouring the wine.

I sipped from my goblet. "If I had stopped to answer the phone, before dashing over to Marty's house, things would have turned out differently," I said, sighing. "But, as usual, I was in a big hurry to talk to Marty about the news article relating to Kathleen DeWitt's car accident."

She reached for the cheese and cracker plate on the coffee table and passed it to me. "You've probably listened to the voice mail message I left for you, but I'll tell Nick and Marty about it. The craftsman in Pipestone remembered that Virgil was the one who bought the boots we saw in the Rendezvous parking lot photo. When I think of how close you came to—"

"Even if he'd been successful in killing Shaw, Marty and me, that information you doggedly acquired would have identified him and the police could have conducted a statewide search, Anna." I blew her a kiss.

"That's small comfort," she said, wagging a well-manicured finger at me. "You put yourself in danger."

"I know you didn't trust me, Cassandra," Marty said. "You weren't sure if I was involved in killing Eric or not. I don't blame you. Virgil masterfully hid his identity, posing as the Willis I had grown to admire and befriend. For a businessman from Wisconsin, he had skills in hatchet-throwing and could talk reenactment with the best of us. I had no clue as to his real identity." He swirled the wine in his glass. "No one in our Rendezvous Society had reason to suspect him of being a killer. We wholeheartedly accepted him."

"Now that we all know the murderer was Virgil, I wonder why we couldn't put two and two together," I said, washing down the cheese and crackers in my mouth. "The first murder involved a tomahawk, the second, a frontier knife, and the third, a handmade rope."

Marty shrugged. "Those clues could have applied to anyone who was into Rendezvous reenacting. If I hadn't been so concerned about my own defense, I should have thought of him. He was big on justice and how it was served up in the old days. Some of the men in our group were uncomfortable with his conversations about on an eye for an eye. Hindsight certainly makes it easier to understand."

I reached for the wine bottle and refilled all our glasses. "According to the newspaper article, he quit attending the Wisconsin group's meetings after his daughter was killed. He must have devoted full time to plotting his vengeance on Eric, Randy, Jim, and Marty."

"He seemed to understand all of us and how we were likely to explain events. It was a masterful plan to kill Eric with my tomahawk." Marty rose from his chair and paced the floor. "He had easy access to my tomahawk and knew where I kept it, but he's the last person I'd have suspected stealing it from me. I had no witnesses to confirm my innocence." He scratched his head and peered directly at me. "One big problem law enforcement had was the lack of evidence at the crime scene. No fingerprints. No footprints. A lot of blood, but no blood of a second person. No bloody clothing. All they had was Frank's hat, which he swore he had left there the night before. Deputy Shaw couldn't even figure out how the crime was accomplished."

I nodded. "As time passed, I was convinced Strothers was responsible."

"When did you first suspect him?" Marty came to sit beside me on the couch.

"When he scuffled with me in the coffee shop that night and then found out Eric may have been blackmailing him in return for writing favorable review of his proposed building project."

"Which turned out to be true. How did you find out?"

"Intuition," I said. I wasn't going to admit to any law-breaking by either Jack or me, not to anyone. Ever.

Marty chuckled. "You thought Strothers trashed your studio, too, didn't you?"

"Shows how we can leap to easy conclusions, when we're experiencing stress. Now we know it was Virgil. I had told him about having Rendezvous photos when I saw him at Jack's cutting class for young riders. He wanted to see if they incriminated him, I suppose."

"Well, it's all water under the bridge now." Marty started to rise from the couch and perched on the edge of a cushion. "Everything came down to that one article you copied at the library. Think of it. And all because you wanted to talk with Kathleen's father about buying her horse. Amazing. You tracked her down, found the article about her accident, saw that Eric Hartfield had driven the car, and that Randy and Jim and I were involved in the same incident. You're one smart cookie, Cassandra. Your intuition—or whatever you want to call it— saved a few more lives. Thank you." He leaned toward me and planted a kiss on my cheek.

I glanced at Anna and Nick. Both were thoroughly involved in the story, both content to simply listen.

Marty arched his eyebrows and shook a finger at them. "The parking-lot photo unhinged Virgil. That's not to say he wasn't already unhinged. With Strothers closing in on him, he escalated his scheme, vacated the apartment, set up a meeting with him in Madison, and after doing his damage there, returned to get me. He was set on cleaning up all the loose ends. Anything and anyone connected to Kathleen. He was paying board for her horse and keeping up the rent on her apartment."

"How did you find out about that?" I asked, and then kicked myself for opening up that topic.

"His landlady called the police when Virgil canceled the lease after someone broke in one night. He asked her to clean it out for him and put the place up for lease. She thought she'd better report it. The police checked it out and put two and two together, *after* he was incarcerated."

Anna swept cracker crumbs from the table. "I heard on the news they found an airline ticket in the vehicle Virgil was driving. He was planning to leave for France from the Minneapolis/St. Paul airport. No return ticket."

"Yep," Marty said, "And they found scratches on his SUV, left in the garage in Wisconsin, that are likely to prove he's the one who tried to push Cassandra into the ditch that day in the storm. I can't imagine Virgil was that kind of man. The poor soul lost all perspective after the tragic death of his daughter. His mind was affected. I know what that's like."

I noticed Marty's sadness, as he thought of his own behavior after finding his son and wife missing, and changed the subject. "Shaw said he'd found a hair at the scene of Eric's murder and insinuated it was mine. I wonder if he really found one, or if it was a ploy to get me to help him solve the mystery."

Anna spoke through pinched lips. "That man would say and do anything to elevate his importance and career. There was no hair. I don't believe him."

"Has anyone heard from Jack?" Marty asked. "I expected him to be here tonight."

"He's in Minneapolis for another interview," I said. "He's our most famous citizen now." Two hours later, we had finished a dinner of pork loin and au gratin potatoes. We were all talked out. Marty said his goodbyes and Nick walked me to my Jeep.

"Your place or mine?" he asked, taking my hand.

"Yours," I said. "Last one there buys breakfast in the morning."

From the Author

A RENDEZVOUS TO DIE FOR grew out of the intersection of my wide-ranging interests and my 25-plus years as a newspaper and corporate magazine reporter/photographer/editor in the Minneapolis area. Before spinning this mystery novel, I was an award-winning short story writer, and also won numerous awards in the field of journalism. *A RENDEZVOUS TO DIE FOR* has been a finalist in mystery-writing contests.

I love the idea that *A RENDEZVOUS TO DIE FOR* takes place in a small Minnesota town and centers around the fictional Prairie River Trappers' Rendezvous, a weekend reenactment festival involving local citizens and Indians from the nearby reservation. It was a great setup, just asking for a mystery story.

I hope you enjoy rooting for Cassandra as much as I enjoyed creating her.

Betty McMahon